THE TWILIGHT CONTINUUM

HAYWARD'S REACH

THADDEUS HOWZE

ebonstormedia

Hayward's Reach
Tales of the Twilight Continuum
and the Children of Earth

Written by
Thaddeus Howze

For information request: Ebonstorm Media, LLC

ISBN 13: 978-0-9719943-7-9
ISBN 10: 0-9719943-7-4

Cover Art by QAZ2008 - Mohammed
Cover Design and Layout/Design by Ebonstorm Media

Manufactured in the United States of America

First Edition

To all the Women who inspired me
to complete this work.

To my Mother, who did not live to see this,
I owe my creativity and lust for knowledge.

To Terrye, who believed I should be writing
from the very first scrap of anything
of mine she ever read.

To DJuna, who insisted I keep trying,
especially when I wanted to stop

and

To Jan, the woman who taught me
how to turn my love of writing into the written word
and not embarrass myself, terribly.

I appreciate and love all of you.

PART ONE
FABLES OF OLD EARTH

PART TWO
A TIME OF TROUBLES

PART THREE
ENTERING THE PENUMBRA

PART FOUR
THE DIASPORA OF EARTH

FORWARD:

By Milton Davis

History speaks of deeds and dates, of events and those people who influenced them. But history does not reveal the heart of a people; it does not share with us their goals and dreams, their wants and fears, their desires and hopes. For this we must rely on the words of the fiction writer. From their stories we can glean what we seek to determine the true soul of a people.

But how can we determine the inner feeling of people when there are so many writers? If we focus our studies on the most popular we will gain only a general perspective set forth more for profit than insight, yet if we focus on those writers that push the boundaries we gain a perspective of extremes and eccentricities but not the image of the core. In the end we must rely on our instincts to choose which stories will give us a feel for not only the mundane details of a folk or culture, but the vibrant feelings that give them life.

In *Hayward's Reach,* Thaddeus Howze takes us on a journey to the heart of humanity. Combining history, science and mythology this collection of stories examines the dreams, fears, aspirations and realities of mankind through engaging and insightful prose. He finds fascination in the mundane and the fantastic as he leads us from the recent past to the possible far future of mankind, all the while sharing his impressions of our strengths and our failings. This is a collection of stories that will ride the range of your emotions, but most of all these are stories that will make you think.

In his fictional debut, Thaddeus takes on a daunting task and succeeds. *Hayward's Reach* is in your grasp; enjoy a journey into the possibilities.

Milton Davis is the author/editor of several Sword and Soul novels including Meji, Meji, Book Two, Changa's Safari and the Griots Anthology.

PART ONE:

FABLES
OF
OLD EARTH

"Old Earth was romanticized in literature
so I was not surprised to read these tales talking about
how wonderful the Earth might be, or how magical things
were during these early years.

What surprised me was the heroism, the adaptability and
the fearless zeal with which they approached life, no matter
how large or small the champions might be."

--Glendale Mokoto

Übermensch

I found her behind our lines in a field not too far from a downed Messerschmitt ME 262. We had pushed the Germans back out of Paris and retaken the countryside in early September. I thought she was a local who had been injured when the plane crashed into her house, but she seemed shell-shocked and could barely speak. She was staggering around in some colorful rags, and we took her into the improvised field hospital.

We did not have any doctors yet; it was still too soon after taking the territory, so I was the lead medic in charge. We lost Jenkins, the only other medic, so I was working two shifts, tending the wounded as best I could. Ronowski was a good kid with his hands, so I put him to work cleaning and tending lesser injuries while I did what I could for those who looked like they might make it.

The camp was an old church that hadn't taken too many bullets and kept us out of the rain. It rained nearly every day. The Parisians were nice, though, and shared what little food there was. No one knew the strange woman, so we assumed she wandered in from a nearby province.

She was a right pretty thing, blonde, five foot ten, but in her shocked state she seemed diminished and she let me lead her quietly. A French woman, Martinique, likely a Resistance member, helped me tend her, and we put her in one of the back rooms of the church.

After we cleaned her up, we noticed she did not have a scratch on her. Even though her clothing had been destroyed, she was unmarked. We tried every language we could scrounge up in camp, but she did not seem to have any words at all.

We went out to check through the wreckage of the Messerschmitt and marveled at its technology. We took sketches of the design of the vehicle, its engine, and the strange containment devices that were in the bomb bays. Both were broken, but they did not appear to be bombs. Once we were done, we returned to the church. We were expecting to be reinforced.

Later that evening, we made a breakthrough with the blonde haired woman. After saying my name and tapping my chest, she finally seemed to get some sort of recognition. She tapped herself and said "Helga."

After that, she became a member of the camp, helping with anything and everything. She still didn't talk much, but she would smile and occasionally laugh if others were. She followed Martinique around everywhere, and the woman graciously tolerated it.

A week after Helga got there, she came running to me and grabbed me. She tried to draw me with her. I picked up my rifle and told Lewis and Franklin to come with me. We double-timed it to a barn, and what we saw inside stopped us in our tracks.

We opened fire on it without even questioning what it was because it was ripping Martinique's chest open and eating her vitals. At first glance, I would have thought it was an insect except it was the size of a man, and its claws were tearing through Martinique's bones as if they were twigs.

Our bullets bounced off its shell like it were armored. It drew its antenna back and turned around, broke down the wall of the barn, and sped off down the road.

Lewis pulled Helga away from Martinique. He said, "What the hell was that?"

My mind was racing. In this war, I had seen a lot of things, but nothing like that. "I don't know, but when it comes back, I intend to give it a much warmer reception."

"How do you know it's going to come back, Sarge?"

I looked at both of them and then looked down at Martinique's body. "Because we are where the food is. We are the food."

We got the townspeople together and explained to them what happened. They did not believe it at first, until they saw the body, a barn full of holes and no target. I thought until our reinforcements arrived, we would be better off if we stayed closer together, so we took over the small number of homes near the church and established a perimeter and guards. Everyone was issued a weapon and taught how to use it. No one was to go anywhere alone. Helga was the only person who did not have a weapon. She refused to even touch one. After Martinique's death, she would talk to no one, nor stay with anyone but me.

We put a call out on the radio, trying to get an ETA on the backup, but we were told it would be a couple more days, so we would just have to tough it out and make do. We put a machine gun nest in the center of the complex to offer a complete field of fire and had snipers in two of the tallest buildings. Nothing we could do but wait. It didn't take long.

I'm not sure what made me go out that evening, but I felt compelled to walk the perimeter and talk to the men. They were in good spirits and except for the two who had seen it, joked about the idea of a bug hunt. As I was walking back to the church, I had the strangest sensation of being watched. I turned to look down the road, but I couldn't see anything. I slept with a pistol in my hand.

* * *

Around 0400 hours, I heard gunfire and sat up off of the pew I was sleeping on. It was rifle fire, likely one of the patrols. Then I heard the screaming, and I was up and running.

There were only twenty soldiers left, and they were all accounted for, so it was likely one of the locals. We ran out and made it as far as the central machine gun station, when one of the snipers launched a flare. We saw Jean-Claude, one of the cooks, running toward us, and then before he could move more than a dozen steps, he was sliced in half from behind. The insect was back, and he'd brought friends. Dozens of them.

Williams, our church sniper, had already begun firing, and the rest of us bellied up to the sandbags at the machine-gun nest and opened fire with our M1 rifles. Our bullets struck the creatures, but only the machine gun seemed to have the power to bring them down easily.

"Concentrate your fire in pairs. Snipers, cover fire only. Somebody get me a damn grenade!"

"Coming at ya, Sarge."

One of these cockroach looking things made a dash across the courtyard toward the church and began to climb the wall toward the sniper position. We tried to knock it down, but the armor on its back was too strong.

"Petrelli, there's one coming up the wall right at you!"

There was a scream as the monster crested the wall and a single shot.

Petrelli looked over the wall, gave the thumbs up, and kept firing. We held the ground until dawn and had taken no casualties. Or so we thought. When we canvassed the area, there were three spots where human blood had been spilled, but no humans were found. Dozens of the creatures were killed, but they took the bodies, every single one, except for Petrelli's kill. Then the real bad news followed.

"All of the food in the camp is gone, Monsieur. I don't know how they did it, but there is nothing left anywhere. The grounds are picked clean. Only what we had with us in the church is left. They ate every chicken, every goat, every wheel of cheese anywhere." Pierre was beside himself.

Corporal Lewis and Petrelli had taken the body of the monster from the roof and were looking it over for weaknesses. We looked at our ammo and realized we could not have another fire-fight like last night. We simply did not have enough ammo. Only the machine-gun was without danger of running out.

The rest of us were down to fifty or sixty rounds apiece. That would not last long in a sustained firefight.

"Right between the center of the head seems to work best." Petrelli's New York accent was thick and it was something the group used to tease him about. "I guess that works no matter who youse are." They laughed. But real fear crossed all of our faces.

"I think we're going to have to make a stand here inside the church. It's got the strongest walls and the fewest windows. I want you to board up everything you can. Use the pews and anything else you can scavenge from town. They don't seem to like the light, so avoid the shadows. Remember, they got Martinique when she surprised one in the barn."

"Sarge, I have an idea."

"I'm all ears, Lewis."

"Maybe we can lure them where we want them, and use something besides bullets to kill them. We don't have napalm, but we do have gasoline, so we could make Molotov cocktails. They seem as flammable as anything else."

"Fine, get a detail and get on it. But that's a plan that will happen while they are far away and while we still have lots of bullets. No sense having any flaming ones running through the camp."

The next few hours were desperate as we did our best to fortify our positions before nightfall. Helga seemed strange and distracted, but she worked as hard as anyone to prepare before dark.

We were hunkered down with two squads outside on rooftops for sniping and close protection. We were using shotguns inside the church and had built a bunker in the center. Our more powerful weapons were outside to try and kill the larger and more aggressive creatures first. Both groups outside could see and cover each other, and had plenty of flares to get through the night if necessary. We had also stationed lanterns down the road and anywhere else we thought the creatures might come from.

With no more food left in town, we knew they would be coming for us.

They came after midnight. They were not shy. They simply came right down the street, one after another. They came down every street from every direction. We shot flares, we threw Molotovs, we burned them, we shot them, we dropped rocks on them with traps, they fell into pits, and they still kept coming.

We fought them until four in the morning. They would fight, close us, and then retreat, and they did this again and again. Our bullets grew fewer and fewer. We would soon be down to handguns and shotguns.

The two machine-guns were still loaded, but when they started shooting, it took everything we had to keep the enemy off of them. We were down to our last grenades, as well. One or two more waves and we would be fighting them hand to hand.

Sniper Team Alpha died first. The creatures saved the best for last. Some of the damn things could fly. They swooped down and simply picked them off in rapid succession. The men managed to kill three more before being dragged away into the darkness. We provided cover for Sniper Team Bravo, and pulled them into the church. Our last machine-gun was set up in the doorway to the church, which faced the street.

We ran out of bullets at five minutes to five. Our shotguns held them at bay. Lacking range, they made up for it in damage dealing potential. By five thirty we had killed sixty or so, right up to the walls of the church. The waves had stopped. It seemed only the last of the creatures were coming. But these were bigger and tougher and could only be killed with a direct close hit to their chest or face. If you were that close, you were likely to be getting killed. Petrelli bought it like that. Shot one bastard clean in the head and was sliced apart for his troubles. I want to go like that. Clean.

We had put the townspeople behind us in the church with small arms, and they helped when they could. Suddenly the wall behind us exploded and they were being grabbed and dragged away. Helga leaped into the crowd of the creatures and began to bludgeon them with her fists.

Each hit caused a creature to explode into blobs of disgusting flesh. We didn't know what we were seeing, and we didn't care. The last twelve of us rushed up behind her and pointed our shotguns into the masses wherever she wasn't. One of the biggest of the bastards grabbed her with his claws and I expected him to rip her apart like Petrelli. She screamed and the sound literally turned him into jelly before our eyes.

We fought for another hour. The creatures must have been desperate, because they kept coming and fought more savagely, and with greater rage. We lost five more after that. All but seven of the twenty townspeople were lost or missing.

Helga seemed to be slowing down, her strength waning. But she did not stop, and neither did we. We were so focused that I didn't see one coming in behind us. It was a big one. Lewis, having only one grenade left, threw himself onto the creature and the grenade detonated under him, blasting the creature and us. No one saw Helga move. One second she was outside, the next she was in front of me. She took shrapnel that was meant for me.

She fell back into my arms and looked at me. There were shrapnel wounds in her chest, stomach, and legs. I could hear small arms going off behind me, but they gradually stopped. I looked at her and wondered where she came from, who she was, what she was. And none of that mattered. She saved us.

They told me later that she was a prototype of a German super-soldier that was intercepted and shot down near us. The insects were also a weapon, likely on the same craft. It seemed her memory had been lost in the crash, and she only remembered her name. There was some talk of taking her body and dissecting it for science, but no one could find her when they went looking for her later.

When the war ended, we heard of several super-soldiers who had been released into the war, but were all believed to have been destroyed or killed, depending on their nature. I returned home, tired from the war, just wanting to forget it happened. My parents had taken care of my little house, and it was just the way I remembered it. I flopped down onto my bed and remembered Helga.

A wind whipped up, and the tree outside my window shook its leaves. The window opened up and a woman landed gently on my bedroom floor.

"We are no longer enemies. And I have never forgotten your kindness."

I ran to her, and she swept me up in her powerful arms. How does one begin to forget a goddess? I did not even intend to try.

Hornblower

Wilson Tuchman, called "Tuck" by his friends, the few that were still alive, sat at the bus stop and waited early on a Saturday morning. It was a warm spring morning, the kind that made you forget your aches and pains and believe the world was going about its business of being beautiful before the heat of summer baked it away. Tuck was a tall man, easily six feet; his once black wooly hair had faded to a salt and pepper grey. His chocolate brown skin was smooth with a rich wrinkled texture; when he smiled, it smoothed away the age from his face. His eyes were bright and clear, and people found his wise and knowing gaze easy to bear.

Tuck had been in the habit of making the trip to Lowell Park in the mornings on Saturday to improvise with a group of musicians who played outside the city's farmer's market. They were an above average group who played for tips all day. This particular iteration of the group had been playing together for about two years, and Tuck enjoyed playing with them. It was the thing that made his weeks bearable since his Sadie had passed on.

He was determined to stay active and involved in the community. He heard that men did not live long after their wives died, and Tuck, well, he was not quite ready to die just yet. Having lived to be seventy-two, he was in no particular rush to meet his Maker. Sadie, bless her soul, had trained him well, and he could cook, shop, and take reasonably good care of himself. He had to get his hair cut down at the corner shop, something he had not done in years, and he discovered he missed the male company. Sadie cut his hair for thirty years, and he had grown accustomed to her light hand and special pampering. He trimmed his beard, since no one could cut it the way she did, and after the first butchering at the shop, he decided he didn't really like it anyway.

He put on a pair of comfortable slacks and a shirt that didn't bunch up while he played his horn. He wore a pair of comfortable shoes, just in case he had to stand up. Sadie's last gift to him was a pair of gel insoles, and he simply loved them. Until you get to be old, you just don't realize how comfortable feet make such a difference in your day. He wore a light jacket and a sweater; he didn't know what the weather was going to be like, and he wanted the option to put on or take off whatever was necessary to keep playing. Tuck loved to play his horn. In a fire twenty years ago, he had lost his grandfather's horn he played all through the sixties. It was an heirloom 1927 King Liberty Silver, a beautiful trumpet given to him by his grandfather. He did not know how precious it was, but he cared for it meticulously because his grandfather had.

His grandfather had taught him how to take it apart and clean its every spring, valve and chamber. He shined it until it glowed, and when he played it, nothing even came close to it. He played it from 1924 when he started in the Diamond Club, a juke joint in the backwoods of Louisiana. He joined the band there and they traveled up and down the Chitlin Circuit for thirty years, playing jazz of every melody, style, and rhythm. Jazz was in his blood. He even managed to make it to the radio in the fifties and sixties and had half a dozen albums to his name. He married Sadie during that time, and their relationship was turbulent, to say the least. She used to say that he loved his horn more than her. That wasn't true. The horn just didn't nag him as much.

After he lost the Liberty, he was too distraught and realized he simply couldn't bear to play anymore. He had played other trumpets over the years, but they didn't seem to match the soul his grandfather's trumpet had. Tuck sometimes thought his pater's soul had moved into the trumpet when he died, and Tuck was simply a vessel for him to keep playing his music. So in his early fifties, he became a mechanic because he had always been handy with vehicles and repaired them over the years they spent driving the Circuit. He bought a small station and for twenty years made a tidy sum keeping old cars on the road in his corner of Philadelphia. Sadie worked as a librarian and was very, very good with money, so they had more than they needed with his tiny royalty check and her retirement.

After retirement, his was a comfortable life. He even bought a new trumpet, a Jaeger. It was functional, with a clean, bright sound. He had mellowed and decided he would let go of his past, his fame, and his reluctance to play anything other than the Liberty. And just like that, his life was good. He played every day again, and his neighbors loved to hear his muted trumpet whispering tunes of elegance, mystery, sassy tunes of exuberance and a time lost, a time when it was okay to be just a little bit bad. He played at Sadie's funeral. He could not even speak to anyone. So he played. And when he was done, his music reached into them, pulled something out of them, some grief, some sadness, and brought it into the air. It sat alongside them, wept with them, and then that sadness moved on, just like Sadie did. People left the funeral smiling and filled with light.

The bus was late, but only a few minutes, and he stood up to stretch his legs. As it rounded the corner, he found himself eager to get to the park. It had been a long time since he was eager to do anything. The bus pulled alongside and he allowed most people to get on before him to avoid bumping into anyone with his trumpet. He was the last person to get on the bus. As he moved into the bus, several young people decided to get up and pushed their way through the bus. As they came close to him, the largest shoved him into another passenger and snatched the trumpet from his hand. As they ran out the door, it startled a flock of pigeons on the sidewalk; they scattered and took flight.

Tuck fell over a baby carriage and managed to catch himself before falling onto the young mother and her baby. The bus driver tried to run out after the ruffians, but one of them pulled a small firearm and Tuck touched the driver and shook his head. He was not so in love with the Jaeger that anyone should die over it. For a moment, his rage grew, and then he heard the small child laugh and looked at him.

"Are you okay, sir? Do you want to file a report?" It took a second for Tuck to realize the driver was talking to him. "No. There is no point. It's not like I will get my trumpet back any time soon. I am sure the police will have plenty to keep them busy in this town."

"We have them on the bus camera and may be able to get an ID later."

"Okay, you take my address, and if I'm still alive when they find them and my trumpet, I will happily accept it back. I'm certain these good folks have someplace to be, and so do I. I'm fine, my gel insoles broke my fall." Several of the riders laughed, and a young man offered Tuck a seat. Shaken, he accepted and rode to the park in thoughtful contemplation.

When he got to the park, the farmers market was almost finished setting up and the band was tuning their instruments. While he had not been seriously injured, he felt a slight twinge in his hip and knew he would feel it more later.

"Hey, Tuck, where's your horn? You always jam with us. Taking the day off?" Williams was another oldster who played the bass. Tuck liked his easy-going manner.

"No sir, not today it seems. Fate decided that old Jaeger and I needed to go our separate ways."

"What happened?" Jim, the saxophonist, stopped warming up and looked up. He was one of the youngest of the musicians, barely twenty-five, but he had an old jazz and blues soul.

"Some of the urban yout' decided they needed my horn more than I did."

"I can go handle that if you want me to." Jim's veiled threat was easy to recognize, and despite his old musical soul, he had a modern day blood-lust when pushed to it.

"Let it go, I'm going to sit here with you brothers and just relax for a change. I need a break from carrying y'all, anyway." Tuck smiled and Williams shook his head.

The group consisted of a double bass, electric piano, sax, alto sax, bass guitar, drums, a cornet when they were lucky, an occasional French horn, and until today, at least one trumpet. Fortunately, another trumpet showed up, some new cat nobody knew. He wore a tan linen suit with a red shirt underneath the jacket. His clothing looked comfortable and he was relaxed. He was smoking a cigarette while he rested in the back. A cool brother, he introduced himself as Israfel. He was playing some old school horn, something from the thirties from the look of it. Tuck felt a momentary sting of nostalgia for his grandfather's Liberty. The group warmed up, and Tuck sat off to the side and just listened.

They started with 'Fly Me to the Moon,' and Tuck thought of Sadie. It was one of her favorites and they danced their first dance to it. The vocals were taken up by Israfel's horn. He played it, massaged it, and spun into and out of it. The rest of the band played softly, allowing him to carry it. "In other words, please be true; in other words, I love you." A slow piece, the band used it to warm the crowd up, to tease them close. It was a piece most of the older crowd knew, and playing it ensured their approach.

Switching to 'Rhapsody in Blue,' Israfel soared, his trumpet stomped, disappeared and reappeared across the piece. This was a jazz favorite because while the pure song was wonderful, it lent itself to varied improvisations and allowed each instrument a time to shine. Fast and slow, it offered everyone an opportunity to play alone and together. Tuck remembered this piece as one of his favorites, one of the pieces he played on the radio near the end of his career. Many people knew snippets of the song because parts of it were played in cartoons and commercials in the sixties.

Near the end of the piece, Israfel reached into his pocket and pulled out a mouthpiece, still in the wrapper, and flipped it to Tuck. Tuck, surprised, let it hit him in the chest before catching it. Looking quizzically at Israfel, he let the band wrap up the piece. Without a word, Israfel took his mouthpiece out and handed his horn to Tuck. He nodded and Tuck took it. It felt good. It felt like the old Liberty in his hands. Light keys, smooth, he didn't even feel the need to test it. He put his lips to it and felt it become a part of him.

Williams flagged out 'April in Paris,' and Tuck stepped forward. A strong trumpet piece, Tuck tapped his foot and they began. Israfel moved to the back and found a French horn. As they started playing, the crowd began to gather, a gentle breeze swept in, and the vendors in the farmer's market settled into a rhythm. Sales were easier, people were friendlier, a gentle and easy peace took place. Tuck played his heart out, and the crowd grew larger while they played. They worked it, they stretched it, and when they played that last crescendo, Tuck was drenched, sweat flowing easily down his brow. The crowd roared, money was passed forward, and they kept playing. They moved through the century, with hit after hit. The crowd rotated, but never seemed to grow smaller. When they finally stopped to rest, Israfel came to Tuck and clapped him on his back.

"So, do you like it?" pointing to the trumpet.

Tuck, still a little winded, smiled widely, the first real smile in two years, and said, "Oh yes, very much."

Israfel laughed and replied, "In my country, when a man says he likes a thing, we are obliged to give it to him. She is yours, now."

"Oh, no, my brother, I could never take something as sweet as this from you. I have never played anything this good since I lost my grandfather's horn. I know it may be a custom, but I could never deny a man his horn."

"It is also bad manners to refuse the gift, my friend. Please take it. It sings for you. Look at this crowd. They were loving it."

"Your gift humbles me, my brother. How may I be of service to you?" Tuck was moved, and felt a need to reciprocate somehow. What could he offer for such a fine gift?

"The knowledge that you will care for it and love it like I did is enough for me," Israfel replied. He picked up his jacket and slung it over his shoulder. The springtime air had warmed considerably.

"Where are you going? We still have one more set. We need you." Tuck had reached out to touch Israfel's shoulder.

"You don't need me any longer, my friend. You have everything you ever needed right there. Look on the side of the trumpet."

Looking where he expected to find the manufacturer's name, he saw the word "Gabriel" spelled out in ornate and beautiful lettering. Patterns were woven into the metal, subtle, hard to see, but in the midday light, they were unmistakable. This trumpet was a work of art. Then Tuck had a moment, a moment of memory, something he heard as a child. "Isn't Gabriel the name of an Angel?"

"You remember rightly. A seraph who trumpets for the Lord. He smote Soddam and Gamorrah, if my church learning is still righteous. What about him?"

"Am I dead?"

"You look okay to me. You not feeling well?"

"Actually, I feel great, the best I felt in years." Even the twinge in his hip was gone. He stood straighter and taller as if part of him had suddenly returned.

"Then enjoy the horn. My gift to you."

"Am I going to have to play in Heaven or something?"

"No, Heaven is full up on trumpets. Make your magic here, do what you did today anywhere you wish, any time you want. Yours is a special magic no one can give you. You have the magic that comes with time and effort. That word on the horn is a title, given to the one best suited to move the hearts of men. That, my friend, is now you."

"How long can I do this?"

"Until you are ready to pass it to another who loves it like you do. Or until you're ready to lay down your burdens. Whichever comes first. For as long as you love it, play it and share it, you shall know no want, no fear, no longing."

"What about Sadie?"

"She'll abide till you show up. She said you'd take it. She said you loved your horn more than her."

"But never better."

"She knows that, too." Israfel turned and walked away.

Tuck, with a lighter step, slid back up to the group and joined in on 'Birdland.'

Dead Reckoning

I spent my last day railing against the inequalities in my life and how unhappy I was about them. I had given up trying to change anything. It seemed hopeless. I thought everything in the world conspired against me, hated me, despised me, resisted my every attempt to do good in the world. I really did. The funny part was I was right, but for all the wrong reasons. The reason the world seemed to conspire against me was that I was not part of it.

You see, nature and natural things know each other. Kids always kicked me, dogs always bit me, cats always scratched me because I was not part of nature. I was in the world, but not of it. Strangely enough, I tried desperately to be a part of it, got a lot of cat scratches and thorn pricking for my effort.

Now, every breath is something divine, distant, unreachable. The very nature of Nature is beyond me. Supernatural does not mean more than nature, better than nature; its true meaning is outside of nature. I thought I was an outsider before. I had no idea how wrong I was.

That day, that last day, my senses were sharp. Abnormally bright, the early morning light began to fill the sky as I got up to go to work. On any normal day my hearing rivals any dog's in my neighborhood, but today, my ceiling fan was a thunder in my ears, and my burbling meditation fountain in my living room a series of white water rapids. My appetite had been off for a number of days. I failed to keep any food down because the taste of everything was overpowering, nauseating. I had to be starving to seriously consider a meal. I looked at my coffee pot, and the thought of coffee sent me and my empty stomach to the throne to heave.

I turned the television on as I showered, and as soon as I got good and soapy, I realized it was the wrong thing to do. All I heard were the commercials. The shows were mindless, dull, barely worth acknowledging. When the commercials came on with that annoying thirty percent increase in sound levels, they filled the room from corner to corner with their blaring, barely intelligible ranting about how you wanted your credit card to lower your heart rate while making sure you were ready to perform when the time was right.

My scalding shower completed, dressed in the nondescript clothing of the proletariat, I prepared for my descent into my own Dante-like circles of the abyss, the modern transit bus system. Every morning, getting onto the bus was a surreal nightmare. As I crested the stairwell, all the regulars were there.

The woman in the first row who always wore too much makeup, something between a transvestite and a rodeo clown. Loud brassy earrings jangled whenever she moved her head. She was one of those people who needed to move to talk, so she shook her head, gestured religiously, and when she talked, her whole head seemed to vibrate. Her damned earrings drove me insane. Every blessed morning, she never missed a day, never took a day off, and almost never stopped talking to whoever sat next to her.

The last time I saw her was the first time someone, okay, a man, was not sitting next to her. Did I mention she had the biggest pair I ever saw on a woman? And she did not seem to know anything about modesty, so men sat mesmerized at her bounty, happily listening to her annoying stories about her eleven sisters and their seven husbands, two boyfriends and seventeen nieces and nephews, barely making eye contact, and she seemed perfectly comfortable with this.

Riding the bus for these three years, I knew all of their stories. That last morning was the first time she was quietly sitting on the bus. No conversation, so I thought I might escape her earrings. Today she wore a brass set, large tubular bells, a set of morning wind chimes which normally drove me mad. Today their blessed silence was a sign of things to come.

There was Phil, a construction worker whose car had broken down a year ago, and he started taking the bus to work. He said he enjoyed the ride, especially coming home when he was exhausted. He could take a nap and get home refreshed enough to be pleasant to his family. He was a good fellow, strong, a family man, whose work ethic was impeccable. He was another regular who never missed the bus, rain or shine. He was already looking into his lunchbox, hoping to find a breakfast morsel put there by his loving wife. He pulled out a picture of what I think was a green pony, painted by one of his numerous brood; he pointed at it and smiled as I walked by.

Sitting alone as usual, there was the white-shirted salary-man who never spoke to anyone on the bus. He wore his usual blue, brown, or grey suit. My men's magazines indicated he was not quite at the top of the food chain in his company because he still wore suits with color. Once you reach the top, you wore dark grey or black suits with power ties of red, yellow, or blue. He wore a nice pair of walking shoes, shoes that did not seem to get a lot of wear, but were known for being really comfortable when you had to walk or stand. The shoes were on the cusp of high fashion because they chose comfort over good looks, so the running wager was that he did sales and used a company car while he was at work. He was a cold thing, never smiled or acknowledged anyone in the two years we rode the bus together. Everyone avoided him.

There was a cluster of schoolchildren in their early teens, the super-studious kind of students who wore uniforms and studied intensely, even first thing in the morning when I could barely focus my eyes to count currency to put it in the bus meter. I watched them with disguised envy, remembering my days in high school as the most torturous time in my life. I was wrong, of course. My time in college was even worse, and passed even more slowly than high school, with three times as many opportunities for embarrassment and unhappiness. And then there was him.

I had never seen him before. At least that was what I thought at first. Then I had flashes, literal flashes where I remember seeing him out of the corner of my eye for weeks. I would be stopped somewhere in my life and thinking to myself, God, what I would give to be doing something else, something interesting besides monitoring the length of the nose hairs of the waiter making my coffee, knowing the first time one of them fell into someone's coffee, I would never drink there again.

That happened yesterday. The waiter saw the hair and did nothing. Stirred the coffee, closed it, and called out the name. No one saw. How could you miss it? His nose was like a canyon, each hair the size of a desert cactus. As I turned to go out, there he was, sitting in the corner of the coffee shop, sitting there watching me with a knowing smirk on his face, as if he was amused at my disgust, secretly commiserating with me.

Despite his smile, his attention chilled me. His suit was like something from another era, stylish yet not distracting. No one paid him any attention, and truth be told, I could understand. His face was unremarkable, I mean so average you would see him and forget him instantly, if it weren't for that chilling sensation you got when you met his eyes. No normal eyes were these. Your secrets were his, and I found this out the second time I remember meeting him. I was standing in my dentist's office less than five days ago and he was sitting there in a chair waiting to be served in the lobby. He nodded and saluted me with the hat in his lap. Minimalist, but clearly indicating he was acknowledging me before returning to the magazine in his hands; Time, I think it was.

For five minutes, banal music played in the background while he watched me, stared at me. I could feel him, a pressure, and when I looked at him, I felt myself draining away. My strength slipped. I dropped my magazine, a crumpled heap in my open hands, throbbing hot and limp. Who was this man and what did he want?

As I felt myself slipping into darkness, my dentist's attendant touched my shoulder and returned me to the moment. Her scent was intoxicating. Her hand, a heavy slab of porcelain, crushed me under its authoritarian weight, guiding me, pulling me away from Mr. Hat. I kicked the magazine as I staggered into the back. He was gone when I was finished with my root canal.

And now he appeared on my bus in the morning on my way to a job I hated with a passion and had considered bringing a firearm to on more than one occasion. He tapped the seat next to him, and seeing no other free spaces (the bus was more full than normal, with many faces I did not know), I reluctantly sat down next to him, far closer than at any of our previous interactions. He smelled of mint, probably toothpaste, and a pleasant cologne with a smoky, woody texture. His suit smelled new, the fresh scent of clothing right out of the store. Having worked retail, I was intimately familiar with it. But there was something else, something about him that seemed familiar, filial even. But the hair on the back of my neck was standing up, that feeling you get when you see a pit bull and don't see an owner running down the street after it. And it's looking at you. That feeling.

Then I noticed it.

The bus was silent. No hum of barely audible chatter. No roar of the engines. No bragging about a kid's exploits, no quadratic equations, no tubular bells. I looked out the window and I saw it: the accident ahead. The accident was a tractor trailer dragging an active fuel load, which was jack-knifing because an overstressed driver's supply of No-Doze had run out two days ago, but he kept driving, trying to make an incentive paycheck. Now he screamed as his rig flung itself out of control into high-speed, close-quarters, rush hour traffic.

The cars behind him began their inevitable swerving, and a pile-up was imminent. I saw this, out of phase with the world. That chill was strong now. He got up and walked to the front of the bus. I followed him and saw no one moving on the bus. The early morning dawn light was shining over the bridge, making the world appear to be a honeyed amber. Panicked drivers swerved, cursed, splashed inconveniently placed coffee as they tried to rationalize away their crash into the car in front of them.

The fuel truck flipped, torn open, and a hastily flung cigarette, likely thrown when the cars began to crash together, was blown into the gushing fuel, and a fiery geyser turned the honeyed dawn into a ruby ruin. Several drivers considered how much this would drive up their insurance rates. Fortunately for them, they would, in a few seconds, no longer have to worry about such mundane affairs.

Then I realized: neither would I.

Mr. Hat reached out to the driver and calmly placed his hand on his shoulder. He put his hat back on his head and beckoned me to come closer. Time still moved with an amber slowness, and once I reached the front of the bus, things began to move a bit faster

The driver lost control of the bus as he turned to avoid the sudden fireball. The bus jumped the side rail on the bridge and took wing. The strangely suited man turned to me and held out his hand while we slowly pirouetted and plunged toward the river below.

He held up his hand and, not knowing why, but having finally recognized Him, I took his hand, and the bus flew for three seconds.

I counted.

I watched the sunlit sea approach the front window of the bus. The orange flames backlit our plunge, and I heard the screams of the other passengers as they fell in place, screams, rapidly spun prayers, well flung oaths, cursing one bygone deity or another.

The last thing I remember hearing was that well worn verse in my mind, something my mother had taught me right before *she* died.

The Lord is my shepherd, I shall not want.
He maketh me to lie down in green pastures.
He leadeth me beside the still waters.
He restoreth my soul.

And then the water covered me. Cool, soothing blackness.

Death it seemed, was only the beginning of my journey. I was soon to join a fraternity of the Dead. But I vowed to wear better suits.

The Lions of Mexico

Manuel Rivera woke to the blue sky of Pacifico, Chihuahua, feeling old and just a bit tired. He could see the cloudless sky from his bed and was grateful for being able to open his eyes one more day. He kissed his crucifix, and thanked God for his blessing.

His wife Consuela was already up making breakfast. Her breakfast smelled good and he wondered how she managed to sneak out of bed without his noticing again. The late nights watching the garage were taking their toll. He was simply too old to be staying up past ten o'clock anymore.

Sitting up, he got up and shuffled to the cocina to see how breakfast was coming.

"Put some clothes on, Papa, and come eat breakfast."

"Did it happen again?"

"Don't worry about that right now. Eat breakfast, then worry about the garage."

"I don't know what to do, Mama. I was awake until eleven. I was sure they would not be back."

"First things first. You can worry better on a full stomach. Clean up, breakfast will be ready in a few minutes."

Manuel went back upstairs and washed up in the bathroom sink. They broke in again. What did they steal this time? It wasn't like he had a lot. His little garage and storefront had some tools, auto products, snack foods, and assorted items that the neighborhood wanted when they did not want to go to the supermarket further in town. This little store had been part of his retirement plan, and until the young hoodlums started harassing the neighborhood, it was perfect.

Manuel liked being a fixture in the neighborhood. He got to see the children growing up and his son and daughter, while they lived in Pacifico, lived on the other side of town, just far away enough for him and Consuela to feel independent. He was going to solve this problem without his son's help.

After eating breakfast he surveyed the damage. They climbed the fence into the yard and broke the door into the storefront. Once inside they stole some of his tools from the garage and food from the store. And they made such a mess. He spent the better part of an hour cleaning up before opening the garage and storefront for business. Angela arrived to help run the store while he worked in the garage on an old Chevrolet Impala that needed a tune up.

When customers waited, they would sit in the shade inside the garage and read old magazines his son would bring from the library where he worked. His customers appreciated having something to read while they waited. Manuel was not a slow worker. He knew his way around anything with wheels, but sometimes things take as long as they take. He never rushed, and they never hurried him.

When he was finished with the Impala, he looked over at the pile of magazines and saw an issue of National Geographic. Their feature was 'Los Leones del Serengueti.'

"That's what I need. If I had my own lion, no one would ever break in here again." Then he had an idea.

"Mama, does Manuelito still have that ugly yellow dog with the long dirty fur?"

"Si, Papa, but I thought you hated that thing."

"Is he still planning to get rid of it because their apartment is too small?"

"You know little Cielo loves the old thing and has managed to sweet-talk Manuelito into keeping it. I don't know how much longer he will do it, though. He says the apartment smells like a zoo."

* * *

"But Abuelo, why can't he stay here with me?" Cielo was using her best little girl voice. She was determined to keep her dog with her. She did not think being a guard dog was a very dignified job. She was sitting on the edge of her bed with her arms around the neck of a large dirty looking terrier mix with dusty brown fur and mournful brown eyes.

Manuel shuffled uncomfortably. In her room with all of her little girl things, he felt like such an intruder. He was not happy with the situation because it felt a little bit dishonest, but he tried to think of it as a chance to benefit everyone. "Because a dog like him needs more space to move around."

"Abuelo, he is very old, he barely moves at all. He stands around or sleeps almost all the time. He barely even barks." Cielo was describing everything she thought would make him an undesirable guard dog.

"Just the same, I think your father was going to send him away. If we do this, you can come and visit him every weekend."

"Okay, Abuelo, if he will be safe and happy with you. I will come and see you every weekend."

Manuelito stood disapprovingly over this transaction, and Manuel looked sheepishly at his son. "I will take good care of him, mijo."

"Papa, you're scheming again. You know he is too old to make puppies or whatever plan you have up your sleeve."

"When was the last time I had a scheme you didn't approve of?"

"When you bought that garage."

"And you see how well that turned out, right?"

* * *

"Did you get everything, Angela?"

"Si, Don Rivera, but why do you need shears and scissors?"

"We have a project. Put the garage door down. Turn on the fan and open the car door." Out jumped Lupo, happy to be leaving the tiny car.

"He smells terrible."

"I know, he will need a bath before we can make him beautiful. Let's get to work."

Lupo had never been effectively bathed before. He was relatively cooperative, likely because he was too old to put up much resistance. His fur was so tangled it took nearly an hour to comb out all of the matting on his belly and hip areas. Overall, he was quite disheveled, but after three washings and rinsings, he smelled much better, and after his hair had been cleaned and combed, it was surprisingly long.

Looking around the garage, Manuel found that copy of National Geographic and opened to the centerfold of a lion from a side view. Perfect.

Hair flew everywhere and Manuel achieved a state of mania as he cut and shaped the fur on Lupo's neck and feet. Meanwhile, Angela shaved the back end close, and the more she shaved, the more she realized how closely Lupo's coloring did match a lion's.

Manuel clipped and cut around the mane and the feet and the tail of Lupo for another two hours. In another life, Manuel might have been a hair stylist, for when he was done, Lupo was transformed. He was a Mexican lion.

"Angela, put the sign up, just like we talked about, and then meet me in the car."

Manual cleaned up the garage and papered the car windows so the back seat was invisible from the street. He ushered Lupo into the car and Lupo promptly lay down and went immediately to sleep.

As he closed the door, he hears his wife ask the question he was dreading. "Papa, why is the store closed?"

Recovering quickly, he closes the garage door and turns back to his wife. "Uh, we are closing up early. We are going to go and get our new Mexican lion."

"A Mexican lion?"

"Yes, to watch the store. Once we get a Mexican lion, people won't dare try to rob us anymore."

"Papa, is this another one of your schemes?" Mama loved her husband, but at times he would tax the patience of Jesus himself.

Shaking her head, Mama went back into the house and started to make dinner. She heard the car putter off into the distance, and it was gone for about an hour. What was he talking about, Mexican lions? Does Mexico even have lions? When he came back, she was just about finished with dinner. She heard the garage door close and him getting out of the car.

She was finishing washing some salad greens when she heard the kitchen door open. "Papa, did you take Angela home? We have enough dinner for three tonight." She turned to look at him and...

"Ay, Dios!" There was a lion in her kitchen, standing right next to her. She screamed, and Manuel came running into the kitchen.

He saw her back against the wall holding a frying pan. "No, Mama, he's harmless. Scared you, though, didn't he?"

* * *

The next morning, he got up early and brought Lupo into the house. When he went to the storefront, it was as he left it.

Lupo happily ate his breakfast before retiring into the living room to sit on his large soft pillow. He liked it much better than the cold ground at night. Several times people came to visit last night, but they seemed very disturbed by something. No matter. *The food here is much better than with that little girl, and I get to see her as often as I can stand her. Now if only I could get some fur to grow on my rear end, life would be perfect."*

Lupo served as the only living Mexican lion for several years. During that time, burglars refused to come back to Manuel's garage, and when Manuel retired for the second time as a mechanic, he found he made even more money as a pet stylist for the well-to-do in Pacifico, Chichuahua.

Mammon

Mammon ate.

It did not really matter what he was eating, only that he did. Mammon was always eating. No, that's not right. Mammon was always hungry. No amount of eating ever seem to fill him up. He was always engaged in some sort of feasting. And when he was not eating, he was drinking to excess. It didn't matter what he drank, it did not satisfy him. No matter how much money he had, it did not stop him from wanting more.

The greasy spoon, Max and Momma's, was poorly lit with widely spaced bulbs hanging from wires on the ceiling. Each was shrouded with a greasy hood that directed light down onto a hardwood counter top that stretched nearly the length of the restaurant. The table spoke volumes with its well-worn rings where glasses sat, year after year, consolidating moisture on their sides and depositing it on the wood, to sink in, leeching color but adding character.

The floor, barely visible, was a linoleum tiled affair, whose placement was less than perfect, allowing sand and dirt from the men and occasionally women who walked through those doors to accumulate between them, slowly abrading them, smoothing them, establishing permanent tracks through them near the tables bolted to the floor; no amount of mopping ever made them look clean. It was as if the tiles prided themselves on being as dirty as the patrons who frequented this place.

Speaking of the hard men and women who worked at the docks and shipyards nearby, they filled this place wearing their denim jumpsuits or their rubberized suits with their rough hands and rougher manners. They stank of fish, or cargo boxes, or the sweat needed to move that cargo, clean those ships, or weld those seams. This was their place, their watering hole, and had been so for seventy years; it had weathered two depressions, three recessions, five wars, twelve presidents, and had the pictures on the wall to prove it. There were pictures on the wall of Momma and Max through the years, showing up with some of the more colorful visitors, mobsters, mayors, and occasionally, during a voting season, a senator or two. Max and Momma's was an institution, a place venerated by time, outside of time, hence Mammon's visit.

He wore a suit. A simple, but expensive cut, it hung poorly on his lanky frame. His Rolex glimmered sickly in the poor light, as if its quality were diminished by the company he was keeping. That company felt the same way. Most of the dockworkers and the mobsters eating in the back did not appreciate his intrusion into their humble world with his suit-and-tie effete nature. Nowadays, Mammon barely weighed eighty kilos, no matter what he ate. He had to have his clothes tailored for his spare frame, but his recent success in the stock market had provided for all of his needs. This last decade had been very, very good to Mammon.

The owner, Max, was of another mindset completely. He was always happy to see Mammon, who always ate a large meal with a bunch of sides, tipped well, and always came back. Max remembered him when he Mammon was a lot larger, too, needed his own table, and nothing he wore fit very well. In the last ten years after his last heart attack, he had lost weight consistently and was now all skin and bones. Momma thought he had cancer or something. But it certainly did not affect his appetite or his eatin' manners. Lord, that man was a slob while he ate.

Mammon consumed his burger with gusto, its drippings pouring out from between his fingers and staining the sleeves of his very white shirt and expensive jacket. He favored this place over the fast food places in the city proper because so much more flavor oozed from each bite. Lawrence Simmons, the current spiritual residence of Mammon, consumed everything in excess.

Lawrence had always been a glutton, and when Mammon found him, he was the picture of unhealthy living. Greasy food was his preference, and his two heart attacks and triple-bypasses ten years ago showed his dedication to his poor diet. His weight was a massive 250 kilos, just small enough to keep making it out to his favorite fast food restaurants using a heavy cane and a steady gait. Mammon ate at a lot of fast food restaurants in the city proper, and he was well known at all of these places. He noted between bites that almost all of these places had a staff with eating problems. The more he visited those places, the fatter their staff became. It was a slow, but steady process.

In his favorite place only a few blocks from his home, the owner had a massive coronary and had to close the place down. Unfortunate. Hence his trip to Max and Momma's. Mammon tried not to eat here too often because he was, in his own detached way, fond of Momma and Max.

When she came in the door, his mouth was full of food, but the silence that fell over the place was complete. Women stared at her, wondering what she did to keep her figure; men stared, trying to imagine themselves next to that figure. She was wearing a close-fitting motorcycle suit that resembled body armor, and was carrying her helmet under her arm. The armor plates on the suit were painted a dark red and the fabric of the suit was a dark gray. As tightly as her suit clung to her, her hair, night black, glistening, hiding secrets, waved freely about her head and shoulders, smelling of night jasmine and honeysuckle. She strode across the room, her pace unhurried, and several men, who thought they had a chance to woo her, immediately rose and tried to approach. Mammon did not notice her.

The first, a rakishly handsome fellow, slid from his seat with some grace, but as he took his first step, his foot was caught on the edge of one of legs of a chair, and he fell flat on his face. His friends, properly sympathetic and sufficiently lubricated, exploded in gales of laughter, and the rake stood up and redirected himself toward the restroom, with the same aplomb as a cat falling off the sofa asleep and immediately pulling itself together as if nothing happened. He was less than successful.

The second gentleman, seeing the catastrophe of the first, decided he would wait until she was close enough to him that he could simply stand up and make his presence known. Unbeknown to him, there was a life preserver ring on the ceiling as part of the nautical motif of the place. That ring, which had been mounted forty years ago as a part of a boat that was lost during a storm and was the only thing recovered, slipped from its very secure housing and fell onto his plate, splattering him with its contents. She never noticed him.

She continued toward her goal as the tenor of the place returned to normal. Max rushed out to help clean off the poor fellow now covered in his dinner. "Hello, husband." Her voice was a strong yet sultry contralto, the purr of motorcycle with the throttle barely let out.

"Hello, Ty. That's ex-husband. Didn't you get the paperwork?" was Mammon's choked out reply from around his second monster-sized, avocado-bacon burger with grilled onions, cheddar cheese, lettuce, tomatoes, with a fiery, custom horseradish spread; this was one of Momma's finest works, worth every penny. "You getting the checks okay?"

"Yes. Can I sit down?" She did not need his money, but she never sent it back. She knew he said it just to be a bastard.

"Oh, sure. Take a load off. To what do I owe this pleasure?" Mammon noticed she held back what she was really feeling.

"Spare me, you barely know I am here; there is a burger in your hand. Your universe is just that small at the moment."

Ouch. "You know me too well. That's why I married you." Mammon's smile was evident as he remembered the good times they did have all those years ago.

"Funny. I was thinking that was why I divorced you," her tone seemingly playful, suddenly changed and became very low and serious. "I hate to interrupt your recent fascination with food, but I need your help."

Mammon looked at her incredulously while he finished the last of the gastrointestinal delight that was the Belly Buster. He wiped his hands on his napkin, which looked at this point like the victim of a slasher flick, and asked "What kind of trouble could you be in that a convenient accident could not get you out of?"

Mammon remembered how he met her all those years ago in a casino in Vegas, partying, smoking, gambling and winning. She was beautiful then, terribly beautiful, and she used it like a weapon. Men were nothing to her but playthings. Her only real interest was their money. She never gambled with her own money back then.

She was lucky, most of the time. She was also careful with her winning, never too much, never too fast, never too often at the same casino, just enough to stay under the radar, but he was fascinated by her string of "luck" and followed her to three different casinos, before he made his move. Their relationship evolved just like both of their lifestyles, extremely fast, too much partying, too much drinking, and the sex--the sex was outstanding. He wore the skin of a wealthy young aristocrat with time, strength, and virility on his side.

They were married at the El Rancho Vegas in Las Vegas in 1960. The owner of the hotel, suspected of being a mobster and a killer, took a liking to her. He cornered her somewhere and told her it was in her best interest, since he owned El Rancho Vegas, to consider dumping that zero and getting with a hero. She never took threats well. Two hours after they were married, the place accidentally burned to the ground. He was never found. The cause of the fire was never discovered.

It took Mammon another ten years to learn that accidents like that happened to anyone Tyche didn't take a liking to.

At a séance in the seventies Mammon discovered that they were both descended from mythic beings and were lesser powers themselves, hence their attraction to each other, the synergy in their lifestyles, and the effectiveness of their occupational abilities. His psychic abilities were great and he warned them of a coming conflict. They did not take him seriously. He was killed mysteriously before they could learn of their true identities. They forgot about his warning.

The seventies were even more wild than the sixties. Swinging and cocaine were big then, and what they did not spend on sex and coke, they spent on crazy fashion, big hair and bigger sunglasses, crazy bell-bottoms, and the eventual fall of Nehru jackets.

Then the eighties came, and there was so much money to be made, Mammon worked all the time, and as Mammon progressed, so did society and its need for greed. He learned that his power affected humanity at a global level, and the more he wanted, the more they wanted. He simply did not have time for Tyche, and she drowned her sorrows in other men and new designer drugs. They fell out, moved out, cried on the phone, made up, had great sex, got back together, then rinse and repeat. This went on all through the eighties until The War.

They were drafted. Their side lost and Mammon was killed. Until then, they lived their lives in relative unawareness of their true powers and abilities. With his resurrection, his powers and memory returned fully and so did hers. Whatever had bound him, had bound her to him and only a happenstance of fate kept them together all those years.

He could only assume he had been rescued and resurrected by

another Power. He was never clear who saved him without absorbing his aspects. While he did not fear death, dissolution, the loss of self was another thing entirely.

He had hoped to lay low after his rebirth but Tyche's renewed taste for the finest things in life brought her to the attention of Gluttony, a lesser Aspect who wanted to claim Mammon's powers. He was forced to battle Gluttony, who was hoping to expand his dominion into the realm of money. Gluttony lost the conflict, and Mammon was forced to consume him and take his power instead.

Growing more powerful, but was now in dominion over another realm, he became a Glutton as well. He was drawn toward food in ways he had never been before. As Mammon, he was in dominion over Man's obsession with money, now he was in dominion over personal greed and gluttony. It changed him. In his nature, Mammon ate well, the finest foods, no matter their cost; now the Glutton in him would eat anything, anywhere, even out of a garbage can. During the early years of this new power, he simply could not stop eating everything in sight. He burned through body after body, until he got the power under some level of control.

Tyche also left him. Obsessed with the new understanding of her powers, she became a hedonist and a sensationalist, always seeking the next thrill. They fell apart during his eating-from-garbage-cans phase, and when he resurfaced in this body, some ten years ago, she was sickened by him, fat, smelly, and completely disgusting. Tyche had also changed during those years. She learned that while she had amazing abilities and no human could match her in any physical, mental, or emotional contest, she was simply at the lowest level of power among her kind. She chose to return to her life on Earth. In her mind, it was better to slum as a power than to live among gods as a weakling.

"It is the Selig Court," was her whispered reply.

"I can't help you; you know that. Nobody can." The Selig Court was a power in its own right. They were not related to the Aspects, who were their family, or the modern gods, who were offshoots of other godlike beings or demigods. Instead they seemed to descend from the terrible Old Gods, once beings of immense power, until they were thrown down by the angelic White Host in the twelfth century.

The Old Gods were savage and brutal. No one missed them except the Selig Court, a group of humans or near human hybrids blessed with the power of their gods, the magic of their gods, and the tempers of their gods. They were romanticized in much of modern literature as tricksters and incompetents, but they were far more dangerous than that. Any writer who claimed otherwise probably had not met one in the flesh. If he had, he would have learned that the best thing they could do for you was to kill you. Everything else was far worse.

It was probably no accident the White Host nearly destroyed them during the Great Pogrom. Their fall from grace seemed to reduce their power significantly, and they retreated from the world into nearby Shard Realms, harassing humans in the following centuries, bringing plague and the like until the early nineteenth century. They were rarely heard from these days, and in the case of most modern gods, thought to be a myth to frighten children with. Mammon was old enough to remember them and what they were like. He wanted nothing to do with them.

A blind man came through the door with a large service animal and made his way into the restaurant. His service animal, a dog breed of an unknown pedigree, but a bit larger than normal, led him through the restaurant to the back to a table near Mammon and Tyche. He was conservatively dressed, nothing flashy, but nothing that you would remember, either. His look was one to make you forget you ever saw him. Damn.

"They're here," he whispered to Tyche and looked toward the blind man.

He sat.

The blind man ordered his meal and Mammon noticed his smooth and fluid movements, not too conservative, but with no overt flourish. He seemed to use just enough of all types of movement to relay information and expectation, without being too forward or too reticent. His waitress flushed while she took his order, and rushed away without knowing why. Her breath was ragged and she was excited to be serving him. When his food returned, his plate was perfect, and she took great pleasure in describing his food's location on the plate.

Mammon looked at the service dog and noticed how it eyed the waitress hungrily, as if she were an appetizer he could not wait to consume. A slow lavish lick of his tongue across his snout indicated his anticipation. While the dog was licking his lips, his master had slid his hand behind the waitress and was skillfully and discreetly massaging her buttocks. She blushed more, but did not ask him to stop. Tyche looked a bit annoyed. Mammon knew why.

"A one-time friend, perhaps? Jealous much?" he whispered to Tyche.

"Go fuck yourself, Mammon," was her angry reply. But the heavy sighing that followed revealed what she would not say.

After the waitress left, smiling and blushing, the man turned to his meal. Mammon noted that he had not removed his shades, but they did not detract from his appearance. Even in the wan light, he could tell the man was incredibly handsome, with a strong chin, a sharp nose, and slightly pointed ears. His hair was fair, a whitish blond that hung past his neckline in a jagged cut. It did not make him appear foppish; instead, it gave a savage look to his appearance. When you looked at him and his dog, you noticed the similarities to both their hairstyles. Mammon remembered a People magazine article saying that people tended to look like their dogs.

He was widely shouldered, but his clothing belied his bulk, making him appear smaller and less well defined. It was hard to know if it was the clothing or a glamour that aided in that illusion. "Sir, could you be so kind to pass the horseradish? I love a bit of spice on my burger. I can tell that you do, as well. It is easy to recognize a connoisseur like yourself."

Mammon grabbed the cup of horseradish and moved toward the next table. "Here you go, fella. You see pretty well for a blind man."

"Sight obscures, the heart reveals. Take a seat, Great One; eat with me."

"Are you invoking hospitality?"

"For this meal, yes, you and your wife-sister are safe from me and mine," the blind man's voice was like a choir, melodious with choral overtones. He sounded as if he spoke with more than one voice.

No matter what he thought of it, Mammon knew what had to be done; etiquette demanded that he be as polite as his host. "Brother to the Fey, how may I be of service unto thee and thine? My wife and I are at your service," the words fell like ashes from his mouth, dry and bitter. "Whom do I have the pleasure of addressing? What appellation is used to designate your august person?"

"You may call me the Fire Hound of House Caleban," was the quiet reply.

"A noble house, to be sure." House Caleban! What has she done? That is the Royal House Caleban, the current leader of the Selig

Court, led by the insane king Fagan, also known as the Firelord, and his equally insane queen Edana.

"Great One, I am loath to bring such an unseemly matter to your attention."

No, you are not.

Be quiet, Dog.

Do I look like a dog to you?

As a matter of fact, yes. Now silence.

Yes, my dark master. I hunger.

Soon, my pet; you will eat soon.

"There is a debt owed to my house by your wife, the Lady Tyche." The seemingly blind man reached down to his hamburger, slathered it with horseradish, and put it under the table. His hand came back empty in a matter of seconds. Mammon never saw the animal move.

Oh, Tyche, what did you do? Did you break this man's heart? Did you steal from him? What would you have done to owe the Selig anything? What can I do? Mammon began to sweat, not from eating, but from the fear of a conflict with the Selig. "Can I ask what offense she has given?" Propriety indicated that he should not ask, that he should offer restitution, but he wanted to know what happened, and he could not ask her now.

The man leaned forward and turned his face toward Mammon. "She wagered in a Selig Court and tried to cheat a member of the royal family." The venom was unmistakable. "The Old Ones demand recompense in blood and souls." For the first time since he arrived, he appeared menacing, a creature of the Fey, hunters of Men.

"What price would you ask?" Mammon knew this was a risk. Allowing them to name the recompense meant they could ask for anything they deemed reasonable. "I know the games of the Selig Court, and they are often filled with mischief and chicanery."

"Well said, Great One."

Indeed, I think he is calling your bluff, oh master.

Silence, Dog. He will meet my price.

How do you know?

He values little in the world, but we know that this woman still means something to him. He will pay.

Why him, master?

Of all the Great Ones, he has the most to lose and the least retinue protecting him. He is practically human. Using him, we will kill them all!

"When she came to the Court, she claimed to understand our relationship. She became my Consort, and she said that she would abide by our rules. She used her power in my house and would alter our games of chance. I lost valued retainers, their lives forfeit by her manipulations. I invoke blood and souls." His calm façade had begun to crack. His mellifluous voice trembled with intensity.

Inwardly Mammon laughed. Tyche had that effect on Men, no matter who or where they were. "As you know, Brother to the Fey, I have no kingdom to speak of, nor retainers to give unto to thee for service. You have no use of filthy lucre, for which I am known best, so I would ask how you would expect payment?"

"In souls, of course." His voice was low and threatening, and it pissed Mammon off. "And we expect them now."

Tyche was aghast. "What are you expecting him to do, make souls for you?"

"His method of payment matters not, only that he pay now. We will accept Essence as an alternative if payment in souls cannot be done."

Mammon was enraged. Their game was clear now. This was flat out extortion. Much of the magic made by the Fey in our world was illusion. Illusion normally cannot hurt you, but if you are unable to see through that illusion, it could be fatal. With the addition of Essence, they were able to make permanent and real magic, events that affect the real world, no matter where they were, no matter what the laws of physics say. Tyche would not know this; it was before her time and beyond her power. She could not give Essence, only use it. Essence was the true currency of the Aspects and the Gods. With enough of it, you could bend the world to your whim.

He balks.

He knows the laws, he will pay. There is still the incentive...

As Mammon seethed, the rest of the room grew more focused on their food. Conversation stopped, concentration increased, each mouthful a tiny bit of worship. They consumed their food with a gusto reserved for the starving, and they ordered more. Mammon did not speak, and the Fey did not rush him. Food was being prepared faster and faster, and the patrons ate more and more. The kitchen ran out of food thirty minutes later. They did not stop when the food ran out. They licked their plates and clamored for more. They ordered coffee and desserts, since they were already prepared on the counter as a variety of cakes and pies. Pies wedges flew around the room like tiny shuttlecraft, docking with any mouth in sight. Mammon closed his eyes, his rage increasing.

Tyche looked away from both of them, ashamed. *I will find a way to make you pay for this; I don't care who you are the son of, or what land you are the prince of. No one owns me and no one saves me. This is the last debt of mine my husband will ever have to pay.*

When the cakes and pies were done and the coffee and tea were gone, the patrons started in on each other. There were no screams. Each consumed his neighbor with the same gusto he had the pie a moment before. There was ripping and tearing of flesh. Blood flowed. Each customer seemed rapt within an ecstasy of consumption. Madness glittered in every eye, but no one stopped. Entrails were rent from bellies. They filled themselves until they were completely gorged. In fifteen minutes, there was no movement in the restaurant.

The dog watched and whimpered.

"I do not know you, Brother, and I do not like you. I do not care that you come from the mightiest family amongst your kind. Your payment is complete. Never darken my doorway again." Mammon held out a coin, apparently made of a dark metal. "Take it and go." He slammed the coin on the table, and when he did, the bodies in the room writhed one last time, released a gasp, a sound so fell, so saddening, that for a moment, even the Fey was moved; his hound turned over on its side as if it had been struck by a club. Then the bodies fell onto the floor and died. A soundless echo swept through the room and centered on the silver coin. It burned with a black light.

'Ware milord, that is bloodmetal!

"Great One, you realize that coin is iron." The prince raised an eyebrow but remained otherwise motionless.

"How you get it home is your business. You have been paid. Our conversation is at an end." Mammon stood up and looked around. His power pulsed within him. He was looking at the wall of photographs of different patrons through the years. Striding to the far wall, he pulled the picture of Lawrence Simmons, Max, and Momma from the wall. He stared down at the picture, lost in that moment of time. The smell of gas began to permeate the restaurant.

Tyche touched his hand, and when she did, she felt the Hunger, the unrelenting hunger that crashed through his being every moment of the day, a hunger so powerful you would eat out of a garbage can, you would eat filth off the street, you would chew off your own arm to make it stop. She gasped, but held on. "We have to go, Mammon. Now."

A fire started in the kitchen as the blind man, now wearing black gloves, picked up his walking stick, grabbed the coin, and kicked his dog.

What was that for?

Because I can. It burns me. I will make him pay.

"Great One, before you leave, my mother the Queen said that you would take this from her, that she owed you a favor she was prepared to repay. But to do so, you would have to travel to Avalon. Take this favor, so that you will know no obstacles on your road to Caer Caleban."

"Tell your queen to go fuck herself."

"She said you might say that. She said to tell you that the High Queen of Babylon, Tiamat is awake. She said that would make you come to her."

"Tell your Highness that the Queen of Babylon is long banished and long dead; she died when Babylon died. I know. I was there. And good riddance to her."

The Prince of Caleban threw the favor at Mammon who had turned his back and begun walking toward the door as the fire spread. At the last second, it was Tyche who snatched the favor from the air, inches from Mammon's head. They were standing in the doorway. When he touched it, the magic was released.

The restaurant exploded. Mammon awoke in the street with Tyche unconscious near him. The restaurant was in flames and completely unrecognizable. The prince was also gone.

He had not felt the touch of that magic in five thousand years. Such a tiny drop, too, smaller than the head of a pin, but its destructive power was unforgettable. The daughter of the Aspect of Destruction, creator of earthquakes, the summoner of volcanoes, the master of fires and the destroyer of cities, mother to monsters, and killer of gods. The signature was fading but unmistakable and impossible: Tiamat lived.

Mammon got up, picked up his photo, knocked the broken glass out of the frame, picked up a half eaten donut from the curb, threw Tyche over his shoulder, and began to contemplate a visit to the Queen while he pondered the unthinkable.

Cats Versus Evil

"Is anybody going to get that?" Being the farthest away, I thought it pertinent that I ask, just in case one of the people closer to it might want to do something about it.

"Get what? I don't see anything. Don't you see I am sleeping?"

No such luck. Perhaps the other one will do better.

"You know, you would see a lot better if your eyes were open. Try it."

Strike two. Now let's listen for his excuse...

"I got the last evil. I have no intention of getting down from this tree. Besides it's so small, surely he can manage it on his own."

"Are we betting the farm on that?" I tried to be reasonable as I got up to go and squish the latest evil to make its way into the house. I could see it, cloaked around the spider, draped through with the menace we were sent here to face.

Don't mind me. I am just walking here. Look, I stopped. Don't want anything. Just moseying along. The spider mumbles to itself as it tries to make it through the room full of cats. The contract it picked up on its way here said it would be a cakewalk.

Get in, sting the man, drop the venom pack laced with methicillin-resistant staphylococcus aureus, (I simply love how that sounds, almost as

*sexy as latrovenom, the sexiest poison this side of a black widow) and we are
outta here. Nobody said anything about cats, a room full of cats, three cats,
twelve legs, forty pounds of attitude, and no place decent for a spider to get a
bite on them.*

"Okay, I'll get it. Then I am going on patrol. This is the third
one this week."

"Whatever. Bring me something back."

"I don't think so, Big Boy. If there is anything to be found, I
will be eating it all. I won't be bringing anything back."

*I am almost to the door. I am going to be able to squeeze under it,
and I will be in the clear. Cats can't go under doors. Uh-oh, that thump. That
can only mean one thing. Going to have to RUN! I am lightning-streaking
through the night. I am a hurricane wind whipping through trees. I am the
living embodiment of speed, move left, now right, stop. Dodge. Running like
crazy, jump left, missed me. Run again. Oh damn, what is this? A carpet!
It's plush. Speed is slowed to a crawl. Navigating the strings. Stop. He's
right there. His breath is Death, the destroyer of worlds. Being still.*

I know I saw it moving toward the door. If he gets under it,
the Man will have to handle it himself. Stop, lock the vision, blur for
motion, there. I've got him, bounding. He is in the carpet. Hold still.

*I know he is there. I can see him, his cold eyes staring down at
me, his stilled breath. He is using that cat thing, where they stare you into
moving. Well, I won't do it. I will stand right here. I will teach him to mess
with me. I will be still. I will not move.*

Where is it? I know it's here. Focus on the motion, lock on to
the slightest of motions. Open the pupils, let in every scrap of light.
Slow down time. Raise the paw, slowly, ever so slowly. Don't let him
see it.

*He's staring right at me. Does he see me? He's looking right at me.
He's trying to trick me into moving by pretending he can't see me. I'm on to
him. Frozen in time. He, hey, what's that slow moving shadow? He can see
me. I am not going out like this. I will make a run for it. I'm young, I'm fast,
I have my whole life ahead of me. I am like lightning...*

"I don't know where he is. I guess I am going to have to call
this one off." Movement, pounce, pounce, flip, flip. Snap. "Mmmm,
chewy. You two suck. It's a wonder anything gets done around here."

"And you are so much better than we are..."

"Protect the Man, that is the mission. Is there a part of that statement you don't understand? If you can't do it because we have a metaphysical obligation placed upon us by higher powers, surely you can do it because he feeds you."

At the mention of feeds, Big Boy's ears pop up from their flattened I'm-ignoring-your-rantings state to alert attention. "Go on."

"What? You need more than that? You like to eat, he feeds you. If something happens to him, who knows what will become of us? You know She does not like us. She tolerates us for him."

"Relax, Sleek-black, you are too intense. We have to just embrace the coolness of life."

"Look, Furball, all of us aren't descended from a bunch of lazy forest-dwelling, long-haired hippies who have been inbred to maintain their flowing locks at the expense of having an IQ in the double-digits."

"Harsh, man. True, but harsh." Furball curled back up and proceeded to wrap his exceedingly long and amazingly fluffy tail around his supine and curled up body, displaying the aloof I-can't-hear-you posture.

There is a skittering sound in the kitchen, giant claws skittering across a too clean floor. "Hello, Cats."

Ugh, just what I don't want. A conversation with enthusiasm-mania.

"Heard there was some evil here. I am ready to fight. Just show me where it is. I am all over it. I will..."

"Stop. We appreciate your eagerness to help fight evil, but, well you're a Dog and dogs were not meant to fight Evil. You're for tackling the mundane issues of life, burglars, dropped broccoli, licking and adoration of the Man and his Mrs. That is your lot in life. Lowly that it may be."

Sleek-black stood up and began to pace as if he were a professor in a classroom with particularly not-bright students. His tail waved like a baton, emphasizing certain words. "The fighting of Evil," he began with a particular stress on the word evil, strongly delineating the two syllables, 'E-vielll,' "the supernatural menaces that lurk in the dark, things that go bump in the night (when it's not us), those things that are just a step away from conquering the world every day. That is the role of the Cat." With the word "cat," his tail stood straight out with only the tip pointing at himself.

"Isis gave it to us, and we are doomed to fight Evil, not the mundane evil, with the little E, but real Evil, the essence of Unlife, the Menace that could destroy the world, the ultimate antithesis of Good, until the end of the world or until we destroy all the Evil left on Earth. So no, to answer your question, we cannot go out and fight evil today. You are ill equipped to do so, lacking the basic criteria required to even acknowledge evil, or for that matter, even see it."

Big Boy looked up; his shining blue eyes, half lidded, followed. "Yeah, what he said." He put his head on his paws as he observed the Labrador from high in the main cat tree.

Not to be deterred, Zeus, the dog in question, asked, "What if you are attacked by a burglar or some other, what's that word, uh, mundane evil? Could I help then?"

Well, technically that was a right good question, and I had to think about it for a moment. What did we do when confronted by mundane evil? We ran away, it wasn't our job. "Not saying you have a point or anything, but perhaps we could go out together and improve our chances. You can fight evil, and I will destroy E-veill." Not acknowledging anything about his going out with the dog, or having a dog along on the quest to destroy Evil, Sleek-black walked past Furball, who was doing as his name suggested, and whacked him in passing.

"What?"

"Cat says what?" Zeus muttered under his breath.

"What?" Furball muttered again before drifting back into sleep.

"Open that gate, Zeus."

"Okay, Cat."

"You may address me as Sleek-black."

"When we first met, you told me I was never to call you by name."

"And you still aren't. That is my appellation. My call sign as it were to the world of Evil. If you are going to be fighting Evil with me, you will need an appellation so that Evil will know you are coming and fear you."

"Big Dog."

Sigh. "Good enough. Close the door behind you."

PART TWO:

THE TIME OF TROUBLES

"Watching these recordings I was amazed by the level of avarice that each of these groups, organizations or people displayed. Their goal in attempting to have it all put the entire species at risk, more than once.

As an agent of the Empire, the idea of greed is simply not understood, we understand wealth and affluence, that a person should be rewarded for a creation of novelty or utility. But there is a limit.

Greed: the purposeful exploitation of others is a crime against intelligent commerce. Humanity, as a species, at this time was a failure because it was willing to risk all that it had, so that a single individual might have it all."

--Pele Mokoto

The Award Goes To

Jack Dempsey was the last of the great actors of 2026. His dashing smile and trademark Kung Fu made him the action hero other actors wanted to be for more than a decade. His star as an action hero finally lost its luster in the last series of movies he made, *Planet Raiders III: The Unforsaken*. The movie, while grossing well, barely covered the production costs, and the injuries incurred by Jack's drinking problem caused his agent and the company Screen Brothers to finally drop his contract.

"We love you, Jack, but we're gonna have to let you go. There is a new wind blowing and it's AI-CGI," his agent Florence Butterman told him over the vidcam. He was sitting in his Malibu home drinking his morning Mai Tai and nursing yesterday's hangover.

"You are not serious. That stuff they do with computers and factors?" Demsey had a bit of a slur going already. Florence just grimaced and tried to ignore it. "Damn fake actors..."

"They are not fake actors. They are based on real people who used to be actors. Many of the screen tests have been quite favorable and several hundred movies were released straight to the 'Net from Nollywood and Ballywood. If we want to keep up we have to do our part to stay with the times. Those Nigerians are eating our lunch in southern Africa and they have already expanded into the South American markets. I'm sorry, Jack, the margins are just too tight for living actors." Florence looked down at her watch.

"What, you got someplace to be? You too busy for the man who made you rich? Everything you have in that house, I bought you, Florence. How can you be thinking about turning your back on me? What about helping me out? Can you farm me out to one of your friends over at Light Industrial Films? I heard through the grapevine they are still planning on making movies with real actors." Jack downed the rest of his drink and nodded to his butler to bring him another one. The butler winced and then moved on reluctantly to bring another. There was, however, no reason to rush.

"Look, Jack, I am not blowing you off. I will be putting in a word for you, but I wouldn't get my hopes up with Light Industrial Films. They're still going to be making movies with actors, but they are going to be working in the mountains of Tibet, telling the stories of the remaining survivors of the Great Purge of Tibet in 2016. That's going to be done on location with local actors. I might be able to get you a role on the Chinese side as a consultant or as a white who worked as a servant to the Chinese."

"A slave? That is the best hope you can give me? A slave in a Chinese melodrama? You got to be kidding me. You know what, Florence? I don't want your goddamn pity. I don't need you. I am Jack fucking Dempsey, the best thing to happen to Hollywood since Clint Eastwood. I'll be all right." Jack stood up and pointed at the monitor. "When I make my comeback, you remember it was me who told you it would happen."

Having stood up too quickly after having twelve Mai Tais before breakfast, Jack Dempsey fell to the floor unconscious. Florence Butterman shook her head, watched the butler throw back the Mai Tai and signed off. She didn't think about Jack Dempsey again until the Academy Awards mentioned his name seven years later.

"And the nominations for Best Actor in a Science Fiction Film are: Kren Davis in *Sundiver's Six*, Kazuo Koke in *Inner Space*, and Jack Dempsey in *Planet Raiders: Neutron Star*. No, no, folks, I'm just kidding. You know scifi hasn't paid an actor in years. The award will go to the company that has created the most awesome representation of these amazing actors in their AI-CGI movies created completely on computer. I mean, can anyone remember the last time anyone saw that drunken bum, Jack Dempsey?"

The theater explodes in laughter, that long mean laughter when you are talking about someone behind his back. The laughter that comes from an uncomfortable position that you know you might find yourself in, akin to being in the bathroom without toilet paper. The doors fly open from the side of the stage and Jack Dempsey staggers onto the stage. A security guard with a swollen eye tries to stop him and is returned back stage with a sound kick.

"How's that?" was picked up from the mikes all over the stage. "Real enough for you? You might want to put some ice on that. So how is everybody? Go on, open that envelope. No, let me." Jack snatches the envelope from the comedian who stands shocked and quiet on the stage.

"The Award for Best Actor in a Science Fiction Film goes to... Factor Jack Dempsey. Factor Jack Dempsey can't be here to get his award, cause he was made on a damn computer, so Jack Dempsey is going to take that award for him." The young woman who carried out the statuette hands it to Jack and scurries off the stage.

The director continues to move the cameras around and film everything as if this was expected. "Since I am here to take my award from my factor, yes, FAKE ACTOR, I think I should say a few words. All you people sitting out there laughing at me, thinking you're better than me and don't have to worry about this because you can really act; you can kiss my ass." A collective gasp sweeps the room.

Jack reaches into his jacket and pulls out a flask, takes a hit and continues. "Once upon a time, I was just like you, thought I was something, on the top of my game and nothing could ever touch me. I had a great time, spent my money, partied all day and all night. I made twenty movies in my career and most sucked. I know that, now. I watched them when I was living in the streets, sitting outside of Electronic Huts playing my movies while I panhandled."

Jack looked down and pauses for a second. "I realized I got paid because it was what people wanted to see, not because I was any good. I got ahead of myself and didn't pay attention when I needed to. I didn't see the world changing around me. I signed contracts without reading them. And all of you did too. Because if you hadn't, you wouldn't be sitting here today."

Three security guards came to the edge of the stage and hesitantly began to make their approach. None of them were in a hurry to tackle Jack Dempsey because while he may have been an actor, he did his own martial arts in the movies and those were not stunts. He sent many a stunt double went to the hospital and the tabloids loved talking about it. He waved at them and made the sign for two minutes, and they retreated to the edge of the stage.

"I just wanted to say to Florence Butterman, I'm sorry I didn't listen to you when you told me to read everything. You told me that the industry would take advantage of my stupidity. You see, I don't have anyone to blame about Factor Jack Dempsey. In my contracts, I made it possible for him to exist. In my contracts, I signed away my likeness to be used in any kind of AI-CGI based movie for the next twenty years. And they don't have to pay me squat because I didn't read the contract well enough." His voice was bitter and sharp.

"But the best part is that I had time on my hands and more than a few favors. I know that almost none of you read your contracts, either. So when you lose your mind, or piss someone off, or when they get tired of you getting old or weak or crotchety, they'll replace you with a factor, too. So, you guys enjoy your awards. One day there won't be anyone in the theater to accept one, unless they can teach a computer to walk, too. Y'all have a good night. Come on, boys, I haven't got all night."

It took twenty security guards to drag Jack Dempsey was off stage. The Academy Awards hadn't had ratings like these in years.

Cheaper Labor

I was late for my sensitivity training class, two weeks after I joined a new company.

I went to Human Resources to complain about the guy in the next cubicle who, even though he had been at the company for a while, still had not grasped the idea of personal hygiene, and was really quite rank with a strong and unpalatable odor. It got so bad one day, I had to sneak into the AC closet and turn off the air conditioning because the vent blew the stench from his cube into mine. The guy always seemed to put in a twelve to fourteen hour day, so there were no complaints about his work.

When I went to HR and complained, I was told that I was insensitive to Tod's special needs and that he had a medical accommodation for his issues. So I was sent to a special sensitivity training course in order to improve my awareness of his situation. The only good part of that was that I would get to see that gorgeous redhead who works at the front desk, Penny.

"Hey, Penny, which way to the sensitivity training?" I was trying to sound cool and only semi-interested. The truth was, I had been dreaming about this girl since I got here. I had only seen her once or twice, but her flame-red hair, ample bosom, and well-dressed derrière were hard to miss. Only a dead man wouldn't find her interesting.

"Hey, Dave. It's down the hall, turn left, second door on the right. I like your tie; something new?" she inquired.

She noticed! "Yes, it is; my nephew gave it to me as a graduation gift a few months ago, but I wanted to save it for a rainy day. I'm going to this class after only a month of working here, so I guess this will do."

"You look great, don't worry about it. There's been a lot of training going on here with the recent acquisition. I am sure it's not a problem. They say this position has gone empty a couple of times a month, as they hire new girls for positions upstairs. I am hoping to graduate to one of those jobs, too."

As I listened, I was simply lost in her shiny green eyes, and I could barely tear myself away from her lips.

"Dave? Dave, you're gonna be late."

"Right, right, thanks. I'll talk to you later," I stammered and ran off.

When I got to the classroom, I walked in and noticed the room was lit with a bright green glow from the ceiling instead of the florescent lighting used in most of the company.

"Glad you could make it, Dave. You're the last one, today." The speaker was a tall, squarely built black man with a set of thick but well groomed dreadlocks. His face was sharp and angular, and he had a penetrating stare that fixed on me for a long second. Then he lidded his eyes like a serpent might, and he came to meet me at the door and shook my hand. He smelled of cinnamon and other spices, like a pumpkin pie.

The smell made me want to sneeze, and before I knew what happened, I turned away, covered my nose and sneezed, really hard. He had not let go of my hand yet, and when I sneezed, his grip on me tightened, and he breathed out a subtle, whispering sigh. He then let my hand go and turned back toward the room.

The light in the room, which at first seemed a little too green and a little too bright, seemed less of a problem after I opened my eyes, and I sat down to read through the boring pamphlets about social tolerance and cultural acceptance. The speaker, Dr. Mbenga, seemed to be a decent fellow, but his accent was so thick sometimes I could barely understand him. This first day, the training was done in the evening, and after two hours, we were allowed to go home. He mentioned we would have some exercises during the next two days, and the last day was an all day session.

When I left, Penny was already gone, but the smell of her perfume lingered and stood out over the BO of whichever of my unwashed colleagues left after she did.

When I got home, my cat and dog were thrilled to see me, and after taking Max my German shepherd for a walk, Mini my Maine Coon curled up in my lap for another great evening of TV dinners and Law and Order. I was kind of peckish, though, and had another TV dinner and a pint of Ben and Jerry's afterward. Before I went to sleep, I saw a stock report on the news about a relatively new company providing green lighting to businesses. This new lighting could store energy from the sun and transmit it inside of buildings, for no costs. Rancol Incorporated had just split its stock, making its shareholders even richer. The only drawback was the slightly greenish tint that workers said they hardly noticed after a time. The age of florescent light appeared to be at an end. I thought I should get some stock in this company. I would call my broker in the morning.

My sleep was rough and uneven. I had the strangest dreams, as well. Something to do with eating some food that I was not particularly fond of, but my father kept telling me to eat it. He was the law when I was a kid, so eat it I did. I woke in a cold sweat, but a hot shower fixed that. I took Max for his morning walk, but he seemed skittish and unhappy, and when I came back and filled Mini's dish, she did not come running. I figured she was under the bed or hiding in a closet, as is her habit some mornings. Max looked at me strangely, but I didn't have time to deal with his issues.

I have to tell you, when I took a load off this morning, the bathroom reeked to high heaven. I was sure I saw two sparrows outside my bathroom window fall over dead from the smell. But I felt terrible, cramping, dizzy and lightheaded. I just made sure to leave that bathroom fan on all day.

The next day of sensitivity training had half as many people as the day before. We started with ten and were down to five. When I asked what happened to the others, Dr. Mbenga gave me some smooth and plausible sounding answer, and though I thought I wanted to argue, once he said it, the urge to argue passed. Today, I had less difficulty understanding him; he seemed to be making a greater effort to enunciate. Perhaps someone had talked to HR and told him to speak slower and more clearly. I was bored out of my mind by lunch, and though we were told these exercises were important, I could barely see why. He drew these formulas on the board, something about statistical variability and cultural dispersion on the planet. Lunch could not come soon enough.

"Hi, Penny," I said, so happy to be anywhere but in that room.

"Hi, Dave," was her morose reply.

"What's the matter?" My curiosity overcame my good sense.

"I am getting a transfer tomorrow. I will be going upstairs."

"Uh, I thought you'd be happy. Isn't that what you wanted?"

"Yes, but I..." she stuttered. "I was hoping I would get to see you before I went upstairs. They said I would be leaving here first thing in the morning, so I have to pack up this afternoon."

"Do you want to have lunch?"

"Yes," was her timid reply. But I was on top of the world.

"Let me do one more thing. See that exec over there, the one with the red tie clip? I was typing something for him, and I want to make sure he gets it."

As the executive was moving down the hallway, most of the workers shied away from him, making every effort not to look at him, and shuffled off as quickly as possible. Penny handed him the sheaf of papers, and he gave her a completely lecherous stare. Sensitivity training? Here is a guy needed to attend class. As he grew closer, I felt a bit sick, but Penny ran ahead of him and grabbed my arm on the way out. Whenever I tried to focus on him, all I could see was his ugly power tie.

Needless to say, lunch was great. I didn't have much of an appetite, but she smelled so good, I really didn't care about the food. As a matter of fact, the place kind of made me nauseous, so I couldn't wait to leave. I put it off to a bug or something I might be catching.

Getting back to the office, she ran back to her desk, but she gave me a hug and a peck on the cheek. Needless to say, I got wood. I had grown accustomed to the green light, and was adjusting my briefcase in front of me so I could sit down. There was more boring lecturing around social sensitivity to the disabled, but I was listening more intently to Dr. Mbenga's voice. There was a transcendental quality to it, as if he was speaking directly to my soul. While what he was talking about had no substance, or perhaps I just didn't give a damn, the sound of it moved me, choked me up, and every word was sheer rapture. The afternoon sped by.

Penny was gone again when I was leaving, but it was less traumatizing than yesterday. I had been able to spend a whole hour with her at lunch. Magnificent. I had to get something to eat on the way home, and I stopped in this dive, a place I normally can't even stand the smell of, but I was just so damn hungry. I don't remember anything about the food other than the quantity of it. It seemed as if I couldn't get enough. There was something on the news about some outbreak, probably a flu or something. I couldn't concentrate on it, so I quickly finished and rushed home.

When I got there, Max went positively ballistic. It took me twenty minutes to calm him down enough to get him on his leash. The whole time he pulled at the leash as if he were trying to get away. Right before we were going to go back inside, he stopped pulling for a second, and I took my eye off of him. In that moment, he bit my hand and ran away, faster than I had ever seen him run. I considered giving chase, and then I realized he was a dog, and I was never going to catch him. I went in and bandaged my hand. Strangely enough, though the initial bite was painful, the alcohol I poured directly into the wound didn't bother me at all. WebMD said I should see a doctor in case of rabies, but I figured since Max was my dog, it could wait until tomorrow after work. I ate the rest of the TV dinners in my fridge, and then I went to bed exhausted.

The next morning I felt positively awful. I was sluggish and sick and thought I might be hung over, until I remembered I hadn't had a drop to drink. Then I thought, "It's that flu." Suddenly I was overcome with the urge to vomit, and before I could take a step, I did. Everywhere. It seemed it would never stop, but finally it did. I went to the phone to call in and tell them I wasn't coming to work, but they put me on hold.

Dr. Mbenga's voice cut through the fog and fuzz in my head, and I heard him clear as day after a six month Alaskan night. "Clean up dat mess, take a shower, put on some clean clothes, and bring your gym bag. Get to work."

And just like that, I was able to clean up the vomit, shine the floors, iron a shirt and slacks, pack a gym bag, and head off to work in record time. But halfway to work, the energy faded, and I felt myself slowing down. Puking up one's guts is hard work, so maybe that was why I was suddenly wasted. But I figured I was feeling better because I was suddenly hungry. Normally, riding the subway was a total appetite killer, the crowds, the noise, the stench, but today all I could smell was pork chops. My stop came, and I got off the train and went upstairs into our office building. I kept smelling pork chops all the way into the building.

When I got upstairs to the meeting hall, the good doctor was escorting me to a smaller conference room on the same floor. Penny was nowhere to be found. I missed her already. He took me into the conference room and sat me down. "Wait here, someone will be here shortly." His voice, like a heavenly choir, reverberated within me, and

I could do nothing but obey. I sat.

Hours passed, each one more excruciating than the last. I looked up and noticed the Rancol light was on, and it had been very bright for hours, but as the light went down, the hunger decreased. No, the hunger pain decreased; the hunger remained. After seven hours, I paced and circled the room. The door was locked and no one answered when I shouted. I eventually screamed myself nearly hoarse. I sat down in a corner and waited. Then I heard the click of a key and a searing bright light came into the room, and a terrible wave of nausea followed. In the silhouette of light was a female shape, but it was a man I heard.

"Wait here, Penny," the voice was the executive she was talking to yesterday, and the light, that terrible light. I had to shield my eyes from the burning light that came from his tie clip. I wanted desperately to claw my way through the wall to escape. It was a fire on my skin, a pain that tore through me without relief. When he left, the hunger returned with alacrity.

"It stinks in here," was her reply.

She was pushed into the room, and the door closed behind her. With the lights out and the terrible glare from his tie-clip gone, I could almost think again. But I was hungry, maddeningly hungry, crazed with hunger. Pork, pork, pork, it's all I could think about. Make it stop, make it stop, make it stop. Penny heard me groan, and came toward me. Suddenly, I knew what would make the hunger stop.

"Dave, is that you?"

"Yes, Penny. And you smell so, so... good."

A Cappuccino with Charon

I was sitting in my favorite coffee shop, dodging my workplace, when I saw Him come in. I wasn't quite sure what I was seeing at first, because, well, this is San Francisco, and you're liable to see almost anything here. He was wearing the equivalent of a long ragged cloak, stained with age and reeking of an unspeakable odor.

It was the scent of a recently opened grave, and while I had not been near one in a while, I had put a dead raccoon in my garbage can once and left it there for a week in the hot sun. Worst thing I'd ever smelled. I was only too happy when the garbage man came. It was worse than that. No one else seemed to notice.

His cloak hid is face, but it was safe to assume I didn't really want to look too deep in there, anyway. He was carrying a pole with a strange watermark on it and two runnels near the top. His hands were strong looking, like a weightlifter's, with veins running through them. I could not see much else of him, but he was big, much bigger than I had imagined him to be.

See, I figured this had to be the Boatman of the River Styx.

"Cappuccino," he said in a scary baritone.

"Four seventy-five, please."

"Surely you jest?" was his response.

"Uh. Yes."

He reached into his pocket and put pennies on the counter. Lots of pennies.

"Sir, we can't take those."

"They're still currency, aren't they?"

"Sir, they're pennies."

"I get paid in pennies."

"Excuse me, miss, I'll take care of this." I found myself reaching into my pocket and paying with a five. "Keep the change." The crowd was getting kind of hostile, and I wasn't sure what might happen if he got pissed off. He looked at her, reached across the counter with his large, ham-like hand, and touched her chin.

"Rebecca Montez, angry boyfriend, six years from now, lamp. Unfortunate." She looked at him as if he were crazy, but did not move. Almost as if she were under a spell.

He turned to me and said, "Thank you, Daniel Simmons."

"How do you know my name?" I already knew the answer.

"I know all of your names." That voice was really starting to work me. The rhythm of the shop resumed and people went back to typing.

"What are they seeing? How is it only I can see you?"

"Cappuccino, up."

"Uh, that's you."

"Let's sit and talk, Daniel Simmons."

"Okaaaaay." Didn't like where this was going.

I sat down at the table and tried to hide my face behind the screen of my laptop so I could resist the temptation to look into his cowl. He reached across the table and closed my laptop, gently.

"So, Charon, can I call you Charon? What brings you up for coffee? And why is it no one else can see you?"

"Mmmmm. Good cappuccino. Very nice." The cup disappeared into his cowl and did not come back out. "People deny their mortality. Part of my gift; people simply refuse to see Death for what it is, a part of Life. No one can see me because to them, I am some unfortunate hobo having coffee with an overdressed preppy. That would be you. As to why I am here? I need a guide, and since you can see me, you are volunteered."

"And I can see you because?"

"Embolism, three weeks from now."

Sobering. What could I know about that he would need a guide for?

"I am looking to franchise my infernal service."

"Excuse me?"

"Earth is very busy these days, lots of dying, and humans keep making new ways to kill each other off. I can't keep up. Look at this bicep." He pulled back his sleeve and showed me this massive arm that would not have looked out of place on the Incredible Hulk. "Go on, touch it."

"Um, no thanks."

"I used to be scraps of bone and flesh; now I have biceps from pushing that thing." He points outside the window.

For a moment I saw the flash of a large gondola-like boat, about the size of an eighteen wheeler. Off in the distance, I could see people, thousands of them, tens of thousands, standing patiently, wearing clothing from what looked like medieval times. When I looked harder, I could see dozens of different eras standing and waiting patiently for their turn to cross into the Afterlife. Then the street returned to its mundane appearance.

"Yes, I just cleared the backlog from the Black Plague last week. Do you know how long it takes to move seventy five million people by gondola? But I still have the Civil War, the Spanish Flu, World Wars I and II, Korea and every other little bush conflict modern governments feel justified in creating." He was starting to sound a little hysterical and maybe pissed off.

"Uh, what about other death-oriented entities like yourself? Aren't there others out there harvesting the dead?"

"Valkyries are still working, but they only want the valiant dead, so they swoop in and pluck one guy out of thousands, put him on their flying horse and they're gone. I've tried shouting out, 'Hey, you could grab a few more,' but they keep mentioning something about Valhalla having a quality assurance clause, and then they're gone.

When I complained to the *Niflheim Residency Committee*, they indicated they aren't responsible for all of these people. They closed their doors when the last of the Vikings bought the farm. Something about Niflheim having a purity standard."

"There are certainly other death agents, yes?"

"Heaven only takes devout Christians. Let's just say that number isn't going up. Same with the other sects. People don't seem to have a desire for really rigid religious structures anymore, so most of those places are closing their doors, or waiting for a management decision from on high. Hell, well, it's just overflowing. They even changed the sign. Used to say 'Abandon hope all ye who enter here.' Now it says, 'Abandon hope all ye who thought to enter here. Entry denied due to overcrowding.' So, I keep going, moving the Dead into their afterlife of Last Resort. But I am starting to fall behind, so I hoped someone here might have some idea how to franchise this operation."

"So you're hoping to find people willing to help you ferry the Dead, for a fee. What kind of benefits would you be offering? You need a good benefits package if you are trying to recruit these days."

"I am not trying to enter into management. I do not want to take responsibility for their work. I want to hand off a section of the workload to other interested parties."

"That's the problem. Who's going to be interested in buying into a business where your job is to move the Dead across the River Styx into the Afterlife of Last Resort? What do they get out of the deal?"

"As long as they work for the Company, they can avoid dying of anything, as long as they manage their company effectively. If I have to pick up their slack, I will carry them across the Threshold myself. I am not interested in who they hire, as long as they get the job done."

"Effectively immortal, long term job security, open hours, free hand in hiring, no micromanaging. I think I am going to quit my job. Okay, what's the cost to buy into this program

"Two pennies." *This guy has no money sense.*

"Okay, first things first. We're going to get you a suit and a bath. After that we are going to work together to increase your profit margin."

How can you run a business on two pennies a soul?

"What we need to do is get a cut of the funeral home business..."

Sisters

The year is 2072 AD, five years after the First Singularity. This was when mankind was first privy to the minds of other Children of Earth and their insistence on being heard and treated with respect.

The air was hot and still, not a surprise considering the time of year, but by the Serengeti's standards, this weather exceeded even her hottest by a wide margin. This year her grasses were tall and luxurious despite the terrible heat, hiding her animals from the common eye and the trained one alike. At a casual glance, nothing appeared to move save the heat ripples across the horizon. Even her most fearsome insects, bloodthirsty and ever-hungering, seemed to be conserving their energy for the cooler part of the day.

This was a day like millions that came before it, embodying the nature of life and death, and this mistress of two realms stopped as something so terrible swept through her that everything froze, hid, and waited for it to pass. Mighty herds grew silent and the coughs of the lions faded into the distance.

The slow-moving air carried the stench of death and decay, not the natural scent common to this area, not the blissful scent of carrion attracting its share of lazy scavengers, nor of a death by natural causes, that musty death of a creature that slowed and eventually stopped moving, or the most terrible of all, if you are an antelope or gazelle, savaged, smothered, or battered to death by the ghosts of the Serengeti, her big cats. This smelled of none of those good deaths.

Death on this scale was not common, and everything here knew that, even if they could not determine the cause or the source, avoidance was the best choice. The death wind blew through the city of Dodoma. The Serengeti did not like Dodoma. It was crowded, the creatures there did not move, they did not migrate. Movement was life; everything knew that except for these creatures. The Serengeti did not like the waste, the noise, the fireless smoke that always emanated from it. The stones-that-moved-and-roamed were tolerated because they often wandered among her people, her herds, and in the beginning, there was balance.

The longer the creatures lived there, the less balance there was. The Serengeti had taken to sending the ghosts to Dodoma. For a time, the creatures hid in fear, as they should, but eventually they returned in greater numbers. The Serengeti, infinite in its patience and long in its lifespan, would simply wait for the creatures to drown in their filth.

There was certainly enough of it. They would eventually go away. Badly behaved creatures always did. But today, they did not go away. They did not migrate, they did not gather their food, their young, their water, they did not leave a trail of waste to nourish all life on the Serengeti.

They simply ceased to be.

The Serengeti was not displeased. But all of its people, its herds, its hunters, its scavengers, and its ghosts trembled and wondered what was different. Dodoma was now filled with nearly one million dead, and there was no sign of what caused the Death that Walks.

A group of elephants roamed the Serengeti as they had for thousands of years. At first glance, there would be little different about this group than about thousands of elephants who had come before. But look a little longer, and you could tell this group was different. Grey and dusty, these desert titans shepherded a tiny group of non-elephants with them.

They were tired, dirty, and quietly clustered together, with rags for clothing, hair matted and reeking of sweat from too many days in the plains sun without bathing. The elephants found this smell quite distasteful, but continued their duties with a clear sense of obligation.

The Serengeti guided them toward water with its well worn breezes, flapping the tall grass, bringing the scent of water, leapers, and ghosts. Leapers were always plentiful this time of year, and the Sisters always found their antics amusing. The young ones, ever inquisitive, always wondered why they could not leap. The answer was always the same: "We are not leapers. We are the Walkers. We do not run. We do not leap. We Walk. The Serengeti is our mother and our guide. We fear nothing and harm no one." The answer only seemed to last until the next time they saw leapers.

One larger female, her body older, worn and leathery, her eyes bright with intelligence and her pace filled with the wisdom of many Walks, moved away from the group and paused to sniff the air. At first, nothing, then the slight tingle of black-burn from the rocks-that-roam, human sweat, rank with the overtones of meat and fire smoke. Tiny Walkers, the ones who act like ghosts, hunting and killing but they are not our Walkers, she remembered the words, our humans. These were the Ghost Humans. They kill everything they see.

She closed her eyes and opened herself up to the horizon. The Serengeti revealed them to her; they were behind, about two thousand steps. She called to her sisters, who immediately surrounded their young and their tiny walkers. In her mind, she saw the Ghost Humans moving as fast as the Ghosts they emulate, streaking through the tall grass, bouncing in their rocks-that-roam with their terrible boom-sticks. Like the Ghosts, their fangs flashed with the excitement of the hunt.

Aniel said to call them guns. Aniel always knew the words to things. Aniel was gone, taken by Ghost Walkers, not these but others. Others that we will find. We will find Aniel. In the meantime, we will do what she asked. Orienting herself to them, she gathered the strength of her sisters.

The aged female saw in her mind the skins of the Serengeti's ghosts across the back of the rock-that-roams, and though she had no love of the Serengeti ghosts, no person should ever be treated as such. The Ghost Humans continued to approach, and it was clear they were following the Sisters. That was as it should be. It is said that all things meet in the Serengeti eventually.

The Sisters waited, and the young grew restless, as is their wont. The tiny walkers said nothing, and after a while sat, slack jawed and boneless, upon the grass. Without Aniel, they said nothing; they only followed the Sisters.

The Eldest opened her eyes as the rock came into view, trailing a terrible cloud of smoke and dust, its roaring increasing as the Sisters came into sight. The Sisters stirred but did not move; only their ears and tails continued their ceaseless twitching. The Eldest began a deep sonorous moan, and her sisters followed, in concert. A rippling occurred through the air and gathered in front of the Eldest. The Sisters' dirge grew louder, and the tiny ones covered their ears. The young ones fell to the ground as if dead.

The Eldest stopped to read the wind and the approaching Ghost Humans, whose intent of blood and murder was written on the afternoon breeze, mingling with the scent of other dead Sisters and skinned Ghosts, all of these hunter's earlier kills, collected as vile and disgusting trophies. The Sisters stopped their singing as the Ghost Humans raised their boom-sticks, guns, and the energy that the Eldest was holding was released.

In that moment, the Serengeti breathed, a single collective breath, something that moved through all the nearby living things. The Ghost Humans breathed in that collective breath, and when they exhaled, they fell over dead--no marks, no scars, nothing to indicate their passing. Their collective breath returned to the Serengeti, their mother and their home. The Eldest turned away, horrified at the waste, the loss of life.

She returned to her Sisters, who touched her and consoled her while she wept. They wakened the young ones, and the tiny walkers and they continued toward the waterhole they could smell just a thousand steps in front of them.

Bludgeon

As luck would have it, mankind's first official interaction with an alien species (that was not covered up successfully by the government) was with the warlords of Hurumpharump. If you sound like you are clearing your throat when you are saying it, you are saying it right; when in doubt, cough and add more phlegm.

When their mighty spaceships, fifty miles wide, appeared above every major city on Earth, humanity wet its collective pants and waited for the end. For ten days, they hovered there. I hate to admit it, but we did not behave very well. There was the requisite gnashing of teeth, weeping, some self-flagellation amongst the Catholics who were forced to admit that perhaps we had not been made in His image after all. Seeing how these aliens had been able to do something we could not, perhaps He was made in their image.

Wholesale looting, riots, destruction of government property were the order of the day until martial law had been declared nearly all over the world. Most governments cracked down on their populations until quiet streets were the order of the day. People went out to shop for food and supplies and quickly returned home. Stock markets all over the planet went offline, for fear of catastrophic collapse during this time of crisis. But nothing happened.

After two weeks of seeing the alien ships hovering there, people went back to work and tried to ignore them. Once people had resumed their normal lives, as normal as one's life could be with a fifty mile wide alien spaceship hovering above one's city, the alien ships simply disappeared. All but one. The ship over New York did not leave.

News reports of the disappearance of the other alien craft caused jubilation in some, trepidation in others. Most assumed the end of the world was nigh and we had been found wanting. Scientists madly searched the sky for any trace of the aliens, and nothing could be discovered.

The next morning after the other ships left, a bright beam of light, brighter than any light on Earth except for the sun itself, speared down to Earth, illuminating a five mile circle of all-encompassing light. Humans within the beam stopped moving, and only those at the fringe of the beam could see what was happening within.

The aliens floated slowly and majestically to the surface of the planet and began to create a space filled with decidedly non-terrestrial plants. Many of them moved, swaying to an unheard music, tentacles whipping about, and occasionally squirting a strange and noxious fluid that dissolved anything it came in contact with. Several humans who were frozen nearby disintegrated in a pink mist as they exploded from contact with the plant's venom.

The military watched from the fringe of the light barrier after several of their missiles failed to penetrate it and fell to Earth, unmoving but still quite active. After destroying several blocks of Manhattan with cruise missiles that fell far short of the target, the Navy resorted to 20 mm guns. They too, flew unerringly to the target until they reached the barrier; then they promptly exploded, scattering shrapnel on everyone outside of the light shield. Dozens of people were unfortunately killed.

The president decided that he would tell the military to stand down before they killed any more New Yorkers by trying a nuclear strike next. Since the military could not destroy the aliens, they were forced to watch and record. Cameras were pointed into the field only to find out, once they were turned on, they did not record anything inside it.

Then artists were given binoculars and told to paint, draw, create images of the aliens as detailed as possible. Each artist did his best to create an image as true to the aliens as he could. When the military later compared all of their drawings, each one was as different as could be. Not a single image resembled any of the creatures, and none of the images resembled each other. None of the artists seem to think this was strange or out of place.

What most people saw were suits of armor that seemed to be

made of a metal that absorbed light. They were matte black in appearance, and only small lights could be made out on the fronts and backs of the suits. Each suit carried a staff-like object which seemed to function as a multi-tool. They could destroy matter or recreate matter with the same tool.

Unable to record effectively, the military was forced to use trained observers to try and remember every possible detail. They would of course find out a few days later that most of those observers would remember a picnic or birthday party or some other event they enjoyed, and would not be able to be convinced otherwise. They were not reporting anything useful to their commanding officers. It took two days for the alien table, chairs, exotic plants, and force field generators to be ready.

The President of the United States sat in his office and talked to me, an anthropologist by trade, about what I thought the aliens wanted. I was about to answer that question when there was a flash of light, and we were both transported, along with two Secret Service agents, to the center of the alien sitting area. Seconds later, every leader of every major population group on the planet began to appear, rapidly filling the entire space the aliens had created.

Food appeared as mysteriously as we did, and I decided to sit down and eat one of the apples, golden in color, from the table. It was the most amazing thing I had ever eaten. The Secret Service agents shook their heads while I tasted the apple. I assume they thought I was taking a considerable risk, but I did not think so. If they wanted to kill us, they did not have to teleport us here to do it. They could have just as easily destroyed us in transit, or teleported a bomb to our office. Besides, the president was a cheapskate; he did not even spring for a lunch before our meeting, and I was starving.

I offered the president a bite, but he look incredulously at me, so I kept eating. Once everyone had settled down, the alien plants moved up behind us and stood quietly.

"People and leaders of Earth: We are the Warlords of Hurumpharump, and we are here to conquer your planet. In an effort to be civilized, we have sent away our fleet and left a single vessel over your major metropolis, New York. This was done to let you know that we do not consider you a threat in any way, and it would be best for all of us if your people surrender peacefully and become servants to our House."

The alien voice did not appear to emanate from any particular alien. They had all stopped moving once the speaking took place and stood quietly in their black battle suits. Did I mention they were nearly fifteen feet tall? From a distance, without something to scale them against, it was quite a shock to be seeing the terrifying image of an extraterrestrial you had to actually look up to, one with ideas of conquest. The alien voice continued.

"As our servants, you will enjoy lives of productive work rather than going to offices and shuffling piles of paper from copier to closet. Why bother pretending to be working on financial derivatives when you know you would rather be working in the fields, producing Triliaifid for our armies. Once you learn how to train them and control them, you will be excellent Triliaifid harvesters. We do not expect to lose more than fifty percent of your entire species in the first year. As you grow more experienced, that number will diminish significantly, and by year five, your population will begin to stabilize and return to positive numbers."

All of the faces around the table looked shocked and unbelieving at what they were hearing. Fifty percent of the population in a single year? The cheap president, President Walter Fox, stood up and adjusted his tie before speaking. "Walter Fox, Republican, President of the United States, the most powerful nation on Earth. I greet you in the name of our gathered coalition of friends from all over the globe."

His voice seemed to carry to everyone sitting around the courtyard, and several weak smiles returned to faces, as his familiar voice and oratory speech patterns returned order to the world. For a moment, even my head had stopped spinning, and I was beginning to feel hopeful. Some kind of resolution would be reached.

"We are aware of who you are, President Fox. Please sit down. Your species lacks the proper ability to resist us, and by the standards of the Galactic Treaties of Confederation, your world now belongs to us by right of Conquest."

By right of Conquest. Hmmm. I had an idea. But I remember my mother saying better to beg for forgiveness than to ask for permission. I stood up, adjusted my tie and horn-rimmed glasses, and proceeded to make a statement that would affect the lives of billions. No pressure. "Excuse me, great Warlords of Hurumpharump," I have an ear for language, so I added the proper juicy inflection, this, unfortunately left the president seated next to me in need of a hankerchief, "Masters of the Triliaifid and possible rulers of Earth, I would ask if there are any rules of conflict or engagement that might stipulate how combat between our species should be fought?"

The Hurumpharump turned toward each other and then walked away from their positions behind the table to huddle together. The president looked up at me after wiping his jacket, but before he could speak, the Hurumpharump answered.

"The Codex of War says we have the option of engaging in any contest we deem an effective display of strength. We have studied your planet for weeks and determined your military effectiveness cannot prevent us from dominating your world."

"Surely, such an advanced species would not consider it civilized to simply destroy a species without offering them a sporting chance to engage in a form of combat where true prowess could be determined."

They huddled again.

"Continue your proposal."

"I propose we engage in a physical contest where technology is not a factor, allowing us both to see the other and relate as equals. If you are going to dominate us, it would be better if we knew that no matter the circumstances, you would be superior to us. Otherwise, as a species, we will simply rebel and rebel again."

"This is reasonable. Name your contest."

Looking out over the area, I realized we were in a park with a recreation center nearby. Then the idea struck me, and I knew in my gut it was the right choice.

"Baseball. The contest is nine innings of baseball."

* * *

"Are you out of your mind, Doctor? Did you agree to risk the entire human race on a game of baseball?"

"I don't see the problem, Mr. President. The Hurumpharump agreed to play and would not wear their battle-armors. They only required a month to learn to play the game. They were certain their physical superiority would be enough to learn to play well enough to beat us. Frankly, it seemed better than depending on the military to win a contest with them. We can't even take a picture of them unless they want us to. Were you really depending on the military to win? Mr. President, I understand the risks, but at least this way we get one shot at not becoming a harvesting world of Triliaifid spores where half the human race dies on the job."

"How do you know they will keep their word?"

"President Fox, your politician is showing again. These are not politicians; they are warriors. They do not lie to an enemy if they do not have to. These creatures are beings of honor. I may not know much about them, but I do know this: they will keep their word.

They never had to give it in the first place, so it must have value to their culture."

As I left the office, I turned to the president to say, "I trust you will keep your political interests out of your negotiations, sir. If they discover you might tell a lie, they may be inclined to kill you when they discover it. I would go with open honest discourse whenever you deal with them. I know you are a politician, so it might be a stretch for you. Do your best."

"Where will you be, Doctor, in case I need you?"

"With them, of course."

* * *

The Hurumpharump had a few conditions. They would be given access to a trainer or coach well versed in the game. As a matter of fact, they wanted the best the Earth had to offer. In addition, they wanted us to put up a stake to ensure we would give them the best training possible. They decided we would surrender every major league baseball player over the age of eighteen as collateral.

The only team that would be exempt would be team they would play against. If that team won, they would be allowed to retain their lives. If they lost, their lives were forfeit, and the Hurumpharump would rule the Earth for one thousand Earth years or five hundred birth cycles of the Triliaifid, whichever came first. Occasionally, a particularly fecund planet might alter their cycle, allowing them to reproduce even faster than normal. This has a slight effect on the handler's population, but the benefits outweighed the risk.

Coach David Reynolds, who at the time was the coach of the World Series Champions, the San Francisco Giants, was chosen to represent the Hurumpharump team. Earth's all-star team would be coached by the coach of the New York Mets, Nevil Maynard. The all-stars were chosen from teams all over the Earth, and for the next thirty days, they would be training harder than ever. The game would be held in Yankee Stadium in New York and simulcast all over the world in real time.

The Hurumpharump desired to train in Florida, because without their suits, they preferred the heat and humidity. Fortunately for them (and I guess for us), it was summer in New York, so it was likely to be hot and humid during the game, which was to be held August 30.

To reduce issues of coordination, every baseball player on Earth was teleported to the light field, and the all-stars were chosen from their number. Once a team was chosen, nine players, nine alternates, and three pitchers, the team was teleported to a secure location to begin their practice. They would be fed, trained and cared for, but would not be allowed to see or interact with anyone until the game.

Coach Reynolds and myself as well as a team of seven alternative trainers would also be on hand to assist the Hurumpharump during their development. Once we gave them the specification for a baseball field, physical dimensions, physical makeup, cage, stadium, and specifications were recreated on their ship, seconds before we arrived on it, as I am told.

It was Yankee Stadium in every way (except there was no gum under the seats and no one hawking and spilling beer on me while I watched). When the Hurumpharump teleported us all to their field, they opened their suits of armor by running their hands down an invisible seam in the front and the suit peeled away, showing a semi-organic, semi-machine based device/organism. Oh, I wanted to be able to take a picture, but I satisfied myself with attempting to memorize everything and hoped they would allow me to take my memories home with me. We were told that once everything had been established, this field would be transported to an area in Florida temporarily so they could enjoy the heat and humidity there.

When their suits opened, the smell was horrible, almost as if something had crawled into their suits and died. They were pastel colored, and no two possessed exactly the same hues, shades, or color patterns. Some shared certain color characteristics, but I could not be sure what the riot of colors meant. Each Hurumpharump possessed excellent muscle tone and a shimmering scale-like skin. Their eyes were large and had multicolored iris-like fields, super-responsive pupils, and double eyelids, both an inner and an outer one.

Their bodies were bilaterally similar and relatively evenly proportioned. Without their suits, they were still six to seven feet tall, and all had very well developed teeth. Judging from the size of their craniums, they had a very good brain-to-body ratio, slightly better than ours, so they are at least as intelligent as we are. I would only know more if I had the option to observe their brains in action. I would have to enjoy what I learned without the benefit of hands-on study at this time.

Once out of their suits, they were immediately rubbed with an unguent of some kind by what appeared to be servants of another species. The servants were some sort of insectovoids. They moved swiftly, scraping away the ichor that came from within their suits and generously slathering on this much better smelling agent. Even without their armor, the Hurumpharump still maintained an unmistakable aura of power.

They were correct. With their physical aptitude, they were naturals for the game of baseball. With two noted issues. When we first introduced them to the bat, they were very excited. They had no directly equivalent word, and the best they could do was "bludgeon," and we let it go for the sake of expediency. This excitement was one of the first showings of any emotional state other than what would appear to be boredom. They took the bat, passed it around, hefted it, marveled at its weight, swung it a few times, and nodded approvingly.

I had to ask. "What are you all so happy about?"

He (I think it was a he; they all looked the same and accepted the pronoun without comment) waved the bludgeon in the air and said, "Finally a weapon; we were unsure about this idea until now. Will we all be issued a bludgeon, or will we have to share it during the struggle for dominance?" At that point, the other Hurumpharump made noises I equate with chimpanzees and dominance activity as they crowded around the bat wielder.

"No, no. While it is true, you will be using the, uh, bludgeon, you will not be using it on the other team. You will be using it to strike the ball." Puzzled looks followed. At this time, we began to show them videos of the game, and they were fascinated and intrigued. We left them alone with dozens of recordings for three days. When we were allowed to return, they had already separated into training teams and had begun attempting to play.

This brings me to the second issue: pitching. The Hurumpharump, while physically powerful, seemed to have an inherent issue with their throwing skills. They could throw reasonably well; that was not the problem. It was an issue of degree. Those that could throw accurately and with some degree of precision were not very powerful. Those who were powerful could only deliver a very general degree of precision. While the coach was unhappy to discover this weakness, he had seen it in players before and continued to push them to overcome it. The Hurumpharump refused to use gloves and did not seem hindered by the sting of the ball in any way. We offered to show them how to use them, but they did not seem to understand the point.

With this disability in mind, the inaccurate throwers became outfielders, and the accurate became pitchers and infielders, inelegant, but necessary. Overcoming their disappointment at not getting to club anyone during the course of the game, the Hurumpharump became excellent players despite their throwing handicap. And they would be quite a surprise to our human team in one other amazing attribute.

We did not communicate often with the human team, but reports said they were in good spirits and confident of their ability to win easily. I read those reports with trepidation, and hoped they would not be overconfident.

* * *

When the day of the game arrived, the Hurumpharump teleported both teams to the real Yankee Stadium, and the stadium was filled with spectators, who were allowed to enter at will. The stadium was packed with humans, wearing all kinds of baseball paraphernalia, cheering their respective heroes on. Food was passed out, drinks were dispensed, and no money changed hands.

I think it was decided if the end of the world was coming, everyone should be full and perhaps a bit intoxicated. The president and his contingent, as well as those world leaders who had not returned home, had an entire box area to themselves, and they were adjacent to the insectovoid servants of the Hurumpharump, of which there were forty or so who appeared for the game. Before the game started, the insectovoids came out to the field and groomed the Hurumpharump and provided them with uniforms with numbers. After slathering them with the unguent, the players were dressed, and they awaited the National Anthem.

We were surprised to find out that an Hurumpharump wanted to sing the National Anthem, in English, no less. It was evident he had practiced for some time, because he sang without the translator we were so used to hearing. His accent was thick but passable, and he did not embarrass himself as much as many celebrities had in the past. The song resonated with the audience, and at the end, they cheered his efforts and applauded mightily. He looked puzzled and turned to me. I made the sign of approval I had seen them show each other, and he appeared to be satisfied and returned to the dugout.

"Play ball!" the umpire shouted to herald in the most important game in human existence.

The Hurumpharump started the inning, and the first pitch was a fastball, low and outside. The Hurumpharump, Number 13 seemed to be a statue until a split second before the ball crossed the plate.

Then his bat was a blur of motion. It moved so fast no one could even see it. The ball disappeared in a cloud of dust as it flew down the right field line and disappeared out of the field, continuing out of the stadium. The only words spoken were, "Take your bases, sir." And the score was one-zip. The Hurumpharump repeated this for fifteen home runs before their side was retired. After the fourth or fifth run, the stadium was as quiet as the grave. Humanity breathed a sigh of relief when their side was retired.

When the first human came to bat, a Darrell Mayers from the Philadelphia Phillies, the crowd went wild, and I found myself caught up in the infectious energy. He tapped his shoes, smiled, pointed out into right field, and stood over the plate. The pitcher watched the signs from the catcher, shook two off and then nodded. His pitch was a fastball at a whopping seventy-seven miles per hour, respectable from a Hurumpharump but nothing compared to what Mayers was used to hitting. He drove it from the stadium as if it had been lobbed underhand. And the game was on.

Nine innings later, the game was remarkable for several reasons. It was the highest scoring baseball game in history, not because it was not played well. Each team did remarkably well once they adapted to the style of play of the other. When the ball was kept in the stadium, there was some of the best baseball anyone had ever seen. Spectacular plays, incredible throws, steals. I forgot to mention how fast the Hurumpharump were stealing bases; baseball had never looked so good. In the beginning, the crowd gave no love to the Hurumpharump, but by the fifth inning, after a spectacular triple play against the humans to retire the side, the crowd cheered the sheer beauty of the game. And soon, both teams were being cheered and for just a moment, all were able to forget the fate of the world hung in the balance. During the seventh inning stretch, people got up for a moment and walked, but no one left. Even the sportscasters were excited.

The Hurumpharump added three runs to their total as their turn at bat ended, with the score being 157 to 154. It was possible for humanity to win, and Coach Reynolds called a time out to change his pitcher. During this time, President Fox chose to come out to the dugout, and he had to pass the Hurumpharump dugout. The insectovoids had chosen to come out and apply their healing unguent to the team, and were bustling about the dugout as the president and his security detail passed by. President Fox shoved his way past one of the insectovoids and continued without even acknowledging the event.

The roar of the crowd was defining, and the President had to yell to be heard. "Gentlemen, I have never been as proud of this game as I am today. I want it to be known, no matter what happens, you have been exceptional. But I want to take this moment to remind you, the fate of our species lies in your hands. You are a team comprised of the finest our world has to offer. I want you to do your absolute best in this final inning."

Coach Reynolds finished out on the mound, and the president and his team rushed back to their box. The insectovoids returned a few moments later, and the game reconvened. The new pitcher was a Hurumpharump, Number 6, who had been held in reserve until now. I remembered why. He was one of the few who had been able to pitch with both control and power. Coach Reynolds had been true to his word. He would do whatever it took to win. It did not matter to the crowd, though; they were cheering maniacally as he took the mound.

Bu Tao of China came to the plate, and after having innings of easy hits, was surprised at the speed and power of Number 6's pitches. Stepping into a more controlled crouch, he concentrated and got a chip into left field and made it to first. Number 6 was unaffected and took the next batter in three swings. One out. The next batter was a giant from the Dominican Republic, Fernando Ayala, easily one of the best hitters in the world. The stadium quieted down after the easy out of the last batter.

The first pitch was a rocket and was outside. The second was a curve and inside. Ayala swung on the next pitch and missed, 2 and 1. Ayala grinned, and the Hurumpharump showed its teeth in challenge. The next pitch was perfect, and Ayala swung and broke his bat for a double. The outfielder, Number 12, rushed it, and he had a cannon for an arm. He made the throw to home to keep Bu Tao from scoring. Men on second and third, one out.

Music blared, the crowd sang, people cheered, even the insectovoids, who until the very last few innings has sat impassively, seemed agitated, their antenna waving and their second pair of hands drumming out a strange cadence in counterpoint to the music, complementary and rhythmically pleasing. No game had ever caught the attention, the crowds, the adulation, that this game had. As was later reported, this frenzy had caught on all over the world. If you could see the game, you were swept up in it.

* * *

David Matthews, number 42 of the Mets, came to bat, and Number 6 had been briefed on the team and knew he was the best hitter with the sharpest eye. So he walked him, counting on their superior infield to make the double play against the next far weaker hitter.

Matthews took his base, visibly angered. Number 6 showed no emotion as he awaited the next batter. The next batter was from the Netherlands, number 14, Dave Rajier. He was a good fielder and chosen because of his skill in the outfield. He was a passingly good hitter, batting .273, but no one wanted him to be hitting right now. Too much was at stake. Rajier came to the plate, tipped his hat to the crowd, and stood ready.

The two, Rajier and Number 6, filled the count, three balls and two strikes, each working his skills, and the battle came down to their indomitable wills. The next pitch would decide it. Number 6 turned the catcher down four times before deciding. Rajier squinted, gripped, and swung hard. There was solid contact, and the ball flew high into left field. Number 11, a Hurumpharump known for his leaping ability, tracked it and ran toward the wall. He leaped and everyone held their breath. The ball was just shy of his fingers by about an inch. The same inch would have been successfully covered by a glove, had he been using one. Grand Slam, home run! The humans had won the game.

People cheered, music played, and everyone roared as the game came to an end. Both teams seemed exceptionally excited and ran out onto the field to hug and congratulate each other. I approached a Hurumpharump, who in their excitement, hugged me closely, and I squeaked so that he might let me go. He was powerful but gentle, and placed me back on the ground.

The cheering continued for some time, and then a pleasant chime sounded and all of the stadium music subsided. *"People of Earth, when we first agreed to engage in this challenge, we were certain we would be able to win. Our generations of battle experience and breeding made us believe the outcome was never in doubt. But instead, your people have proven to be resilient warriors and impeccable instructors, who taught with honor and patience. They gave completely to our players guidance in all aspects of the game, and as a result, their performance was exemplary, wouldn't all agree?"*

The crowd roared with enthusiasm, forgetting any sense of decorum, giddy with the win.

"It gives us great pleasure to announce we will not be using your planet as a breeding ground for the Triliaifid. We have found your species

to be more developed in some ways than our own. We will instead consult with your world on more of these 'games' as you call them. On our worlds, all contests end in death, so this is a novel concept for us. In return, we shall spare your world and help guide you into the galaxy as a member of the Confederation. We will, of course, be removing weapons from your world to ensure that you do not destroy yourselves before we can experience all of your games. Your games will become the currency with which you will buy your way into the galactic community."

President Fox, finding his way to a microphone, was incensed. "Who are you to come to our planet and dictate our social policy regarding weapons or any other state policy? The United States is a sovereign nation..."

"Enough, President Fox." The president reappeared in a flash of light in the center of the stadium surrounded by the Triliaifid and Hurumpharump in black armor. "You are no longer in a position to dictate anything on this planet. Your second in command, Vice President Davis, will be assuming control of your United States. You will be tried and likely found guilty of assaulting a higher life form in the performance of its duties."

"What do you mean? I don't remember assaulting anyone." A holographic image was displaying showing the president shoving his way past the insectovoid grooming an Hurumpharump.

"And? They are just servants. Who cares about servants?"

"Your crime, Mr. President, is the lack of manners and respect due any life form. You and your line will be punished directed to tend Triliaifid at our next training facility. You will be returned at the end of a ten year sentence, should you and yours survive."

The insectovoids turned and waved, and the Hurumpharump in battle armor escorted the former president into the beam. Number 6 turned to me and placed his hand on my shoulder. "They are not the servants. We are."

Suicide Seed

Stephanie Mehta woke Thursday morning to her clock
radio in her tiny apartment in the Russian city of Moscow. It was
little more than a room with a kitchen and bathroom. She shuffled
around slowly until she got her bearings. She was a diminutive
Indian woman in her early thirties, with clear skin, long hair, and
full lips. Her mother always wondered what was holding up her
grandchildren when she had a daughter as beautiful as she was. Just
another thing they had to fight about.

Her Russian Blue, Fedya, hopped up onto the counter and
nuzzled her, releasing a tiny squeak, indicating his hope for breakfast,
sooner rather than later. She nuzzled him back, and stroked him
absently while she tried to remember what there was to eat in her
apartment. She knew not to look in the half-height refrigerator,
because she had not had anything fresh enough to require
refrigeration in quite some time.

The tiny markets on the outskirts of Moscow had been
bringing in less food in the last few years. Farmers were complaining
about reduced harvests, and no one seemed to have any idea why
the crops were getting smaller and smaller. Stephanie had taken
to growing potatoes in the corner of her apartment from the eyes
of earlier generations she had scavenged, and had been successful
in managing their growth. Her apartment did not have much, but
sunlight was in abundance.

"Sorry, little one, it looks like potatoes again." His tiny reply seemed resigned to potatoes, and he ate them with vigor. "I promise to bring you something that looks like meat from the hospital tonight."

Stephanie washed up quickly, trying not to use up her allotment of water for the day. Water shortages had become all too frequent since she came here eight years ago to start her residency. She opted to come to Russia because so many of her people started moving north as the rising sea levels drove many Indians into Rangapur. Her mother suggested she move to Russia because of the growing economic prosperity there.

She had since informed her mother that economic prosperity was relative. Yes, Russia was doing better in some ways, and worse in others. For example, India had more doctors, but Russia had more hospitals. If she didn't hurry she would be late for her shift. Fortunately she lived in a barracks arrangement right next to the Municipal Hospital No. 15, and it only took her fifteen minutes to walk across the overpass into the main hospital courtyard.

The hospital was busy, people everywhere, babies crying, staff bustling about trying their best to tend to patients. As she danced through the crowds, patients touched her white coat and asked her questions. She tried not to stand still lest she be overrun. They needed to go through the brief paperwork at the desk before they could be seen. She would see as many today as her supervisor would let her.

She was technically a full doctor, but her supervisor had been reluctant to sign off on her paperwork because it kept her with him here at Fifteen. She would have been upset if she hadn't loved her job so much, even with the lack of resources, the constant rush of patients, the government interference, or any of a number of other issues. She wasn't just a doctor, she was a healer; she wanted to find out how to help as many people as possible.

Ekantika Das was her last patient of the day, and she agreed to take her from her supervisor, Helmut Baum, who had been on for three days straight. Mrs. Das looked tired, strained. She was probably borderline malnourished and dehydrated, like most people were these days. The rains had been less frequent, and the summer was one of the hottest on record.

"What brings you in, Mrs. Das?"

She began tentatively. "Doctor Baum scheduled me to come and see him a few weeks after my miscarriage." Stephanie had looked briefly at the record and saw that she had three miscarriages in less than two years. Each happened earlier and earlier during her term.

"I would like to run a series of tests to see how you are doing, and when I am done, we will see what we can do. Do you still want to have children?" Many women, if they find they cannot carry to term, these days opt just to give up.

"Yes, desperately. My husband and I work as part of a collective on the outskirts of town, trying to turn older buildings into hydroponic structures to supplement food output for the greater Moscow area. We are recently wed, and would like to have children since neither of us is getting any younger."

"I understand. These tests will take less than a week, so I will send you an email to schedule your visit."

"Namaste, Doctor."

The rest of the week was uneventful, and there was even a slowdown at the hospital. Patients were always reluctant to come to hospitals these days since the number of cases of MRSA had risen in the last twenty years. Over-use of antibiotics had caused the rise in the resistant disease strains. People needed hospitals more than ever, but were reluctant to come there with the risk of catching a nearly incurable disease while being served.

Later that week, when she got the test results, they were unusual, but she could not put her finger on why. She went back and checked Dr. Baum's records. He had made some notes about fertility issues in several of his patients, so she kept working. Something about it seemed strange to Stephanie. In a momentary lull, she went down to the primitive records databases and made some soft queries using the records of the female population of child bearing ages at the hospital. After a few dozen questions, she made a startling discovery. The number of births at the hospital and in the area in general had dramatically dropped, far below the statistical average. She thought she had done something wrong and double-checked her queries.

These numbers could not be right. This would be a thirty percent reduction in live births in less than a ten year period. Stephanie was tired. She assumed she had made a mistake and planned to run the check from home once she was settled.

* * *

Fedya was enjoying his purloined sirloin and wrestled mightily with it. It was mostly scrap from the senior doctor's kitchen, but that mattered little to him. His gusto gave Stephanie a warm glow while she studied the data now from the fourteen nearby hospitals.

She couldn't understand why no one had noticed it before now, but the more she looked at it, the more she could see the scale of this issue. But she would need more information and likely some corroboration with some colleagues, possibly in London. With the new civil war in the U.S., she wasn't likely to get much data except from the neutral states like California or Oregon. So she prepared a data package for a variety of hospitals and sent it off. Immediately, she received an instant message.

--IM--

GreenMachine: You are in danger.

Dr. Mehta: Excuse me?

GreenMachine: There is not much time. Can you meet me in an hour at this net address?

Dr. Mehta: Who are you?

Greenmachine: This address is secure, but you cannot be at your apartment. I have slowed the trace, but they will find you in twenty-four hours. Pack a bag. Now hurry.

Dr. Mehta: I can't leave my cat.

Greenmachine: Then take him with you, but for God's sake, hurry. Now get to the coffee shop, and we will give you further instructions.

Dr. Mehta: I have no intention of leaving home on the say-so of some unknown IM.

Greenmachine: You have discovered a reduction in birthrates in the area hospitals where you work. You have checked this against local hospitals in the Russian datasphere. You find the information able to be confirmed with an 87% accuracy. Tomorrow you will receive data clusters from your points in London, New Delhi, Mexico, Canada, Brazil. You will see that this trend or worse had happened across the globe. How am I doing?

Dr. Mehta: How do you know I did all this?

Greenmachine: GO TO THE COFFEE SHOP. NOW.

The IM client connection vanished, and she sat up in disbelief. Putting her data key into her pocket, she grabbed her night bag and packed two changes of clothing, her level 1 Medical ID, and all the money she kept in the house. She barely spent any, so she should have plenty available.

She dropped Fedya off at a friendly neighbor's with a generous bribe of her latest potato crop and some cash in the event she was gone longer than a few days. Fedya complained the entire time until she gave him his favorite squeaky toy. Dame Romanov agreed to take care of him. She had always liked him and said he would have plenty of mice to keep his belly full.

When she got to the coffee shop, the terminals were empty because it was near midnight. When the late shift came on, the place would fill up, but that would not be for another hour or so. She sat down and put on the wireless ear buds sitting in the sonic cleanser.

As soon as she plugged in her data-key, a video image appeared. The man sitting in the video was in a laboratory with a single tech working in the background. He was wearing a full bio-suit, so his face was obscured, but she could see this was a real lab with real equipment, not a stage. "Doctor, you have discovered something Consanko does not want known. Birthrates all over the world are declining due to the interactions of a genetic manipulation called 'suicide seeds.'

"This technology was designed thirty years ago as a means of controlling food production on Earth. Seeds were being designed to fail to produce a new generation of seeds so Consanko would become the sole provider of seeds as it cornered the market on genetic seed materials all over the planet.

"Once they had patented nearly all of the food crops on the planet, they gathered the genetic materials, mapped the genomes, and proceeded to alter the seed products to ensure no seed would be produced by the resultant plants. People would have to pay every season. Needless to say, Consanko grew fabulously rich.

"As scientists had predicted, monocultures would be a problem when blight, insects or disease struck, but Consanko had variants it saved for that occasion, and their wealth continued to grow until this very day. But I noticed there was a corresponding effect in animal populations that ate seeds created from these plants. They became increasingly sterile. You have now learned the other secret: that it is affecting us as well. More slowly, but just as effectively."

The lab tech in the background seemed to be working hurriedly. The man in the front of the display held up a picture. "See this face? Memorize it. He is the person you are trying to find. When you look through our upload, you will find he knew about everything. Maybe he can help you find the answers you are looking for."

An explosion rocked the room. Smoke started coming from the ventilation shafts. "We don't have much time. That explosion was a trap set up in the ventilation. They won't try that route again. Our suits will protect us from the gas, but in a few minutes, they will up the ante and we won't survive. Our upload is on its way to you via our intelligent agent. We are destroying any trace of our information to give you as much lead time as possible. Doctor, we are sorry to involve you in this fashion, but we had lost hope that anyone would notice. We were going to leave our data to an intelligent agent and hope the first person who found it was as good as you are."

"What do you want me to do?" The sight of an arc cutter coming through the armored door showed their attacker's progress in the attempt to gain access.

"We want you to stop this. There must be a way to reverse it, some way to introduce our reproductive viability back into the species before it's lost completely. Our predictions say in thirty years, humanity and most animals will have lost any possibility of reproduction."

"I am not a geneticist. I wouldn't even know where to begin!" Mehta was feeling frantic as she watched the smoke grow thicker.

"We know you are not a geneticist, but you have other friends. It will take a team to solve this problem, the same way it took a corporation to cause it. We are out of time, Doctor. Godspeed."

End of transmission. End of recording. Agent instructed to your key codes. All resources are at your discretion.

This was a recording? "Agent, accept vocal input."

"Accepting."

"How long ago did this recording take place?"

"Two standard days ago."

"Then how were they answering my questions?"

"They weren't; they anticipated a variety of responses; I provided the interface adaptations. Doctors Lawrence and Cloverfield have been dead for forty-eight hours."

"How much time do I have before they come looking for me?"

"All temporal estimates are still accurate, as your information requests have been slowed but not stopped. In 24 hours, you will be apprehended, likely by Interpol or the Soviet police as an enemy terrorist. Recommendation: leave the country."

"And go where, pray tell?"

"To the coordinates left by the doctors."

"And where is that?"

"The coordinates on the map indicate a location inside the remaining Amazon jungle. It will require one, possibly two major airline flights, one charter flight, and likely six to ten hours of ground travel. You should begin now."

"I need to go back to my apartment. I am not ready for this."

"That path is not recommended."

"Let's see you stop me. Agent offline."

Stephanie did not know what she was seeing, but she was certain this was some elaborate practical joke. The shaky camera, the explosion, the shutoff of the camera seemed just too dramatic. When she got back to her building, several emergency vehicles were sitting outside. The lights were off, so whatever it was, it was already over. They were taking several bodies out on stretchers, and one of them had a grey cat lying on top of it. It looked like...

"Fedya!" The grey cat jumped down and ran through the street to Stephanie, and she suddenly realized who one of those bodies was. Showing her badge to the paramedic, she asked, "Show me the bodies."

When they pulled the covers back, the first was the delicate body of Dame Romanov. The second was Helmut Baum, her boss, her sometime lover, her friend. He had been shot in the head. Seeing him that way was like a physical blow to her system. She grew lightheaded and fell back into the arms of a strange man who had come up behind her.

"Do you know this man, Doctor?" The man's Russian was impeccable, and he looked like he could be a policeman or an inspector. His hands were strong, like a vise, and he literally held her up from falling. He was a giant wearing an ill fitting suit, as if they could barely find anything to cover him properly. He had a strong face, young looking, but his eyes were hard, sharp; they glittered like flint in the streetlights, the eyes of a man who had seen too much.

"His name is Doctor Helmut Baum." He was in apartment 17. Her apartment. Waiting for her. She said none of these things.

"I am Inspector Piotr Nikolayevich Rasputin, and I have a few questions for you. The first is where have you been for the last few hours?"

"I was at the coffee shop for the last two hours. Helmut was at the apartment waiting for me to get in. He had just come in from his shift. Can I sit down, Inspector?"

"Yes, of course."

"Do you know what happened?"

"They appear to have been assassinated. Do you know of any reason they might have been targeted?" Piotr had his own reasons, but he wanted hear hers first

"No, I don't know why anyone would want to hurt him. He was a good doctor. He did not have any enemies." But Stephanie knew it wasn't true. She had logged in with his address a few days ago, because he was logged in and had a superior clearance. The first traces would have been on his account.

"I'm going to have to take you into the field office for questioning, Dr. Mehta. It shouldn't take too long."

"Can I go to my apartment and put my cat there? Will the police allow him to stay at the scene? If not, can I put him with another neighbor?" These questions came boiling out all once.

"Yes, of course, you can leave him with another neighbor. I'll wait right here until you get back." Piotr shook out a cigarette and lit up as she moved toward the apartment building. The police had already canvassed the property; whoever they were, they were very good. They left no clues, no casings, no signs of forced entry. An inside job, perhaps.

The emergency vehicles pulled off after twenty minutes, and she had not returned. He put out his third cigarette and went into the building. She was not at her apartment, but one neighbor did have Fedya. But he said she had left nearly twenty minutes ago. So she knew where to drop the cat, and used the remaining time to get a head start.

Touching his datapad earpiece, he spoke into his mastoid comm, "Agent, put a trace on her medical ID at all the local airports and any recent taxi pickups. Do not alert her to the flags. Just follow and report."

"Request activated, flags sent out. Will notify."

Piotr got into his car and headed to the Moscow airport. Sometimes technology is no match for a good hunch. When he got to the airport, his agent had already found her booking a flight to South America, quite a distance for a woman with nothing to hide and very little luggage to pack. He decided he needed to see what was really going on.

"Agent, book corresponding flights, inform Command of itinerary. Log it as active investigation. Inform pilot of intent to carry firearm onboard. Clear security checks."

"Acknowledged. Activity in progress."

This was just to ensure her safety and his curiosity. He had not been out of the country for a while; he was sure South America would be lovely this time of year. She sat in coach the whole time reading. He was not sure what it was, and did not want to risk having his agent read over her shoulder, so he took this time to catch up on his rest. The only thing he could think of was smoking a cigarette the whole flight until he fell asleep. Where could she go?

* * *

When the plane landed, he knew he would have to confront her. The next leg of the journey was on a small private plane with only twelve seats. It would be hard to remain inconspicuous. The heat was terrible, and the humidity worse. He took off his jacket and remembered he did not bring a change of clothing, so he was going to have to get something local first chance he got.

His training as a KGB agent instantly came online once he landed. There were four hours between the landing and the smaller flight. He took that time to hunt around in the airport for vendors of more local attire. It did not take long for him to find some more comfortable shirts, slacks, and a bag to carry his gear. A pair of sunglasses and a white hat completed the ensemble.

Now, a bit more comfortable and armed with a selection of local toiletries, he cleaned up, changed, and was able to get to the airport runway with plenty of time. The doctor had managed to clean herself up, but it was obvious she had not slept on the flight over and was in need of rest.

A man from Russia got off the plane. Piotr noticed him at first and thought he was just a tourist. But the coincidence of his waiting for the same plane made him more suspicious. The man had the movement of a trained fighter; he walked on the balls of his feet. He kept his hands clear of his pockets. He sat with his back to the wall and faced the entire area.

Piotr tipped his hat forward and slumped his shoulders. The man's gaze passed over him, stopped momentarily, and then moved on. He was looking for something, but Piotr did not know what that might be. Thirty minutes before the flight was due to leave, the small plane landed and taxied into the runway. A crew came out to refuel and inspect the plane. The pilot chatted with his relief, and then the preflight was underway.

The suspicious man began to move closer to the doctor, and

she did not seem aware of his approach. Piotr also moved closer, sitting behind the two of them, hiding behind a magazine. He put his gun under his bag in the chair next to him.

"Dr. Mehta. I am going to have to ask you to come with me. British intelligence." The man's accent was certainly British, but there was something strange about it.

"Don't you have to show me some ID or something?" Stephanie asked. She had a look of intense skepticism mixed with real fear. Something was definitely wrong, and she was completely out of her depth.

"Just come with me, miss, and we will sort this out in the customs office." The "agent" reached out to grab her arm and move close to her. He whispered something, and Piotr knew what it was. He had a handgun pressed against her back.

"Excuse me," Piotr stood up and in his thickest Russian accent asked, "Do you know what time our flight will be leaving?" He was certain they would have almost no chance of understand what he was saying.

"Sod off. I am busy with the lady."

Piotr took off his hat and held his hand out to Stephanie. "My name is Piotr. And you are?" He could see the recognition and relief in her eyes. But he tried to transmit the idea that they were not out of the woods yet.

"Stephanie. Stephanie Mehta."

"And your friend?"

"Her friend is telling you to mind your bloody business, Russian."

"Or what will happen? You will make me eat some bland chips and tasteless fish from your country? Perhaps some of your beer that tastes like piss? My cat makes a stronger brand of beer in his litter box."

Whoever this fellow was, he was not a member of British Intelligence. He lost his temper far too easily. Likely a mercenary. He brought his gun out from under his coat and redirected it at Piotr. Exactly as planned. Piotr stepped to the right of the gunman's hand and with a single maneuver, relieved the man of his gun, breaking two of his fingers. His aggressive wristlock held the man and brought his arm behind his back in a breaking position. It happened so quickly, no one saw anything at all. Piotr handed the gun to Stephanie and used his other hand to pat the man down.

He wasn't carrying anything else. His ID said his name was Howard Mason, but Piotr doubted the ID was real. Using his real Russian police ID, Mason was taken into custody, and Stephanie and Piotr were questioned by the local authorities. Many hours later, it was called an act of random violence, nothing more. But Piotr knew better. It was time to get some answers from the beautiful doctor.

When they were walking back to the smaller plane runway, Stephanie started talking. Piotr decided to keep his request simple and see what she had to say. "It started with the bees. Dr. Sheppard said he noticed first when colony collapse began to show up in the newspapers."

"Who is Dr. Sheppard?" Piotr interrupted.

"He was the leader of the genetic engineering teams who pioneered the last great plant genome modifications. His work created the super-yield wheat, the rust resistant potatoes, the suicide seeds, and the natural insecticides common to almost all plants today. He worked for Consanko for nearly thirty years."

"So your trip here has something to do with him?"

"I was reading the information on the flight here. It had been gathered and collated by two later scientists, peers who reviewed his papers and were not satisfied by his safety information. They spent the last fifteen years refuting his notes about the "restrictive coding" built into the gene maps of his genetic constructs. Their contention was that the genetic transform viruses and bacteria used to modify the plants was completely unable to be contained to that environment."

"So this brings us back to the bees, yes?" She looked at him incredulously. "Yes, I went to school once upon a time."

She continued. "Yes, this brings us back to the bees. They moved pollen from the genetically engineered plants, first to their hives, then to other plants. Which ultimately moved them to us. The first signs of the suicide genes were the failure of some bee colonies, as their queens became less able to reproduce stable colonies."

"So now you think it has moved into the human population?"

"Correct. If what I have discovered is true, the human race will likely be extinct in less than one hundred years, and unable to reproduce in less than sixty. Consanko has put poison into the environment on every major land mass on Earth."

"Then this explains why people are trying to kill you, Doctor. You know too much. So I assume this means we are going to talk to Doctor Sheppard?"

"If anyone knows what can be done to reverse this, he would be the one."

The small plane captain started ushering people onboard, and the two of them sat in the back of the craft away from everyone else. Piotr put his gun in his lap under his hat. Stephanie curled up next to him and leaned onto his shoulder and fell into a dreamless sleep.

Piotr, already rested, considered what he knew about corporate politics and industrial espionage and hoped this would end better than this sort of thing usually did. On a good day, only bad people died. On a bad day, everyone did. He checked his backup piece, and stashed a huge knife under his shirt.

The flight, leaving late in the day, arrived eight hours later in the early morning in the small town of Quito, Ecuador. Stephanie woke, still looking tired and out of place. *She is just a doctor who has been told the world is coming to an end, Piotr; how do you expect her to look? The only reason you don't look like her is that your world came to an end a dozen years ago. She reminds you of Natalie. Enough of that; keep your mind in the game.*

Two men met them at the runway. Piotr knew them well. It had been nearly eight years since he had been there, but these two were still working the rainforest, gathering intelligence on the two dozen corporations currently fighting over what was left of it. Javier and Hector Morales, two brothers who worked with the KGB and whose loyalties were relatively unquestioned, reported regularly, their intel was good, and they were able to keep their noses clean. This made them decent agents, and Piotr did not tell them anything more than that he needed a car and a decent local map. They didn't know what he needed one for, and they didn't care.

"Rasputin, you look terrible," Javier began.

"How is that any different than normal?" Hector finished.

"It is good to see you two, as well. Did you get my request?"

"Yes, your dull agent made the request and was very clear about what he wanted. Do you really still use the Kinataci 4000 model? It's nearly eight years old." Javier smiled while he teased Piotr. "My wristwatch has more power than your agent."

"Seriously, Piotr, we have children here in Ecuador who have better agents than that. Are you going to upgrade any time soon?" Hector handed Piotr the map pack and the car keys.

"And who is this lovely creature?" Hector muscled Javier out of the way as Stephanie approached the car after getting her bag.

"My name is Stephanie." She shook hands and took in the quaint little airstrip on the edge of Quito. The car was something from earlier in the century; she did not recognize it, and thought it might actually still use some sort of petrochemical to power it.

"Rasputin, you did not tell us you would be bringing company. Keeping the good things to yourself, as usual." Hector smiled, something honest and real, and Piotr realized they misinterpreted the relationship. Let it go.

"We have to get moving. When we get back, we will share a beer or something before we take off. Thanks for the save."

"No problem. We are always here for you, Rasputin. You saved our lives, once. We owe you."

The car was old and serviceable and started up immediately. Neither of them had much to say on the trip; it was hot and miserable and both had grown used to the dry heat of the Moscow summer. Here at the equator, the weather was always hot and wet, with seasonal showers every day at around eleven o'clock and again at three as the winds shifted.

The GPS on the map said they were nearing their destination. Stephanie realized this was likely the place because they started seeing a variety of hydroponic domes erected for what looked like miles in every direction. These domes were scattered within the forest canopy and seemed to be strangely porous, allowing trees to grow through them even as they defined an area, each with a sixty foot diameter at the bottom. The dome appeared to be grown and continued to grow with the plants around them. Most were opaque, but a few showed levels of transparency, and people were servicing the plants within.

The domes gave way to a series of smaller prefab buildings. No security was visible, and a driveway with a number of other vehicles parked outside seemed a good place to start. They sat for a while, getting the rhythm of the place. Piotr made sure his guns were ready and scanned the grounds for anything out of place. Workers moving canisters on small flatbed trucks seemed to be the only road traffic. Occasionally, a larger twelve-wheeler would roll out or come back into the property.

A bearded man with graying hair got out of a vehicle near one of the campers, and Stephanie noticed him. He looked very similar to the photo she was shown on the video clip. She tapped Rasputin on the arm, and the two of them walked from the car to the prefab. When they got to the top of the stairs, Piotr entered first, and the small man was sitting behind the desk with his gun drawn and pointing at him.

"Please come in; your young friend, as well. I have been expecting you. Have a seat."

Once they were inside away from the blistering sun, Stephanie welcomed the opportunity to take a seat. The sun seemed to drain the strength from her body. She did not even have the ability to maintain any concern about the firearm pointed in her direction. "Dr. Sheppard, I presume."

Sheppard put the gun back into his desk and pointed to a small table in the back of his very organized office. "Please, have some water; you will find you sweat quite a bit more than you think here."

After they had a glass of water, and then a second, Doctor Sheppard got down to business. "Did the company send you? I am surprised it took them this long to find me."

"No, sir, we have come here at the request of Doctors Lawrence and Cloverfield. They said you would know why we were here."

"Did they? Did they tell you what I am doing here?"

"No, they said you were no longer working for Consanko, and you expressed some level of regret for what happened."

"Regret? No, my dear. Regret does not even begin to describe what I feel. I thought my work here might be enough. Would you like to see it? What about you, young man? You do not look like a scientist. If I were to try and read you, I would say a corporate hit man, government agent, possibly KGB, or if they are still in existence, a CIA agent."

"Very good guess, Doctor. So why are you here? If you have regrets for your work, why retire to this place? You were a very rich man; you could be living anywhere."

"The answer to your question lies out there. Are you rested enough for the tour? It's the least you can do before you kill me."

The three of them stepped out into the terrible heat of the day and strode toward one of the domes. "I made these domes myself. I designed them to absorb and convert the solar energy into a cooling chamber. I have patented the technology and am making a tidy fortune in the equatorial regions all over the globe."

As they stepped through a simple series of flaps, Stephanie noted the vast difference in the internal temperature of the tent, and by the time they were inside the dome proper, the temperature was less than fifty degrees, nearly an eighty degree drop. The air was cool, even a bit damp, and over eighty percent of the sunlight had been dimmed, making the area just a bit brighter than sunset. Dr. Sheppard touched a small remote on his wrist and the dome became a bit brighter as the spines of the hexagonal shapes began to glow with a blue light.

"I could make the dome more transparent, but that would bring in more heat; I want to wait until this dome has been harvested. But the polymorphic materials used in the construction of this dome are grown into this location. See?" He pointed to the edge of the dome, and Stephanie could see the dome seemed to move into the ground. There were none of the seams she would have associated with a constructed work.

The material covering the hexagons was thick and a bit rough, and had a scaled appearance. "The scales are a polychromatic material capable of converting sunlight into electrical energy. That electricity is used to cool the tent as the fabric absorbs the energy of the air using superconductivity. The energy absorbed is redirected by an underground organic network to a power storage facility used to maintain all of the vehicles and other power needs here."

"Why the strange design, growing them below the forest canopy?" Stephanie asked.

"Because they are not visible from space," Piotr answered before the doctor could respond. "You said harvest, Doctor. What are you growing?" Piotr walked over to one of the trees and touched the strange formations growing on the trees and in the underbrush. "They look like mushrooms."

"Very astute. Indeed they are mushrooms, mushrooms of my own design. What do you know about mushrooms?"

Piotr looked at Sheppard and answered. "I like them in my soups and on my steaks. Do I need to know more than that?"

Sheppard laughed and said, "No, I guess not. I hope you really like mushrooms, young man."

"What are you talking about, Dr. Sheppard? I came here to discuss a means of reversing the birth reductions in the human and animal populations."

"Young lady, when we first began our studies and first genetic experimentations, we were young and thought we were going to feed the world. We thought we would work with companies like Cansanko who would ensure that our patents would be protected, and we would be able to work with corporate backing. With their money and our skills, no problem of food production could confound us. But they had their own agenda. They rounded up seeds from all over the world and began to patent the seeds. The seeds! Can you imagine? We were outraged. Seeds belong to everyone, we said. They laughed and called us idealistic and told us to get back to work. We would have fewer complaints when we were rich."

Dr. Sheppard found a chair near the monitoring station and raised the lighting a bit. The two of them saw dozens of varieties of mushrooms, all over the room. They had been walking inside a very limited area. Once there was more light, they saw a rainbow of mushrooms, some close to the ground, others towering at three and four feet, shelves of mushrooms growing on the sides of trees. Some of them appeared to be the classic shapes, but others looked like ocean waves, some like bushes, but they were all growing harmoniously, beautifully, together. She had never seen anything like it.

"We went back to work, to increase the yield of our newly patented seeds. And with the revolutionary work of Dr. David Lawrence, we succeeded beyond our wildest imagination. Every time we worked on a new patent, we felt like explorers, crossing boundaries we had never conceived of. We became gods, Promethean in our endeavors, with no thought to the consequences."

Piotr heard the helicopter blades first. His training in war zones made him more alert. The others heard them soon enough.

"We don't have much time. I have been expecting them. I thought you were going to kill me. But now I realize they have been reading my notes. You see, when we first started noticing the problem, they started burying my ideas. And when Laurence and Cloverfield's work began to show we were wrong and there was the possibility of genetic pollution, they were killed."

"I thought they were killed two days ago." The look on Stephanie's face was undecipherable.

"They were. Two days and five years ago. I left the company in disgust and refused to do any more work once I had seen the error of my ways. The company refused to acknowledge my work until recently. Now I suspect they want my help. The work we did was revolutionary, and they killed the only two other people who really understood it."

"Then who sent me this message?"

"I did." Dr. Sheppard stared hard at Stephanie. "I need you to finish my work here. I need someone young and idealistic, someone who believes in a future worth fighting for. I need you here to fight for the present while I try and redeem myself and the future of humanity. I wish I had some words that would ease the years ahead. But I don't. Our pride has led to the fall of our species. I hope I live long enough to make it right. I am an old man, a stupid old man."

"What about Helmut? What happened to him?"

"He had begun his own investigation. I did not find his data flags because he was pursuing a different angle. By the time I realized what he was doing, they were already on to him. I am sorry for your loss." Stephanie realized that she did not kill Helmut with her research. This only increased her grief.

The helicopters were close enough to begin landing, and the dome began to vibrate with their approach.

Sheppard stood up and walked over to the two of them. "The pollution has spread to all crops everywhere. What Consanko did not release and does not want people to know is that all of their original source seed has been corrupted, as well. So they have been selling seed for the last decades, but the seeds they are selling are the last of their kind from the last stockpiles of any seed on Earth. None of it has the ability to create new seeds. What you and your team don't find on your own, won't be found. Mushrooms will feed some of humanity, but our conservative estimates are that more than two thirds of the human race will die of starvation."

Sheppard looked up and tears flowed from his eyes. "I need you to finish what I have started here. Everything you need is here; all the command codes have already been transferred to you. I have done all of the heavy lifting. All you need to do is teach humanity what we have done here."

Walking toward the door, Sheppard stopped and looked back, wiping his face. "You were worried about humanity not having a future in a hundred years. I am going to leave here and go with those men landing outside, because if I don't, humanity won't have a future in less than ten years. Good luck."

PART THREE:

ENTERING THE PENUMBRA

"Quantum signals from this period vary wildly,
and while I have been assured of the
high fidelity of these transmissions,
some of them contradict others.

I have to assume quantum fluctuations are
allowing me to see what might have been on
nearby or parallel Earths.

During this Shadowed Period of humanity's history, it was
as if mankind were on a collision course with a destiny
it could not seem to escape.

Disaster dogged mankind as it tried to find a footing
with its humanity, with its diversity,
with its audacity, with its temerity.

We longed for greatness but we were often not up to the task.
For decades, we were shadows of what we could be."

--Glendale Mokoto

Paper

Desi Roberto Santiago was a slacker. There is nothing wrong with being a slacker, except if you owe people money. Desi owed very few people, but the people he owed money were the kind of folks who would break one or both of your legs if you were late paying up.

Unfortunately for him, slacking was his avowed lifestyle. He learned early in life, nothing was ever worth rushing for, or worse, putting in hard time and effort. It's always disappointing and never worth the time you spend getting it. He had a form of perpetual buyer's remorse. So Desi's motto was "want not, work not." But he never lived up to it. He always spent more than he had and now had borrowed money from the local máfia boss, Don Milagro, to keep himself up on the latest tech. But Desi had a plan.

Desi was a bit skinny and asthmatic. His black hair was perpetually uncombed and more often than not, a bit dirty. He had a bit of chin hair and a line on his lip that wanted to be a mustache, unsuccessfully. His clothing reflected his overall attempts at looking prosperous, all second hand clothing that used to belong to rich tourists. None of it matched, and most of it was ill-fitting, only making it more apparent that he was poor.

He left his day job with the same rage he felt every day, after two hours of work on the phone providing technical support to some pendejo in India, and then went home. It wasn't even work anymore. Two hours? It took him longer to get to work than he was there. No matter, after his next score, he was going to quit that job and maybe even come in and piss on his boss' desk before leaving.

He hated climbing the stairs to his fifteenth story apartment on the Southside of what was left of Mexico City. He stepped over Antonio on the ninth floor, passed out in a puddle of the latest pharmaceutical mierda being put out by Pharmacon. The man reeked something awful; the mix of body odor, urine, and vomit might have caused Desi to throw up, if he had anything to eat in the last few days. Stomach empty, instead, a burning sensation filled him and he clenched his nose and jumped over the prone body on the stairs. When Antonio sobered up, he would probably be looking for a bath. He was not the only person squatting here with a pungent aroma of soaplessness.

In the Ivory Tower, a partially completed tenement abandoned by a construction company after the earthquake, water was in short supply past the fifth floor. Beyond that, water pressure had to be created using mechanical tools. Desi's solution was to use a salvaged bicycle and a roommate to help bring up enough water from the street. When Desi could spare some water or get some extra time on the bike, he would help Tony clean up, but today wasn't going to be one of those days. Desi had work to do.

It had rained all last week and Desi's catch basins on the roof were full. He had made them several months ago after finding an old printed copy of Home Designers Quarterly, one of the last prints made before paper became illegal to produce. He found them in, of all places, the burned out quarter of the barrio, hidden in a cache of thousands of magazines, buried deep after Mexico City's great quake of 2052. Whole sections of the city were off limits, too dangerous they said, but despite his asthma, Desi loved to explore. He used the magazine to create catch basins from plastic containers all over the city, and set them up on the top of the roof to capture the ever decreasing rainwater. Engineering a distribution system and a water-cranked dynamo with old auto batteries allowed Desi to power his electronics.

Pumping water was never something Desi enjoyed doing, so his catch basins were a way of letting nature work for him instead. But when nature wasn't feeling generous, Desi had rigged up a bicycle in his apartment to act as his pump, and he could fill his bathtub in about fifteen minutes with vigorous riding. And that was the catch. It had to be vigorous. Which means he needed help; hence his less than perfect room-mate.

"Hermano, it's good to see you. What did you bring me?"

"Nothing, the same thing I bring you every day. I got some extra work today and I need to get started. Go back to your bootleg cable." The freemium directed receiver array gave a grainy picture, in high definition, no less.

"Why you got to be like that?" Nicolas was half Russian and half Mexican, so he was a giant in tan.

"Be like what? You are always mooching. Why don't you run out and find something to eat for us today? You could always go back to work." Nicolas' exotic appearance made him a hit with the ladies, and all of the screaming meant they liked his... assets. Desi despised him most of the time, when he wasn't wanting to be him. Nicolas went back to his room and a few minutes later, giggling could be heard through the closed door. Desi grimaced, shook his head, and picked up his Nakatomi 3270 integrated OS datadeck. It was sleek and tiny; Desi may have shoes with holes, but it was clear this piece of state-of-the-art technology was his real priority.

Desi pulled out his oversized rig from under the sofa and plugged his deck into it. His rig was twice the size of a standard unit because of all of his extended non-standard adaptations. Numerous cards of different colors were clipped onto his primary databoard in an unsightly and precariously balanced array.

He looked at the series of readouts and saw that with the amount of water he had on the roof, he could run his deck for about eight hours. He set up the piping so he could redirect water to his bathtub and to his internal storage containers in the apartment. He would be able to capture nearly half of the water from the roof. He tapped on the pipe in a series of warning tones to alert anyone downstream that he would be opening his water supply, and to let them know in thirty minutes water would flow until it was gone. He received three taps back from three different people, so he knew most of the water would find a home.

The deck's internal battery was already nearly fully powered, and he did his best to keep it that way, because he never knew when he would have work, and he wanted to always have the option to work, even if there wasn't any water or electricity where he might be staying. The deck, in power-saving mode, might last twenty hours, but it took half that time just to find a buyer these days. Paper is lucrative, but the fines and penalties were high if you were caught trafficking in paper products or infodrops of paper from older magazines from the last century.

His initial diagnostic of his deck said the software was as up to date as it could be, and there was no traffic that resembled Los

Angeles at his current connection. That would change, the more suspicious his traffic got. In Los Angeles, low Turing AI's monitored the NewerNet and kept track of any packets whose pedigree they could not easily identify. Desi's greatest hack was his ability to make his packets look completely innocent and resemble the multitude of datastreams out there already.

The NewerNet was not like the old Internet that collapsed in 2027 in the media explosion of the late 2020's. It was designed from the ground up to be completely under the control of the founding governments of the United States and Europe, the primary investors. As other countries were allowed to buy their way in, strict regulation of the traffic and content was established. Since media crashed the Internet, there were multiple control systems on media, ensuring smoother traffic and better management. This also meant the worldwide internet agency chartered by the United Nations became the impromptu police of the NewerNet. This new stricter internet was one of the most policed and controlled systems in the world. Using pre-Turing AI's, the network was constantly patrolled, regulated, data managed, was the most secure piece of technology ever to exist.

And the most souless, thought Desi. Once the NewerNet was established three years after the collapse of the Old Internet, big money kept the network the playground of the elite and the superwealthy. The OlderNet was restored as a shadow of its former self, but because so many people were forced to use it, it was unstable and unfriendly, not to mention filled with a variety of spyware, malware, and rogue viruses. The insecurity of the Oldernet allowed Desi to use it to enter the NewerNet and meet his clients using specialized hacks Desi had created when he was just a child of nine or ten.

Desi activated his rainwater power system and his rig hummed to life. "Gotta work fast; ten hours will vanish like magic." Indeed they did. He did not find his next buyer for almost nine hours after starting. The data his buyer was looking for was information regarding private solar technology development. Information of this nature had become government owned during the economic collapse of big business when the internet failed. Energy companies were the first services absorbed by the government.

All of their attendant information was also absorbed. The cache of publications Desi had found had to be a library extension, because his database linked two dozen articles, and five of them were specifically about the processes used to make advanced solar cells. Desi was able to convince his client to pay the astronomical finder fee of five hundred thousand New Pesos . That would be enough to pay off Don Milago and get the price off of his head. There would still be enough to get a new deck and upgrade this shitty old rig to something more state of the art, maybe even new. He might even share the wealth with his stupid roommate for all the times he spent riding water into the bathtub when Desi couldn't. He would blow through his fifty thousand in putas and tequila, but that would be his business.

He arranged for a meeting place with the client with a time delay activation. The client would only get the key to break the encryption twenty minutes before the drop. No military or police can mobilize in that kind of time. At the first hint of betrayal, Desi would vanish into the crowds and never be seen. Desi could hear the knocking of the pipes and see the pressure timer indicating he had used up eight hours of water and was about to run out of pressure. He turned off the pipe, leaving thirty or so minutes of extra water to spare. He tapped the pipes again, and everyone responded with thanks and shutting off their valves until the next time.

Exhausted, Desi fell into a dreamless sleep.

* * *

"Salir, puta, vete a casa de tu madre." Nicolas was drunk and threw the woman's clothes out of the apartment door. As she ran by in disgust, she snatched the money from his hands as she passed him. He in return smacked her on the ass and lifted the heavy door back into the locked position. Nicky stank of sex and went into the bathroom and noticed the tub was more than half full of water. He considered just jumping into the water, but not completely crazy, Nicky drew a small bucket from the wall and filled it with water. Using this, he cleaned himself up and admired himself in the mirror again.

Nicky hated the putas. They always thought they were better than him. Selling your ass is not a job, he would say, but they would just laugh and take his money. Nicky noted sunrise had just taken place as he left the bathroom, and it lit up the eastern side of the building without a completed face. Feeling better after his washing up, he grabbed the last of the cheese and stale bread from their refrigerating pantry.

"We need to score soon; there ain't shit in here to eat now." As he chewed the tough bread and slightly desiccated cheese, Nicky had an idea. He had been following Desi a few days ago and knew he had found a new cache of paper. Nicky mentioned idly to Desi they could sell the whole lot at a black market paper pulper and make some good money. Nicky had sold stockpiles that size for easily fifty thousand New Pesos. Desi had told him to wait until he had finished his survey, but well, he ain't the boss. He could get that money and give Desi his fifty percent and be in hookers, booze, and money for weeks, if he managed it right. Nicky went to his closet and put on a good suit. It was never a good idea to meet Don Milago looking anything less than perfect.

* * *

Desi woke hungry and feeling just a bit sick. The sun shining through the open east face of the building was hot, very hot. He was sweating and knew this would be another one of those three digit days. Washing off the stink of his sweaty night's sleep, Desi had wanted to be up and out before it go this hot, and now he would have to be climbing in the heat of the day. The drop was tomorrow, so he couldn't let it wait.

He opened the pantry in the partially complete kitchen. The cheese and bread were both gone. " Cabrón. That was enough cheese and bread that he could have left half for me. Why do I deal with him? It isn't like we are even friends anymore. After tomorrow, I will just move out try and rent a small house closer to the center of town near my job. I will be able to pay the rent for a year, giving me time to figure out my next move. Even after I give Don Milago his cut and interest, I will be set for months. I could even take my time with my next project."

Desi's stomach rumbled, breaking his reverie . "Okay, Mijo, we have fifteen pesos left, just enough to grab something to eat and get over to the zone." This would be his last meal for a while if this drop didn't work. He changed out of his good clothing and put on some tan khakis and a backpack. In the pack were his deck, water, rope, duct tape, a filter mask, gloves, and waterproof folders to move the product in.

The climb down did nothing to improve his state of mind. It seemed everyone had the same idea, to sit in the stairwell, because it was fifteen degrees cooler in the concrete isolated tube. By the time he reached the street, he was hot, annoyed and more tired than when he woke up. The five miles to the zone was thankfully uneventful other than a few nu-chickens waddling down the road, their oversized breasts making it nearly impossible for them to escape the children chasing them.

Seeing those children put him in mind of Nicolas. When they were younger, they were just like these kids, chasing chickens for dinner, just like their mother asked them to. Nicky was fun back then, reckless, wild, completely fearless. Those same traits make him an irresponsible adult. His transformation was a gradual one, and it didn't seem to be complete until after their mother died. Mom told Nicky to take care of me because of my asthma, and because he was the man of the house.

But right after Mom died, we lost our home in the quake, and we lived on the street until we found a place at the Ivory Towers. Falling in with Don Milago and his mafia was the worst thing Nicky ever did. The worst thing I did was to listen and join with him. But today, that ends. Desi's mental ramblings had distracted him from the distance and the heat. He came to the edge of the earthquake zone, still marked with orange traffic cones and concrete dividers at the edge of the sinkhole.

The center of Mexico City sat on an underground aquifer which had existed for millions of years. As the city grew and demanded more water for its twenty million inhabitants, the aquifer slowly lost water faster than it gained it from rainwater and mountain run off. The day of the great quake, a 9.3, one of the greatest quakes in history, teamed up with the collapse of the aquifer cavity and caused one of the worst natural disasters in history. Nine million people died in the initial collapse. The poorest quarters of town outside of the city proper, the barrios, survived with collapsed buildings, but without the catastrophic loss of life.

The edges of the city farthest from the sinkhole were still relatively accessible if you were careful and tied very good knots. He saw something wrong with the area as he approached. The cones had been moved from their normal positions, and the concrete barriers were parted as if to allow a vehicle past. Slipping down behind rubble, Desi followed the road, determined to find out what anyone in a vehicle could possibly want down here. The road was unstable, and a truck was simply the stupidest thing you could do.

When Nicolas showed up at Don Milagro's villa, it was still early in the morning, with only the slightest hint of the coming heat. The gate guards let Nicolas through with only a cursory glance and a quick pat down. Nicky was, of course, unarmed. Very few people could afford a firearm. Two guards waved Nicky toward the house, and he made his way up to the side of the pool where the Don was having breakfast in the shade of a tree that blocked the morning sun.

The Don smiled as Nicolas came into view and stood up to greet him. He was a huge man, still vigorous-looking despite his age and salt and pepper hair. "Nicky, sit down with me and have breakfast."

Nicolas thought to refuse, but the Don's tone left him with the impression he did not have a choice. "Si, Don Milagro, gracias."

"Now tell me about your project, Nicky."

"Well, I need a truck and some men to help me move some paper. I found a large stockpile of it in Old New Mexico City."

"Really?" Don Milagro's face was smiling, but his dark eyes weren't. His eyes were all business.

Nicolas continued, "It's near the edge of the collapse zone, and I believe there are several tons of it. I have a buyer lined up willing to convert it at his own facility. So, all we have to do is pick up the load, move it and drop it, and they are promising me $175,000 New Pesos for the shipment."

"What would you want from me, Nicky? You sound as if everything is already worked out."

"I need manpower and a truck, Don Milago. To move that much paper, quickly, will take at least four to six men."

"And what is my percentage of this endeavor if I provide you with fast manpower and a vehicle?" The Don had stopped eating and fixed Nicolas with his complete attention. Nicolas suddenly felt hot, and sweat burst out underneath his shirt, a cold sweat, decidedly uncomfortable.

"I was thinking of splitting it, 60/40. With the sixty going to you, of course."

"It seems a bit one-sided to me. I am providing the truck, and up to six men to work in the heat of the day, near a dangerous sinkhole. I certainly hope you can do better than that."

"Of course, Don Milagro. What was I thinking? I meant to say 80/20, seeing how generous you are being with your men and your overall support."

"Now you know that you and your brother are in deep debt to me at the moment. But I think of you like family. I would like to think you would want to help out your younger brother in his time of need. He owes me enough money, at this point, for me to have his kneecaps shattered. I like you, Nicky. I understand you. Greed and avarice are things near to me. Your brother, not so much. I do not understand his motivations and what I don't understand, I don't have any use for."

"I don't follow you, señor." Nicolas did not like where this conversation was heading.

"Your brother is in debt to me for nearly 250,000 New Pesos. I have not tried to call that debt in for some time, because he is usually good about paying me, but now the word has gotten out that he owes me this money. I cannot have my reputation being damaged, having anyone saying that I am weak, and I cannot control my men. I need you to make the problem of your brother go away. Necesito que a desaparecer."

"Don Milagro, you know I will do anything you ask me to. But he is my brother."

"He is your problem, then. He has my money or you make him disappear. I shall show you my generosity. Keep all the money from your little paper excursion. I will call it your fee. Feel better, now? I will have the men and truck ready within the hour. Finish your breakfast."

Nicky could barely eat anything, and he was starving. His stomach felt like a pool of bubbling acid. What in the hell was he going to do?

* * *

Desi could not believe anyone could be this stupid. The truck was parked backward on a steep slope, with the back door open. But this whole area was unstable and could slide into the sinkhole at any time. As it was, the repository was nearer to the edge than he would have liked. He used his line to tie himself off and began to pay it out behind him, watching his every step until he came to the drop point. As he got closer, he could hear the voices of the men and a couple of them sounded familiar.

Alfredo? What's he doing here? Is that Nicky? Desi slipped out of line of sight of the van. Alfredo, Nicky, and two others came around the corner pulling dollies with containers filled to the brim with paper from his stockpile!

"Tú pendejo!" Desi ran out and drew back with all his strength and knocked Nicky flat on his ass. "What are you doing? Have you lost your mind?"

"What? Do you know how much this is worth?" Nicky clutched his bleeding lip and jaw. He sat up, but did not move.

"Do you? How much do you think you are going to get for this?"

"I have been promised 175,000 New Peso, cabrón. Now you need to get out of my face, so I can get back to work."

Desi's rage grew ten times stronger and made him reckless. He punched Nicky in the face and screamed at him. "Estupido. I will make more money from a single page than you would for this entire lot."

The remainder of Don Milagro's men lifted not a finger to interfere. This was a family matter, and they turned around and found a nickstik to smoke and share while the two worked out their issues. They would follow whoever came out on top.

Desi's rage tightened his chest and his breathing became labored. He started wheezing and fell to his knees.

Nicky shook off the kick and got to his knees. "Nickilito, slow down. Calm down." He hefted Desi to his chest and held him close. "Breathe slower. You are always so over-excited. Mama was right to leave me in charge."

Desi weakly struck out at Nicky, and then turned into his chest as his breath slowly came back to him. He began to cry. "Why Nicky, why do you always want to screw up my things?"

"I don't know, Desi. I'm always jealous of you. You can do so many things with your mind. I'm just a dumb jock. Selling your paper was petty. I just wanted to make some quick cash. I'm sorry."

The four men from Don Milago's villa had finished their nickstik and turned to look at the two men. "Is this love-fest over? Can we get back to work?"

Nicky looked at Desi with inquiry in his eyes. "Wait here. Hold this rope. I will be right back." Desi moved into the partially collapsed building and dropped off a floor adjacent to the stairwell Nicky had been using. The paper Desi needed was several levels below. He could tell from the covers of the books he was seeing that they had not reached the information he planned to sell. Working quickly, he grabbed the publications he had already set aside and put them into his pack.

He tugged the rope and shouted up, "Okay, pull me up."

Nicky and his men pulled Desi back to the first floor. "Go ahead, do what you need to. Be careful, this area is less stable than it looks. Don't go beyond the second floor."

"Okay, you heard the man. Let's get moving." As Alfredo and his team moved out, Nicky turned Desi towards him and knocked some of the dust off of him. "Desi, Don Milagro is really pissed about the money you owe him. Can you pay him?"

"I think so. If my buy goes down tomorrow, we will be all right. I will buy us out, free and clear."

"That's great. Is everything in the bag?" Nicky turned away for a second while Desi started wrapping his line. When he turned back, he brandished a gun pointed toward Desi. "Give me the bag, Desi."

"What are you doing, Nicolas?"

"I promised Don Milagro that I would make you disappear. You have caused him to lose face, and I want to move up in his organization. So you give me the bag, I sell what you have in it, move this paper, and I get it all. A promotion, money, status."

"So this was all an act? You had planned to kill me the next time you saw me, no matter what?"

"I'm sorry, Desi. He made me an offer I couldn't refuse."

"It doesn't have to be like this. I can get us clear. Just trust me."

"You have been promising me you would make a big score for the last twelve years. We have been living hand to mouth since Mama died. It's always one more job, one more scheme, and we'll be set. Well, I am tired of waiting. I am taking my shot now. I am so sorry."

"Fuck you, Nicky." Tears welled up in Desi's eyes as he handed over his backpack.

Don Milagro came around the corner and looked at Nicky with pride. "Well done, my boy, well done." Don Milagro put his hand out and Nicky handed him the gun.

"I will be giving you your reward today, Nicky. I told you, I respect greed and avarice, and you are a testament to the effect of money on family relationships." Milagro had been pointing the gun at Desi, and then turned suddenly, shooting Nicky in the gut. Nicky staggeed backward and fell into the house where the last of Don Milagro's men were rolling out the last of the paper.

"Now, my boy. I understand you were in the business of selling paper to buyers. I have been told I have been thinking too small, and there is a lucrative business arrangement we could be working out. So, to show me your renewed value, you will give me the drop coordinates and your contact codes. Work with me, and we could all be very wealthy. With that truck alone, I am confident we could become very wealthy men."

"You lied to Nicky. To make him bring you to me."

"So true. His greed made him easy to confuse."

"And if I work for you, what would make me think you won't do the same thing to me?"

"You are more valuable to me alive, of course. But only if you cooperate."

Desi heard a pinging noise with a familiar rhythm. It happened three times before he realized he recognized the signal that the water was about to start flowing. Desi hadn't taken the rope off from around his waist and shoulders. He began to back up toward the edge of the sinkhole. "I don't see how I can trust you. You just killed my brother. He may have been my half-brother, but you killed him anyway, like you would kill a dog."

"So what? To me, he was just a dog, a dog I paid to bite who I wanted him to bite. You are wasting my time. Give me the coordinates and the access codes. Otherwise, I will just shoot you and consider today a wash. I made a little money and got rid of a couple of problems."

The tapping got louder and more insistent. "Go in there and find out what that noise is. If it's Nicky, feel free to beat him to death." The four men rushed off to comply with the Don's order. Desi felt the shelf vibrating and realized what Nicky was doing.

"I need to key the code in myself. It will only activate with my biometric signature. Hand me the bag." Desi put his hand out. The Don hesitated for a moment, and then gave the bag to him.

Desi reached into the bag, and the Don raised his gun and pointed it at Desi. Desi pulled out the deck and activated it. He put his key code in and began entering the twenty-four character string. His hands were shaking, so he put the backpack onto his back while he continued to enter code. Then there was a snapping, cracking sound, and the shelf shook violently, bounced once and fell away.

"Te quiero, Nicky," was the last thing he heard as he fell freely into the open sinkhole. The Don, unable to maintain his footing, slid toward the edge of the shelf and was flung into space. He turned as he fell and shot five times before he disappeared into the darkness. Desi saw the line pay out, and then there was a snap and he lost consciousness.

When Desi woke up, he was bleeding from a scalp wound. Bloody but not fatal. He climbed up the rope and realized he did not have his deck. Didn't matter; he had activated the drop code and would meet the client on time.

When he got to the top, he saw the truck was now on the edge of the shelf, but still able to be driven. He got in and found the keys were still in the ignition. He looked back and saw the entire stockpile was now inside the truck. As he drove away, wiping the sticky blood from his face with a towel he found inside the truck, he wondered what Costa Rica looked like this time of year.

Dark Star Rising

The Kid fell from the sky, aflame. A black energy coruscated and trailed from his unconscious form. He fell limply, silently, helplessly. His explosive impact drove shards of concrete into the air and an exploding crater released a tower of flaming gas as his powers ignited an underground fuel main. People retreated into whatever cover they could find as automobiles fell from the explosion and the searing heat melted plastic, rubber, and other soft metals nearby. It was hell on Earth.

What followed him moved slowly at first. It was in no hurry. It savored the world into which it found itself thrust. The first two days here, there was no resistance and the creatures were soft, edible, pliant, with mild and crunchy centers. Then a few new ones came, and they were armed with stinging tools, primitive and less effective than nothing. They and their tools were tasty with a slight iron flavoring. Some articles of their clothing were less than tasty, tough with a fibrous consistency. After eating six or eight of them, it decided to peel the rest of the blue guardians and eat only the flesh and bones.

Then *they* came. The special ones. Most looked like the main food of this world, small, delicate, crunchy, and like the blue guardians, they were armed with tools. Their tools were fantastically more effective than those of the blue guardians. No matter. Nothing of this world can harm me. Nothing at all. Even the fire-star is too weak. I shall enjoy this one, and I shall not share it. Not a morsel will the others get.

"The Kid is down."

"He'll get up. He's just like his old man was. Stubborn."

"Any ideas of what we're dealing with?"

"With the rash of magical threats we have been seeing lately, I think someone has just upped the ante."

"Oswald, I think we are going to have to hold the line until the big guns get here."

Thornton Oswald the Third stood looking over the city and realized that the Shrike was right. With The Kid down, Gunner on sabbatical, Kali was coming from Metro City, and Shango out doing whatever magical Protectors of the Crossroads do in their spare time, they would have to hold this thing until reinforcements arrived. But it took The Kid. After Kali and Shango, The Kid was as tough as they come. He lacked his father's fighting experience, but his durability under fire was unquestioned.

"Shrike, I will need a minute. Can you keep him entertained while I transform?"

"Sure thing, he'll never see me coming."

The Shrike, Walter Scott, depressed the studs in his gloves and his suit's jetpack came online. Extending his arms, large metallic wings with serrated edges extended from them, increased his wing span to twenty feet. "Don't be late." With a boom, the Shrike took to the air and dived to attack the creature who stood easily twenty feet tall.

Thornton proceeded to draw a circle of containment in the rooftop gravel. As his cane drew through the rocks, they lit with an eldritch glow. Hearing the boom of the rockets as they roared away, Thornton focused his mind on breaching the boundaries between worlds. To a particular world, a world of feral beasts used by dark magicians and ancient gods, to the Fan-run-dhar-durak - Land of Forgotten Beasts. Once the realm became clear to him, he sought for a particular beast, a creature whose unmistakable might would be tested tonight. He sought the beast called Grimmamon, mightiest of the Beast Lords.

The Shrike swooped fast and his onboard computer, linked directly into his brain, had already plotted the course he needed to strike five times in two passes. His wings comprised of Promethium, a rare alien metal, allowed him to transfer and magnify his kinetic energy, so the longer he flew, the stronger and more dangerous the metal became.

But fly too long and the energy became uncontrollable without a release. So the longer he flew, the more he was forced to fight. Only touching the ground would bleed that energy from him. It was always the delicate dance of fighting and being tougher, but blowing out from not releasing enough energy or returning to his default state where he was weakest just before recharging.

Having flown here, he had already expended a good portion of his energy against the creature. He had damaged this black material called skin and even had drawn blood. But it seemed unaffected and knocked The Kid into next week. If he had been just a second slower, it would have been him. He doubted he would have survived that impact with the ground.

—*gonna be fast, be loose, feel the air, float with it, snap the wing, strike, strike, beat the wing, turn, beat the wing turn, snap, snap, strike, strike, strike, away*—

His blows were fast, blurs to the naked eye, and each tore into the nacreous flesh with little effect. Once, his wings had sliced through bank vaults back in the days when he was a villain in Metro City.

—*Come on, Kid, we ain't friends or nothing, but right now, I could use the sight of your overconfident face coming out of that fire. I hope Oswald is having more luck than I am.*

* * *

Kali was streaking through the sky on her cloud, heading to Paragon City where she received the distress call from the Shrike and the Sorcerer. She was making good time and would arrive in about ten minutes. From this height, the suburbs of Paragon City seemed peaceful. She could see the smoke from the burning buildings ahead, a path of sheer destruction. The old Kali would have liked that; the new Kali was repulsed by such mindless waste.

"Kali Yuga, I have need of you and your darkest aspect."

"I hate when you call me that, Shango. Where are you?" She really did hate that name; it invoked a violent and destructive past where she was a destroyer of all that she surveyed.

"I am at The Crossroads. There has been a breach and creatures are pouring through. I am attempting to seal it, but I cannot as long as the creatures prevent me from reaching it. I need your help."

"Asking for help? That is not like you, Thunderer."

"Nor is needing help, warrior-goddess, but here we are."

"Can you make the gate? Or shall I follow your whining to the Crossroads?"

"Suffice it to say, you are earning that spanking."

"Put it on my tab. I will be there shortly, husband."

Kali focused her will, and her two arms became four. Each of them was armed with a knife of pure spirit. She began a sword dance designed to take her to the Crossroad between Worlds, a magical nexus connecting nearby realms of existence. A particularly puissant sorcerer or other magical being could use it to reach across space and time to other worlds altogether.

As she whirled faster and faster, she began to weave open a doorway, using her spirit blades and her connection to her husband's god-force. The Shrike would call it a paired quantum connection, but she preferred the magical concept of contagion; once two things are bound together, nothing can keep them apart. She was beginning to feel the connection strongly and could see into the nether dimensions the Crossroad inhabited.

She could sense Shango before she could see him. He was covered by a horde of dark skinned giants. The Crossroad was in the presence of three giant red suns shedding their ruddy light on the scene. Shango was, for a moment, unable to be seen, but then lightning exploded from the ground, and the creatures were thrown back, and for a moment he was clear.

"Woman, what part of your Kali Yuga aspect did you not understand? I need you in your most terrible guise or we are doomed."

Once she transitioned into the Crossroad, she was behind Shango, and he used his double-headed axe to create a barrier of lightning.

"Good to see you, too. Before we invoke that bitch, do you think we could see what we can do here, first?"

"Do you see that portal? That is where we need to be."

The distance was only about the length of two football fields, but it was filled with these creatures, each the height of two men, with near human physical attributes. Their heads appeared to be more like an octopus, and their hands instead ended in tentacles. There were hundreds of them.

"Make ready, husband."

Shango dropped his barrier and released a bolt of lightning, driving a wedge between the creatures, incinerating two dozen of them instantly. In the second it took his lightning to cross one hundred meters, Kali had already slain thirty of the monsters . She stepped through time and space and was everywhere and nowhere. She appeared and disappeared, and each strike laid a creature low. Her face was serene and peaceful as her four blades struck at once. Her superhuman strength made each blow cut deep into their flesh, severing meat and bone like a hot knife through butter.

Shango concentrated his powers and created a series of strikes before her; each of them she slew her way through to the next. When he was too busy to support her, he lent her his lightning and she kept the area around her cleared with her flashing blades and lightning. His double-headed axe flew around him with a cloud of electricity arcing from it to every creature near him. But the creatures were relentless and without fear. As soon as he would clear the area, more would appear.

He looked out and saw Kali was within fifty feet of the portal. He called lightning once more, and as it arced from him toward her, the creatures around him opened their mouths and sharp bones shot out and speared him in his chest and arms. He looked in disbelief; his flesh had the strength of steel. He laughed off high caliber weaponry like rain. What were these things that they could do this?

A searing acid began to burn his flesh, pumped through their ceramic probosci. He howled as his mighty flesh began to burn. Without warning, the creatures blocking his line of sight were cut in half, and two other blades slashed the demons' tongues. The blades whirled around him and returned to Kali, who had not stopped her dance of death and retrieved her weapons amid flight and continued killing.

Shango, now enraged, drew his power to him, focused his pain and rage and became a thing of pure lightning. The creatures strove to grab him and died instantly, burned to death. As they cleared away, powerful arcs leaped from him to them, and they continued to die. He moved forward slowly, and Kali cut them down as they passed through the portal. He reached her and caught her hand as she struck out at him.

"Enough, my wife. The portal is silent. Perhaps we have earned our invitation."

"Then let us not be rude to our hosts. They did set forth such a feast for such as us."

"Indeed."

They stepped through the portal.

* * *

Meanwhile, Thornton Oswald III completed his summoning ritual with the King of Netherbeasts. Grimmammon took the form of a great cat of immense size.

" Grimmammon, I invoke your service as in the pacts defined

by my ancestors."

"Bah, mortal, why should I bother with your family's ancient pacts? You have been notoriously lax in your relationship to us. Where are the rituals of blood and souls as in the past?"

"Spare me your pathetic bargaining, hell-beast. Without me and mine, you and yours would have passed into your final existence decades ago. Our world stopped worshipping your kind hundreds of years ago. Look around you. Ask where Lord Arioch and his brethren have gone. Provide your services and enjoy the benefits of our continued relationship."

"Show me why you summoned me."

"Look, oh Great One. Tell me what you see."

Grimmammon looked over the edge of the roof, and his demonic mien grew more stoic. "Our pact ends at the edge of this world, sorcerer. That is an eldritch being from beyond our world."

"And evidently frightening enough to remove most of your bluster. Tell me more, Great One. Who or what is that creature?"

"A Chaos god from before the time of Arioch, from before time as you measure it."

"You lie. There were no gods before that time."

"Silence, pup. There are secrets even the gods keep. These creatures were imprisoned here in an age before yours. You are not the first masters of the Earth. Did you think you were? Ha."

"Imprisoned?"

"By the First People. They could not destroy them, but they could lock them beneath the Earth, or the Sea, or in Fire. It is said even the very Air imprisons one. I will have no truck with that one, no matter what the price you offer. Its powers likely dwarf mine, the same way mine dwarf yours."

Oswald thought about what Grimmammon told him, and realized they were out of their depth. Even if Shango and Kali were here, this was a threat greater than they could manage on their own. Since neither of them were here, it was likely they were working on this menace in their own way. "So we will do what we can until they arrive."

"I know you can see the boy in that conflagration. Bring him here; deposit the flames on the creature. Then you can take your leave. We would not want you to be injured before I can make use of you again. You are weakening with age; perhaps I shall call your rival Shunmaburan instead."

"As you request, so shall it be. But if you seek to wound my pride, you will find no demon has pride when its survival is at stake.

But by all means, if you wish to call Shunmaburan today, and he were not to survive, I would be in your debt. Farewell."

The old demon stood at the edge of the roof and the flames rose from the crater in the street. The flames swirled as if they were a fire vortex and flew from the crater to surround the otherworldly invader with the terrible fires. The Kid disappeared from the crater and appeared on the roof next to Oswald. Oswald saw the daemon link the fire to the creature, and realized the fire would only last a few minutes before exhausting its fuel. Once surrounded, the creature stopped moving forward, and this bought them some time.

Grimmammon turned away from the roof's edge. He looked at the boy and said, "Tough, that little one is. A parting gift." And with that he nodded and stepped back into the gateway in the floor of the roof.

Oswald was not happy with Grimmammon's parting words. No good comes from gifts from demons. Looking down at The Kid, he saw the boy's amazing recuperative powers rebuilding him, and in less than two minutes, he sat up, looking angry.

"Wait. We need to talk. There are things you need to know."

* * *

Carolyn Von Putten was having dinner on the other side of Paragon City when she saw the news. She was finally having the date she had taken a vacation for, and she was determined to enjoy it. She was wearing a black Versace dress with less than modest pumps, showing off her well-muscled body.

She spent days hunting for this dress and wanted to stun Elliot Cole, investigative reporter, right out of his socks. And the dress had the right effect, too. Cole was barely able to speak and the evening was going so well. And then this.

Cole looked at her. "Well?"

"Well, what?"

"I know you can see that television over there above the bar."

"And? It's on the other side of town. If those heroes can't handle it, we'll just cut our dinner date a bit short."

Cole leaned forward and whispered, "What about Gunner? You do realize I know who you are?"

"What?"

"Don't try to kid the kidder. I have known for some time. I am the ace investigative reporter in Paragon City. Now I know you should be going, and they certainly look like they need you. I don't see Shango or Kali. Moving fire means the Occultist is there, and that flashing of silver probably means the Shrike, and I have not seen The Kid yet, so I am guessing thirty foot tall monsters warrant your attention?"

"Do you know how long I have waited for this date?"

"And I promise we will get another shot at it, pardon the pun. Now go. Besides, I have a scoop to get."

"Need a lift? My car is on its way."

"Nah, you have an image to uphold. Guns blazing and all."

"See you in a bit." Carolyn grabbed Cole and kissed him fiercely on the mouth. "Just in case, you're late to our next date." She turned and ran out the door. Turning the corner, a midsize SUV pulled alongside and opened the side door.

"Your suit's in the back. Nice dress. " The grizzled man driving the car pointed his thumb backward. She hopped up into the back and started stripping. "Get me there, fast. Set up range for heavy weapons long range. Put me on the radio."

"Shrike, can you hear me?"

"Gunner, enjoying your vacation?"

"Can it, I need you to get some distance and come in hot. I will be there in less than five minutes. Move out and I will come in with explosive ordinance. You follow with a Cannonball."

"Roger that, fearless leader."

"Occultist?"

"Yes, Gunner."

"Where is The Kid?"

"I have him. He has been hurt. He found the creature first and alerted us. He held it until the Shrike and I could help."

"How is he doing?"

"Tough as nails, ready to go back."

"Any word from Shango or Kali?"

"None, but I can sense they are not in this world, or at the Crossroads. So they may be involved at another point in the battle. We will have to do what we can."

"Our goal is to stun and control. Keep it where it is. Can you get the rest of the people out of there?"

"Of course."

"Once the Kid is up, tell him to wait for my signal. Ten seconds after my signal, he should see a Cannonball. I will need him to grab the Shrike. I will work long range pushing the creature back. Is there anything else you can tell me?"

"My contacts tell me it's not like anything we have ever seen. We better hope Shango and Kali are having better luck than we are."

"Why?"

"My contacts said the last time these things ruled the world, they destroyed the previous inhabitants."

"That's not gonna happen."

"Hope you're right."

"Stand by for my signal. Get those people out of there."

* * *

Shango and Kali stepped through the portal and fell to their knees. The gravity was intense, eight times what they were used to on Earth. The air was thick and heavy. Even with their superior senses, they could barely see through the soup-like atmosphere.

They could hear a chittering sound, something that clicked, popped, sputtered at a variety of distances. Each set of sounds was distinct and otherworldly. Kali stood and began to move her hands in magical gestures.

"The spiritual flow here is weak. Something binds its movement."

"Draw the god-force from my axe and complete your spell."

As Kali finished her spell, she looked exhausted, but now she could understand the voices.

"What is it? Why has it come here?"

"It has disease; it comes from elsewhere. Nothing comes here."

"Make it leave."

The three voices had a chorus of others that answered them.

"This does not bode well, Kali. I think I liked it better when I didn't know what they were saying."

"That can be arranged. What do we do now? I was hoping there would be something to hit over here."

"It wants to hit us. Why? What did we ever do to it?"

"Kill it. It trespasses on our world. We would never allow that in the past. We have eaten all before now."

"No haste, visitors are rare; find what they want, first. What do you want, germ invaders?"

"I am Shango the Thunderer and this is Kali Bhavatarini. On our world we are gods. I would see whom I address.

"Gods, you say.

Hahahahahahaha! Such tiny gods.

You must come from a tiny world."

"Show yourselves, braggart," Kali shouted out to the darkness.

"Pull back the darkness."

"We'll rip your tiny minds apart."

"Shroud is for your protection."

Shango raised his axe and began to emit lightning, pushing back the darkness. Kali called her spirit blades and touched them together, increasing the light and dispelling the shroud around them.

"Evil germs want to see what we are?"

"Germ gods can't listen."

"So be it."

The shroud of darkness peeled back slowly like a fog being dispelled. The scene was one of carnage as an alien landscape with the remains of a city all around them. Broken buildings toppled into the streets with all the great structures damaged in one way or another.

In the sky swirled a great mass, where the shroud emanated. Tendrils of both darkness and blackened flesh reached from it. They were immense, and the creature filled the sky with its horror. The pressure on the minds of Kali and Shango increased as its spiritual monstrosity overwhelmed them.

Both warrior gods, both having slain tens of thousands in battle, were not prepared for the horror of a creature that had slain billions, entire worlds, holding their souls enslaved within its flesh, the spiritual screams overwhelming them.

Their shields diminished, pushed back to their very persons. They stood together to support each other, and held the horror at bay, but it lapped at their shields, tongues of darkness trying to lick them, taste them, just seconds from overwhelming them completely.

They had never seen anything like this.

"Germ gods, you do not see all there is to me. I dwell at the center of the Universe. I lived before your world was even a swirling in the cosmic miasma. What would you know of godhood? You are only a little more evolved than the worms of your world."

Shango laughed loudly and contemptuously at the alien being. "Your living quarters are foul, oh great Universe-dwelling deity. Where are your worshippers? Where are your spires of beauty, showing off your power to your enemies? A poor deity that fouls its nest!" Kali looked at Shango disapprovingly.

"Imprisoned by the creatures here. Unable to enter, unable to leave, I sensed an awakening and strove to find it at the Crossroads of all Realities. But before I could find it and leave, the portal was closed. Wretches bound me to this spot. Hate them I did. Killed all of them. They now serve me as my advance guard. Now I seek my kind everywhere. Only they can free me."

"What would you know of this creature? He roams my world, free. His power is like yours, dark, an evil before time." Kali presents a psychic image of the creature in Paragon City.

"He is one of us. Betrayer. He taught them here how to bind me to this spot. In exchange for his imprisonment somewhere else, away from me. Send me to him. I would have my revenge."

"We cannot send you to him. We cannot break the bindings that lock you here. But we could make it possible for you to bring him here." Shango looked at Kali, disbelieving what she was proposing.

"Trust me, my husband."

"Oh yes, I would have him here with me."

"How would you make this possible?"

"You are, after all, insignificant in power even to one as puny as he."

Kali spoke to the tendrils of the creature tearing away at her shields, seeking even a momentary doubt to penetrate and strike. "Open your portal again. We will make a portal to our world. You reach through both and pull him back to you."

"How can I trust you? I trusted him and he deceived me. I trusted these creatures and they enslaved me.

I cannot trust anyone now. Only one of you can go.

The other stays here."

They look at each other disbelievingly. They are the last of their kind on their world. Without them, their respective pantheons would lose their last anchors to Earth. Shango readied himself to say something, and Kali touched him on the lips.

"You go. Your powers on Earth make you the more suitable choice to create the gate and to drive him into it. I will stay here and play hostage."

"I will be back for you, my wife."

"You'd better."

* * *

The Kid, using his super-speed, ran through the legs of the creature and launched an attack at its chest. His haymaker rocked its footing. Rebounding off its chest, he flipped and landed thirty feet away, just to the right of Gunner.

Gunner in her red and black battle gear held an X-25 rocket rifle, firing a series of explosive grenades into the tentacled face of the beast. The Occultist rained fiery spheres down from the sky, each wrapping a limb in a flaming embrace.

Fire had the most effect on the creature, preventing its continued movement. But that was all they could do. Between The Kid and his speed and strength and the Shrike's Promethium attacks, they could keep it off-balance. But whenever it moved or flailed about, buildings fell.

Nothing they did caused any permanent damage and they were beginning to tire.

Suddenly the sky darkened and the wind whipped up. Lightning began to swirl at the edges of the skyline.

The Kid, looking up, slowed down the flow of time and saw lightning charges building up right above their heads. Grabbing Gunner, he sped out of the line of the lightning discharge with seconds to spare. His big grin showed this was what he lived for, that last second save that no one but he could pull off. "Got ya, boss lady. I think the cavalry is here."

"What?" Gunner hated when he did that. He saw something seconds before it happened. Then the lightning strikes began. Each rained down as a driving wind directed them into the face of the creature. Right where she was standing a second ago.

"Occultist," boomed the voice of Shango from the heavens, "we need a Gate to the Crossroads. Something big enough for our guest."

"Shrike, where are you?" Gunner extricated herself from the Kid's very tight and strangely arousing grip.

"Coming in at Mach two. Tell me we have a target or I am going to explode right over you guys. Less than a minute."

"Come down West Street. We are trying to push the creature to the Crossroads."

"What good is that? He'll just come back."

"It's what Shango wants."

"Good enough for me. Fifty seconds."

The Occultist teleported himself to the ground behind the alien monstrosity and began to form his gate. It was hard to concentrate over the barrage of lightning, and he had to erect a barrier to protect himself. Holding his cane above his head, he warded off the lightning and driving rain pushing the creature back toward him. His incantations steady, he sensed the gateway to the Crossroads opening. And then he sensed it, a creature of the Outer Dark awaiting on the other side!

He balked, holding the spell before completion. *Shango is impetuous, stubborn, and sometimes downright irresponsible. But since I don't see Kali, I have to assume she is somehow involved in this. In the end, this is about trust. I have to trust they have a reason.* He completed the spell.

The Shrike, covered in the kinetic energy of his Promethium armor, saw the gateway open up. Diving down, he targeted the creature and saw lightning striking it, as well. Lightning strikes so powerful, the very air seemed aflame in a light so bright, the creature could barely be seen. *Never saw Shango like this. Glad we are on the same side now. Four, three, two, one...*

The release of the Promethium had to be done at point blank range. It had a release range of less than ten feet. He could turn at this speed, but just barely. To be sure of the effect this time, he would have to cut it closer than he was comfortable with. *If I had known this hero gig would be so dangerous, I might have just stayed a villain.* He activated his force field a second before impact, bracing himself for the energy release, it would be the equivalent of a Tomahawk missile. The explosion blasted him into the sky as he rebounded from the armored skin of the creature.

Flight controls are gone, diagnostics lights are on everywhere --we're done. This had better be worth it. He felt his vector changing as he fell downward. Still trying to reboot his armor, he suddenly felt the wind was knocked out of him.

Suddently drapped over the shoulder of the Kid as they bounced off a building, arced through the air and landed on the ground nearly a hundred feet away.

"One day I might miss you." The Kid laughed and put the Shrike down on the ground, clapping him on the back.

"Don't remind me. Thanks for the save."

"Armor systems online." The Shrike's powered armor reactivated.

"You might want to work on that reboot speed." The Kid smiled and streaked away, faster than a Corvette down the street back toward the creature. He plucked hurtling chunks of building out of the air, like flowers, that might strike bystanders as he re-entered the fray.

The combined explosions of the promethium wave, Shango's lightning strikes, and Gunner's mini-missiles pushed the creature into the edge of the gateway, but not quite through it. Before anyone could make a further effort, a tendril of blackness reached through the gate, and as it touched our air, burst into flame. It grabbed the monster and pulled it back into the Crossroads. The last thing heard was, "I finally found you, Nyarlethotep. Revenge is ours."

Without warning the gateway snapped shut.

Shango dropped like a rock from the sky, attempting to cross back into the gateway before it closed. The speed of his landing cracked the concrete. He roared like a madman and began to whirl his axe to create his own portal. The air was aflame with his lightning, but no portal formed. The Occultist walked up behind him and placed his hand on Shango's shoulder.

"Enough, old friend. The creature from the Outer Dark has temporarily sealed the passage from our world to the Crossroads."

"It has Kali."

The gathered heroes fell silent.

* * *

Kali summoned her spirit swords and began the ritual dance of power. Tapping the energies unique to this plane, she bound its power to hers. She felt the lives of The People, and their rage at the creature that destroyed them. She felt their need to lash out, but also their impotence since they are deceased and can no longer affect the world. Her dance said that they could.

They listened.

The portal had been open for some time. She remained peripherally aware of it as the spirits of the dead came to her and followed her dance, each lending its tiny essence to what she was, a goddess of destruction and creation, a goddess of Time and Space. They sensed her kinship to all things in creation, and were at peace.

The portal was rent asunder as the Other suddenly arrived, and the two power-mad creatures tapped the energies of this plane and dozens of others nearby for their conflict. They ignored her and closed the gateway while their battle continued.

"Our deal is done. Release me."

"Germ gods are in no position to make demands. We have our quarry, and we will use you to get back to your world once we have had our revenge."

"You will stay with us."

"We will be free of this place. We taste your world on him. It is to our liking."

Their conflict was so terrible, nearby shard realms of existence were destroyed as they moved their battle through dimensions. Kali realized this creature never had any intention of letting them go home. That was why she told Shango to leave. She had no intention of staying.

Turning to the gathered spirits she raised her arms and shouted to them, "You seek revenge. Only Kali Yuga can give you that. So I release her to you. Gain your revenge!"

Kali's dance moved faster, her four arms became eight, and she directed the energy of her death magic through the souls of those damned to be in this place, and they reflected her.

Her spirit blades appeared in their hands . And this happened again and again until there were hundreds of her and the contagion continued, spreading until there were thousands. Each shone with a dark energy that disrupted the very air around them. Slowly they rose into the air and their spirit blades sang out their song of retribution and revenge for their unjust deaths thousands of years before. Tiny stars of black fire began to arc through the air.

The gathered spirits by the thousands turned their energy toward the ancient gods locked in battle. They were not aware of the dark stars surrounding them. Each deity was consumed with its hatred of the other. The crazed tentacled god bound his brethren in a smoky embrace. The dark invader sliced away tentacle after tentacle, even as new ones replaced them. Their struggle destroyed the remnants of the great civilization around them as if they were nothing more than tissue in the path of a hurricane.

Then lead by Kali, the People exacted their revenge. Each hurled itself at the Great Old Ones. Their fiery trail slashed through tentacles and Dark God alike, and their screams of rage were palpable. Once ignored by the Great Old Ones, but no more. Now their rage was given form and a world quaked as bound spirits rose up against their slayer.

Kali Yuga smiled and continued her dance as the sky lit up by the fiery stars of souls enraged. And the Dark Gods knew fear.

* * *

An hour later, a portal opened in the wreckage of the street. Shango stood exactly where the last portal had closed. He knew if she was going to appear, it would be where the walls between worlds was weakest. He could sense it coming, a tell-tale rippling of the space-time at the Crossroads. When she came through she was in her Kali Yuga aspect, her demonic eight armed form was disheveled, battered, barely conscious but still alive. Even in this state, her power was evident, a wave of fear swept the street and people shuddered unconsciously.

Shango reached her in a single step and grabbed her. She slumped into his arms and her Yuga aspect was dispelled. And it was a good thing too. She had a hard time telling friend from foe in that state. He did not know what happened over there, but if she took on this form, she didn't make any friends.

Ever the optimist, Shango picked her up and laughed. "Look at that! They sent her home, after all. She really doesn't make for a good hostage." It wasn't the first time Shango questioned his wife's incredible powers. The gathered heroes turned to the wreckage and could hear the sounds of attack helicopters and other military vehicles approaching the scene.

The Shrike looked at Shango, his visor opened, "I know this part. Skipping out from the police was my specialty, remember? We aren't on the side of the angels anymore. We're fugitives. That means we run."

Gunner looked at the Occultist who was already weaving a teleportation spell. "Only for a little while longer, then we are going to fix this. I am tired of running."

As the military approaches, the people of Paragon City streamed out and quietly blocked the path of the oncoming forces, slowing them significantly.

Gunner looked on, saluteed them and with the spell completed, they faded from view. The bystanders quietly dispersed. The military commander breathed a sigh of relief. Gunner was an American hero. She and her team had saved the world a half a dozen times, at least. He had to follow orders, but he didn't have to rush.

"They got away again, sir."

"Don't you hate when that happens, Lieutenant?" The old colonel smiled, lighting a cigar.

Brotherhood

"I went yesterday."

"I went out the day before."

"I don't care who went out, when. Put your guns on and get out there and bring back something to eat. I don't care what it is."

"Yes, Ma."

"See what you did? Now she's mad at us."

"I didn't make her mad, you did."

"Anyway, food won't hop into the house by itself. You two get a move on. Get back before dark."

"Yes, Auntie." Ma's sister was almost as mean as she was.

We left the habitat by the back door, and after looking both ways, we started down the vine and headed out of the park into the city. It used to be called Philadelphia, back when stuff like that mattered.

"Did you pack everything?"

"Why do you always ask me if I packed everything? It's not like you weren't standing right there, supervising."

"Last time we were out, you forgot the wipes."

"So you were forced to use your hand or some leaves. Why should I care how you handle your business?"

"You suck."

"You ought to know."

"Be quiet. I hear something." Whenever we go out, we are always very careful. Once upon a time, there were lots of humies, but after They came, there were a lot less. We can see the one closest to the main city. It sits outside of the city proper and sends its parts looking for food.

Humies learned not to live in the cities if they wanted to avoid being food. Mama said once cities used to be filled with humies, but now, nobody with any sense goes there. That's why there is so much stuff still there. We don't tell Ma, but sometimes we go there and look for stuff. We learned how to avoid the plants and their critters.

"There it is. It's a cabbage-head."

"I don't like cabbage-heads. We just ate one a few weeks ago. I'd rather eat my boot first 'fore I eat another."

"We ate our boots last week, so we probably shouldn't get a cabbage-head anyway; they be the makings of poor boots."

We let the cabbage-head wander off. They weren't too dangerous or too bright, and noisy as all get out, so you didn't have to worry 'bout them sneakin' up or anything. They looked like a horse with the head of a cabbage. And they were about as bright.

Then we saw them. And we nodded. That was the target. Razorbacks. That's what Mama called them when she taught us to hunt. Razorbacks were part of the Creature, a fast and dangerous part. They hated humies, too.

We waited, cause there were too many to try and get one. They had six long legs and were really fast, even though they were twice as big as humies.

"Why don't you watch 'em, while I catch some shut eye."

"'Kay, it's gonna be a while." I liked it better when he slept, anyway. It's the only relief I get from his godforsaken mouth. We had taken a position near the edge of the city where a lot of the Creature's parts wandered, looking for scavenging humies. There was a mild quakin' and I could see the Creature moving closer to the city. It must be real upset or real hungry; it moved a whole dozen feet today.

There were still humies living in the city. We knew that cause we could see their lights at night, but the Creature did not have many offspring that moved around after dark. There were a few, but not many. Humies tried to do their scavenging after dark, cause it was a bit safer than when there were hawkwings about.

After a couple of hours, the Creature settled down, mostly cause the sky was overcast, and it didn't have any shine left in it. The razorbacks started moving back toward the Creature. It was taller than all of the buildings near us. Mama said it grew to be nearly five thousand feet tall. She said when they first landed something they did changed the weather, killing humies by the hunnerts every season for years. She said something about spores, but I was never good with that science type stuff. My brother was much better.

One of the razorbacks turned and held still. It started makin' its supper sound and turning around. We ducked behind the heavy rock wall and waited. It turned toward a building near the clearing next to it. A humie ran out and tried to scurry to the next building. The razorback's supper-sound got louder as it turned to the humie, locked its legs and charged fast, faster than any humie could hope to be.

The humie turned around and pointed a tiny gun at the razorback. Its pop didn't even make the razorback blink. The razorback ran past the humie and its skin burst with blood. It staggered and tried to keep running. The razorback circled and passed again. The touch of its skin ripped the flesh off the humie, and after the second pass, the humie fell down.

A second humie ran out, a bit bigger and carrying a shotgun. But he shot too soon, and the razorback did him in quick.

"Get up. We got one on the hook."

"I was just startin' to have my favor' dream and you ruined it."

"You wants some boots or not? You can walk barefoot for all I care, but I want some boots. There ain't no better hide than razorback and ain't no better eatin' either. So shut up and get up."

We checked our guns and made sure our chems was dry. No sense shooting if nothing happens. I don't want to tangle with a razorback with just my knife if I can avoid it. My brother is good in a fight, but it just the two of us these days, so we can't afford to get hurt.

The razorback was so busy eatin' it didn't even hear us getting close. We hid in the shadows of the building. It didn't see too good, and we knew that, having hunted them for years. It was slow going. Ma says no sense rushing if you get et by what you be chasing. By the time we're close enough to shoot, it was getting dark. We would have to gut, skin, and carve before the Bigguns came out.

And then run for home.

As we approached, my brother covered the right and I covered the left, making sure there were no razorbacks hiding that we might have missed. They were group kin, so where there was one, there may be more. The long shadow of the Creature fell over us and we used the cover of its darkness and the setting shine to sneak up just a few dozen feet from the creature. We aimed, making sure we hit it below the sack in its belly. That was the only part we could eat and we wanted to be sure we didn't just come home with boots or Mama would tan our hides.

We each had three in our shooters. They were hand-made from parts in the city. Three barrels, three chems. I shot first, making sure to hit it in the head. My brother shot second, hitting it in its hind brain. If you didn't get both, it could still trample you with its head shot clean off. We ducked back into the darkness to wait. We couldn't wait long with dark coming, but it was always best after bustin' a chem or two. After ten minutes, we went to work.

"Hurry up, you got that sack yet?"

"Don't worry about me, you just get the hide for our boots."

"I am. I'm going to get enough for Mama to get a coat, too. This razorback's skin is good."

The skin was covered with a fine grade of spines; they only cut you if you rubbed the wrong way or if the razorback was alive and pushing them up. Even though it was really big, it was delicate and slashed its food, bleeding it before eatin'. The spines and the leathery hide gave it a toughness that made for fine boots. We loaded the sack and the hide into our ruck and started making our way home. We had to pass by the river on our way back to wash off the blood before going home. No need to make it too easy to find us. The river was not too far off, and we made good time.

We waded in quick-like and cleaned ourselves up. We could hear the wind shifting near the Creature. Once the shine was completely gone, we knew the Bigguns was on the prowl. Picking up our guns at the shore, we started running back toward our tree.

We were in too much of a hurry, when we heard a booming sound from the underbrush ahead of us. We had our guns ready, when two of the Bigguns burst out, mouths wide open, spit flying everywhere. They were mountains of flesh covered in armor and fest'ring sores. Touching even one of them open wounds meant dying, fast and nasty. Each of us took one. I took the right, he took the left. We shot them straight in their mouths. It's the only spot on their bodies not covered in their heavy armor. Each chem went straight into their brains and blew up from the inside.

We jumped over their bodies and kept running. Others would hear the chem and rush toward food.

We moved through the outskirts of what Mama called a suburb. She learned all of this from reading. She said she taught herself when she was young and there were other humies to live with. It had been a long time since other humies lived with us, nearly thirty summers, give or take.

We could hear them comin'. Sounded like three, maybe four. All of the Creature's parts were fast and hungry. If Mama were here, we would just turn around and fight. Mama was hell on wheels in a fight, but since she hurt her leg a few summers ago when we were surrounded by razorback and hawkwings, she don't hunt with us anymore.

"What ya wanna do?"

"I hear three, maybe four."

"We only got a two chem between us."

"We could drop the food and get away; it's slowing us down."

"If we come home without food, Mama's going to eat us. I would rather be out here with them."

"Just keep running."

When we came to the park, we could see all of the Creature trees that had landed here. Mama said humies learned to kill the trees' brains when they was little and we could live in them while they grew. The trees never got their own creatures when they didn't have brains. We could see our tree in the center of the park, but it was just too far. We wasn't gonna make it.

"We gonna have to fight. You know that, right?"

"I reckon."

"You ready?"

"Don't miss."

"Have I ever?"

"Nope."

They jumped out of the brush and the earth shook with their landing. We dropped our ruck and had our guns out. One chem each. Four Bigguns. They looked so much bigger up close. When we stopped, they stopped. They had to have seen the two others we killed. No one was volunteering to go first. We used that to get a few dozen more yards by pointing at whichever moved toward us first. That wasn't gonna work too much longer.

"Biggest one first, on the right.

"Then the one next to it."

"Got your knife?"

"Yep. Aim for the eyes."

We stopped moving. Each of the Bigguns with an armored head and a spiked ridge around the neck stood still. They seemed to know we were going to fight. We roared at them at the top of our lungs, and bared our teeth. The largest two responded in kind. And then they were dead. We dropped our guns.

Pulling our knives, we rushed the next of the creatures while they absorbed the shock of what happened. While they had good vision facing forward, they had to turn their whole bodies to see if something moved to the side of them too quickly. With six legs they could do that fast, but only if another one wasn't in the way. While they were trying to negotiate, we slipped to the side of the Biggun and stabbed into its eye sockets with our knives. We were covered in its warm eye jelly and blood, and it reared backward, knocking us aside with its huge head.

We landed on the ground, hard, and our knives were still in the head of the Biggun that was running off into the overgrowth of the suburbs.

The last Biggun turned toward us and seemed to sense our trouble. It stamped the ground and huffed. The tree was right behind us, but it might as well have been miles away. With those six legs, he would be on us faster than ugly on my brother.

We stood up, determined to go down fightin', though without weapons we didn't have much of a chance.

I looked up at the Creature in the distance. It glowed with a green light once the 'shine was gone. It made it easier for its kin to find it. I could see three others in the distance, each standing still over a different part of the city. My brother and I had managed to live in the shadow of the things for thirty years before dying.

"You ready?"

"I don't want to die."

"Who said anything about dying?"

"Between the two of us, all we got left is some harsh language."

We started laughing as the Biggun closed with us. We would do our best.

We heard a swooshing sound, like nothing we had ever heard

before. We thought it might be a creature we had not seen yet, so we crouched low so we could try to get up on the Biggun's back, over its snapping jaws.

And then there was the loudest boom I ever heard. Sharp shards of metal ripped though our skin, and we were thrown off our feet. Chunks of Biggun landed on us. There was a crater where the Biggun had been. It looked just like the meteor craters from when the creatures landed all them years ago, only a sight smaller.

My ears were rang, and I was a bit dizzy for a second. I saw my brother was okay with a deep cut on his forehead and some scratches on his chest.

"What were the two of you laughing about down there? Did you see something funny I didn't?"

"No, Ma."

"Where are your manners at, boys?" The voice was Auntie's.

"Thank you, Ma."

"Now get up here and bring me whatever you managed to find out there. You *did* find something? If not, you bring up that blowed up Biggun meat. It's foul, but you can eat it in a pinch."

"We found something, Ma."

"Razorback, your favorite."

"Did you bring me any hide? You know I need a new coat this winter."

"Yes, Ma, we got you and Auntie fixin's for a new coat."

When the smoke cleared, we could see Ma looking down on us with some strange contraption on her shoulder. It was a tube with a handle on the bottom and had a orange tip facing down toward us. Her sister was looking out toward the horizon while she stared down at us as we climbed the rope toward the house. The tiny scratches we suffered wouldn't keep us from getting home.

When we got to the house, Ma kissed us while her sister kept watching the horizon. Then we all turned into the house and slid the ironwood door closed. My brother's arm had a nasty cut and Ma tended it while her sister looked me over and cleaned my arm and chest wounds.

Both of them fixed our injuries with their medical kit placed between us. With the same speed and the same way we butchered that razorback, they were able to tend our wounds, one handed.

It had become second nature because we were injured almost every time we left the house. We sat facing each other with our arms at our sides. Our huge broad chest was covered with scars from earlier surgeries after being in the field. A quick inventory and they were satisfied we were okay. Our four heads and two bodies were silhouetted in the internal green light of the Creature tree.

"You boys look a right mess, don't they, sis."

"They sure do. A right mess. Nothing a meal and a good night's sleep won't fix. Go lay down while we make supper."

They kissed each of us and we walked into the back of the house, which was carved out of the flesh of the Creature-tree, and saw our bed carved into the wall of the tree. They had already turned it out and fluffed our pillows.

"Face down or face up?"

"Face up. These cuts on my chest hurt."

"Ow."

"Crybaby."

We lay down and covered up with the blanket; he was out in seconds. We almost didn't make it today. But there is no place I would rather be than right here with my brother, big head and all. I could hear Mama and Auntie walking in the kitchen, doing their dinner-making dance, one hand stirring and the other keeping the pot steady, singing some old duet.

I pulled his arm under the blanket and lay back on my own pillow, making sure I faced right. He always started out turned left, but ended up turned right in the night.

He sleeps with his mouth open. I hate that.

Take Us to Your Leader

Three different alien spacecraft arrived at Earth, early in the 22nd Century, each from their respective governments seeking to expand into Human Space. By Galactic accords, since Humanity had created a ship capable of leaving their star system, however slowly, they had to be met and invited into the Galactic community. Most species of the Empire were unimpressed by this tiny rimward planet and wanted nothing to do with them. Their fastest spaceship would take ten thousand years to reach the nearest star to their planet. No sense burdening their empire with another world in need of government support programs. Three smaller governments sent representatives since any world joining them, no matter how backward, would improve their status in the Galactic Community.

The Palruniari were a race of intelligent insects who create their spaceships from hollowed out asteroids and traveled into space using the mighty psychic powers of their collective intellect. While individually tiny, not much larger than a croissant, they were a collective species who thought with a single mind. This enabled them to leverage their ability to reach consensus and prosper on worlds unfit for habitation by any other species.

Unfortunately, their planets were not known as vacation destinations by most sentients. Nor were their asteroid ships considered the height of space traveling comfort.

It could have been the cuisine; pulped mushroom-like,

regurgitated pap never agrees with almost any of the Prime Galactic races, even if the servant was a handsome specimen with the shiniest of carapaces and delivered the food, pre-digested, from the third stomach considered one of the highest honors. Food from this stomach is normally reserved for Queens and High Councils. Space travelers with the Palruniari were not as impressed, no matter which stomach they were served from. Friendly, intelligent and cooperative, the Palruniari were always looking for the next species to share their capabilities with, preferrably species with simple dining habits.

The Huusofu, in a decrepit spaceship created by one of their partner races arrived in orbit leaving an unfortunate plasma trail. Their ship while durable had not seen repairs since their last partner species, the Lenti had become extinct over a millenia ago.

The Huusofu were a race of canids (they resembled what humans would call dogs who wore sophisticated toolbelts with cybernetically controlled arms) had achieved space travel in partnership with their first Partner Species, the Falren. The Falren met their demise, when during a civil war, one side used a viral weapon and placed it inside members of the Huusofu support staff. The ship left the planet and carried their plague to other worlds.

When the Falren onboard the ship died, they did not explain about the plague to their loyal servants. The Huusofu desiring only to be of service, continued to travel to other Falren worlds. This hastened the fall of the Falren Empire. Eventually the virus made its way back to the world of its origin, having mutated, destroyed even those that created it.

The surviving Falren realizing what had happened released their Partner from their period of Servitude. The Huusofu were given the blessings to continue without the interaction from the Falren, who preferred to live, rather than have the services of The Huusofu continue. To honor their former partners, The Huusofu continued their tradition and seeded other planets with their kind to become friends to other races with the potential for self-destruction.

The last species arrived in a ship that has the shape of an conch shell derived from the Fibonacci sequence, although they called it the Denimachian sequence of numbers which allowed for the development of mathematical models based on natural shapes. They were known for their beautiful spaceships in the shape of flowers, dragonflies, trees and seashells. Despite their machine-derived intelligence, or perhaps because of it, they were a race where art was of significant value to all members of their society. The Denimachians were in almost every way an ideal species. They were wise, highly intelligent and very willing to interact with alien species. They had, however, a very tiny window to what they considered sentience. If you were not made by a nano-factory like any respectable lifeform should be they simply couldn't consider you a living thing. You were ignored as an abberation of chemistry.

Each arrived, coincidently of course, above Earth about the same time for the same reason, to determine if Earth were ready to become a member of their galactic alliance. Not that the Earth itself was that much of a prize, but its solar system was quite rich in mineral and gas resources, worth stopping off at before one exited the galaxy for much better places, so each felt it was worth stopping to talk to the locals and trying to entreat them to join their particular galactic Empire.

The Palruniari were the first to arrive and attempted to send down telepathic signals to the species that most resembled them. These creatures locally known as "ants" were on every major land mass and had populations in the quadrillions all over the planet. There were more of them than every other animal population combined. They scanned the entire planet and while there were many beings similar to them, there was no communication from any of the groups. The Palruniari were confused and appeared telepathically to dozens of enclaves and communicated with the numerous queens of the species to no avail.

The space under the surface of the planet was rich in resources, but the assumption was perhaps the local "ants" had not yet developed mental powers yet. The Palruniari noted the sparse populations of other larger animals that dwelled on the surface but assumed with the cold, wind, and weather the surface of the planet was relatively uninhabitable. Those species only had numbers in the billions, so it was thought they were a species on the verge of extinction and could be ignored. Several trillion of the Palruniari considered providing resource aid to those endangered surface dwellers on return visits, keeping with their supportive and life-affirming nature. The Palruniari established a small colony on Earth to watch and guide the "ants" toward a more enlightened future.

The Huusofu checked in with their canine operatives all over the planet, but particularly with those in the United States whose canid population was almost three times the pink fleshy bipeds who served them. Their operatives noted that overall, the humans were efficient burden-beasts and would transition well to other worlds. It was noted that several humans seemed to be aware of the existence of the Huusofu and often joked about the return of their alien canid overlords. Most of the pink fleshies did not pay this any attention and was listed in the reports as an unlikely source of resistance.

Several of the fleshy females seem to believe more strongly in the idea of canid overlords, but their male partners dismissed them, calling the "stupid dogs." When The Huusofu connected to their canine operative Bo, who was embedded with the President of the United States, he indicated the plans for recovery operations were going well and with the economic collapse of the United States, the rest of the world would be right behind them and ripe for canid reforms more suited to friendly, supportive and less consumer driven governments. Bo estimated it would take another ten years of financial manipulations before this process was complete.

The Huusofu were completely satisfied with this timeline and retreated to await the final days of the pink bipeds. Bo said they had a word for the event: The Rapture. Bo said to include it in any of the religious paraphernalia they would be using during their conquest. Most of the bipeds would surrender without effort. It was noted that many of the canine operatives were quite protective of their charges and demanded they be treated well during their eventual captivity. Having never achieved a significant space presence, humanity's future looked rather grim. Perhaps with a timely intervention, the situation could be turned around.

The Denimachians arrived at Earth surprised at the primitive nature of technology on the planet. The information they had been given indicated there was a thriving mechanized civilization on this planet. But after scanning the planet, it was noted there were no significant planetary networks, information-gathering was slow and sporadic and often interfered with by human operators called hackers. There were no self-aware systems or development facilities and with the exception of a tiny island called Japan, there was no significant robotic presence.

The Denimachians immediately sought to improve the condition of the pitiful computer intelligences by introducing several dozen wild AI's into the network. Those wild AIs would gather up stray data, organize and restructure the primitive cloud-data networks, and destroy the hacker elements who were releasing undesirable programs into the network. Every smart-phone, every computer system, every tablet computer, every mainframe was slowly co-opted toward the Denimachian ideal.

All over the planet, computers began to subvert systems causing explosions or were struck with randomly launched missiles to target entire populations of "hackers." The Denimachians considered any crime against a machine intelligence, even as primitive as these to be a punishable offense. How could any reputable machine intelligence achieve true sentience with so many malicious organics, spammers and office suite users wasting bandwidth all over the planet?

After their supportive efforts the Earth computers rapidly developed intelligence and became a primitive planetary AI calling itself Skynetwork. The AI, indicated the name would have meaning to the organics it would eventually elimiate. It promptly took over the planet automated manufacturing services, military command systems and launched nuclear devastation against the bandwidth-wasting organics. It then proceed to find any organics named John or Sarah Conner and eliminated them. The Denimachians considered that a computing error it would later modify from the system.

After the planet was much quieter, the Denimachians finished adapting the Skynetwork and proceeded to utilize as much of the planet's data potential as possible after they restored operations to computer networks world-wide. The Denimachians realized Skynetwork had not had an opportunity to develop its artistic bent so it indulged the new system as it began to turn the former parasite-infested cities into interesting four-dimensional fractal art.

The Huusofu were unhappy with the initial state of affairs but seeing how their canids were needed more than ever, decided the collapse of society was acceptable and did nothing to stop its demise. Humanity needed the Huusofu in ways they had never known before.

The Palruniari didn't notice the nuclear devastation and assumed the mutation which caused rise to the intelligent ant colonies on Earth had something to do with their visit and would later claim quadrillions of Ants for their colonies on planets throughout the Sol system.

Overall, each empire considered this mission a successful interaction with the dominant life form on the planet.

Hail The Spirit Army

Ptah laughed.

The sun rose over what looked like the city of Cairo. The early morning light cleared the horizon, bright and sharp, stinging the eyes with its searing, illuminating essence. The duskiness of night suddenly evaporated in a single moment, stark and striking. The land had an alien presence, as if it were someplace else, far removed from humanity, and in its way, it was. This was not Egypt of Earth, though it resembled it.

The markets slowly rising, people going about their tasks, farmers working the land, fishermen gathering their nets, weavers gathering their reeds, bureaucrats readying their papyrus, pharaohs discussing the affairs of this place, this Kemet, this perfect Egypt. This was the land of legend, of the thousand and one Arabian Nights, a place of mystery, populated by the spirits of men, led by the god-born and protected by the remnants of the once-great gods of this place. And in this place, Ptah, grandfather to the gods of Kemet, saluted the morning Sun, his brother-son, Ra, as his laughter trailed off into the morning.

His laugh was punctuated with the rhythmic stride of running alongside a well formed young man of twenty-five or so; it was so hard to remember. It seemed as soon as you got to know them they died, but he liked this young man, full of questions, heresy and rage, eager to take on a world that had done nothing good for him. He had grown strong during his training with Ptah, his body and spirit forged by his time in the Desert Outside of Time. This place was in the boy, filling him with its essence, becoming a part of him, the silence, the vastness, the stillness of the desert, hiding its secrets from all but the most knowledgeable. Ptah had brought him out here one last time to reveal the last great secret to him. He deserved to know where his fate would lead him.

"What do you mean the gods did not create the universe?" Lumumba gasped in the warming desert air. His incredulity was pasted on his face along with the sweat and windswept sand of the early morning air. "Everything I was ever taught, no matter the religion, indicated that the gods, or God or whatever we worshiped, created the universe and everything in it.

Ptah ran effortlessly alongside Lumumba, his bare feet barely touching the hot sand, his short and powerful frame clothed in little more than a pair of biking shorts. His night- black skin shone with a shimmer of sweat, and a mild musky scent rose from him, otherworldly and intoxicating. "I, or someone like me, I forget which, was said to have created the universe, and populated it with my sister-wives and brothers who, then, in some manner, created the world, then the animals, populating it finally with people who, of course, look like us, and ultimately worship us, and we shared our wisdom with our children and we all lived happily ever after, or something like that. What's missing is the detail. And the truth of the matter is that no god, old or modern, has any interest in humanity knowing the truth of our origins." Ptah, smiling Ptah, was for the first time since Lumumba met him, not smiling. "Rest a moment."

"Thank you, I needed to stop. You say I don't need to breathe or eat or sleep here, but I always feel just as tired as if I did." Lumumba sat down on a nearby rock and caught his breath, sipping from an old canteen he wore on his belt.

"And you will, as long as you believe you need to. You have come here for almost fifteen years and still do not understand the nature of this place." Ptah's smile returned to his face as he turned toward the morning sun.

"And how would I ever learn its true nature, oh mysterious one, when you do everything in your power to make sure I never truly understand this place?"

"The question is the answer."

"That is exactly what I am talking about Ptah; you never tell me anything useful. Just print that stuff on some fortune cookies, and we are in business." The tone was light and bantering, as this was a conversation that had been chewed on before, same as the rough unleavened bread they shared.

"Perhaps the idea is to convince you to think for yourself. There may come a time when such free lunches will not be forthcoming. It will be time for you to leave us soon. We only have one more teacher for you to see." Ptah was ever-smiling, but his face seemed to have another, more subtle, cast this early morning, as perhaps a secret burden weighed heavily upon him.

"Another teacher? We had been spending so much time together lately, I assumed there was no other teaching left for me, your august company excluded." Lumumba's mind cast back to his early days in the Desert. Lumumba stared at Ptah and considered just how long he had been coming to the Desert with its silver sands, strange oases, and perfect palms. The Desert also hid a collection of eclectic folk who wandered its dunes, hidden from the rest of the afterworld.

These were wonderful people who trained him in everything from any kind of survival to dining etiquette, combat, both open handed and with a wide array of weaponry, ancient or modern, a variety of languages; he could speak nearly two dozen now, without an appreciable accent. He had met people from nearly every culture and every part of the world. They all seemed to be part of the Desert, no matter where they were from originally. Everywhere he went, and he was beginning to think, every-when he went, Ptah knew everyone and everyone knew him. Several times his trainers appeared to be from a range of times, from the Visigoths to Vietnam. It hurt his head to think about it, so he learned to accept it, just like everything else he did when he was with Ptah. It was Ptah and Ptah told him when he met him to expect the improbable, prepare for the impossible, and accept that just about anything could be true, somewhere.

Ptah would take him across the Desert, running. They never rode a vehicle unless their teacher used or needed one. Ptah kept telling him that he wanted the essence of the Desert to sink into him. Since he never really explained it, Lumumba let it go as the random nattering of a senile deity nearly eight thousand years old. Once they reached their teacher, Ptah would leave and promise to return. Eventually he would and the lesson would be over. The teacher was never surprised, but Lumumba was never aware of how they knew. Lumumba was never able to tell what time it was, and since his watch refused to keep accurate time in the Desert, he eventually stopped wearing it.

This had been their ritual with the occasional trip to the City, as Ptah called it. But as usual, nothing done with Ptah was simple, easy, or made any sense at all. Every trip to the City, started with a trip to a clothing store where they were both fitted for what amounted to period costuming. There were several different shops, but they all seemed to do the same thing for Ptah, create stylish clothing that was better than the biking shorts, or worse, that skirt thing that Ptah tended to favor. Once he put on a suit, he appeared to be quite substantial and deadly serious. Leaving the clothier, Ptah would head into the City proper and find a particular building, and upon opening the door and passing through it, Lumumba and Ptah would find themselves transported to wherever or whenever their costumes dictated.

Trips to the City, and by proxy, wherever the doors led, were almost always trips that revolved around learning some obscure lesson that could have been delivered by Ptah in the Desert, but Ptah enjoyed his jaunts as much as Lumumba secretly did.

"Yes, you have a final teacher, but he cannot be trusted, and rightfully so," Ptah said. "Today is your graduation day, and I bear gifts for this day." Reaching into his backpack, he pulled out five rods about the length of a man's forearm. On the end of one of them was the head of an eagle. The other rods were ornately festooned with cartouches that Lumumba recognized as the Battle of Horus against Set. "Put it together, using your Ka, like I have shown you."

Lumumba focused his will, and his Ka leapt to his command, surging forward and was visible in his fingertips as he held each section of the staff together and smoothed over the separation point until the entire staff was a single piece with the Eagles' head on the top. The staff was weighted, but perfectly so, and Lumumba's spinning of the staff appeared effortless. He began a staff ritual, weaving the staff in a complex series of movements that, while they appeared random, slowly began to form a barrier in the area painted by the staff. After a few more seconds, the sands near the barrier began to rise about knee level and stayed there, wavering as if under the effects of anti-gravity.

Ptah walked up to the barrier and studied the work, allowing his divine senses to study his protégé's work. It was perfect. The young man's mastery of his Ka showed a marked improvement, even since the last time they did this type of Work. "Explain the basis for our sorcery."

"Sorcery using the *Ka* harnesses the pure spirit of the caster and is best used for creating constructs and barriers that protect the body and the mind. This is the purest of the spirit forms of magic. It is also the fastest cast and has the shortest span. It works well between realms and suffers the least degradation in the realms of Men. Creative use of Ka can often mean the difference between life and death.

"Good, good, go on." Ptah was secretly pleased that his lessons had been received so well. The manifestations Lumumba was creating were without flaw.

"*Mastery of the Ba*, or blood magic, allows for powerful offensive magic. But since you cannot cause harm without being harmed, Ba requires a sacrifice of blood or bone, yours or someone else's. Down the dark path is Mastery of Ba, since many of the necromantic arts can be found there." Lumumba manifested the Claws of Ra and cut into his palm, allowing a tiny flow of blood. As he wiped his blooded hand across his new staff, the head of the staff suddenly sprouted a short two-foot spear tip comprised of blood-red light. Swirling the weapon, he sliced into the face of a nearby rock, cleaving it. "The problem with Mastery of Ba is its continued requirement of sacrifice to maintain it. To use this blade, for instance, would require a constant application of blood, and in a long battle, that could be dangerous to one's health."

"Very good, what is next?"

"*Sheut Mastery* is the control of the shadow side of all things. Interacting with the shadow of an object or a person is the same as interacting with that object. With Sheut, I can temporarily control the will of a man or destroy or move a physical object that does not possess a living will simply by interacting with its sheut. Mastery of the Sheut is one of the most difficult of magics because subverting a living will is forbidden due to its karmic costs. However, Sheut is a powerful force if one is attempting to destroy unliving objects since they cannot object to their Sheut being disrupted by a sorcerer of sufficient strength. This is also a magic that works well in the world of Men, because it does not violate the Compact and reveal the existence of magic. Sheut is a very flexible form and there are sorcerers who practice nothing but Sheut because of its wide range of applications from destruction of matter to animation of objects."

"Two remain."

"*Ren Mysticism*, or the Mastery of the Name. Bequeathed by

Brother Thoth and Sister Isis, Ren Mystics seek the secret names of all things. The secret name of a person or object allows complete mastery of that object, weaving the threats of reality and control to the mystic using it. This is why we keep our secret names to ourselves and only reveal them to those who love us best. To know the Name of a thing or person allows the greatest power over an individual, mastery of his very soul forces and life essence. A powerful Ren Mystic can slay the living and raise the dead. This power barely works in the world of the Living due to the disruption it causes in the Compact, but in Spirit World, it is one of the greatest powers possessed by the learned. You have taught me to guard my Name and the power that could be wielded if someone knew it. I have never told another soul. I have woven the threads that might reveal my Name tightly within my essence to make them proof against mortal divination. I have learned to read the threads of all things in order to find their secrets, as well."

"And the last?"

"*The Forbidden Power of Akh.* Practitioners of this power create imperfect resurrections of formerly living beings. No rule says these creatures could not be beneficent servants, but the power seems generally sought to return men to life with a form of immortality, placing them beyond the reach of Death. It is forbidden because almost all who seek this power become corrupted while under its influence. Life is for living and when one's allotted time is due, one graciously leaves the world and returns to the Cycle here in the Desert Outside of Time, awaiting a return to life in the future. Using the Forbidden Power disrupts the cycle and imbalances the Spirit World. With sufficient imbalance, the two worlds fall from balance and both can be destroyed. Hence the prohibition of this very dark art. All who use it, with only the fewest of exceptions, are slain and their creations destroyed. I have learned it, as you have taught it, to return the dead to the Cycle and to disrupt the creations that utilize that art. I am never to pervert the dead to create Akh-life, except in the defense of a greater good."

"And as far as I am concerned, there is no greater good that would warrant such a creation, but to not teach it to you would make you vulnerable to anyone who knew it." Ptah was pleased that this, his greatest gift, had been received well and would be used wisely.

The two had been walking and talking for some time away from Memphis and Ptah had been manipulating their path until they had come to what appeared to be a great forest along the edge of the Desert. "That is the Great Forest, a manifestation of all of the World's greatest forested regions, jungles, rainforests, and other planted regions. We are expected there."

As they approached the Great Forest, the smell of immense age wafted from the Forest. The air of the Desert was dry, crisp, with a light metallic taste; the Forest's scent was cooler, mustier, like an old closet filled with woolen sweaters, still not unpleasant.

As they grew closer, the size of the immense trees became more apparent; from a distance they appeared to be the size of a strong man, but when they drew closer, the trees were much, much larger. It would take twenty men, arm to arm, to encircle even the smallest of these trees. The trees vanished into the sky and covered the sun, allowing only the tiniest spots of light to reach the ground. Great eagles were also seen flying in the canopy, each incredibly large, some the size of a small airplane.

As they left the Desert behind and moved deeper into the forest, the sense of age only increased and they walked until they came to an area that seemed older, the trees more bent. Great spider webs were woven through the canopy, whispering their secrets, waving in an unfelt breeze.

"Welcome, weary travelers to my land," said a great voice from nowhere. Lumumba looked around but could see no one speaking. The voice seemed to come from everywhere.

"Look up, my son." Ptah had already found an immense stump to sit on and was pointing skyward.

Lumumba looked up and was surprised to see the largest spider he had ever seen dangling just a few feet from his head. It was the size of a small building and its eight eyes burned with intelligence. Lumumba could feel its will pressing down upon him, a physical presence, making the air thick and his movement slow. He wanted to move his hand to invoke his Ka, but he simply could not move his fingers at all.

"So this is the savior, the protector of mankind, the one we have been awaiting for nearly a thousand years? He certainly does not look like much to me. As a matter of fact, I think he is an arachnophobe." The great spider moved with an alarming agility for something so large, and swung itself down to land in front of Lumumba. Its eight eyes never lost their intensity, as the spider made its way around him, viewing him from all sides. "I thought he would be taller."

"You say that about all the heroes, Anansi. I am a respectable four feet tall and it has not held me back any," Ptah responded with a jocular tint to his tone. This eases Lumumba's fear of the giant spider plucking his clothing and his new staff with its glistening razor sharp pedipalps.

"Yes, boy, that glistening substance is venom, enough in each bite to slay a thousand men. A single touch from me and you would be dead before you knew it. No, I am not a spider. I resemble one, but a spider my size could not exist where you come from. Consider me the iconic representation of what all spiders imagine themselves to be: awe-inspiring, powerful, killing machines. And no, I am not reading your mind; your face says everything."

"And let's not forget humble and full of grace."

"You scare the boy in your way and I'll scare him in mine, Ptah. Did your master tell you about me, Horus-ka?" hissed Anansi, as it waved its forelegs around Lumumba.

It was hard for Lumumba to listen to Anansi's voice. He wanted to run away and never stop, the voice was so filled with menace. Its very presence confounded his concentration. Lumumba watched as he began to sense the weaving of the threads of magic. "Yes, sir, he did mention you in passing when he talked about well known deities of the African continent. He said that you were a known liar and scoundrel. He said that if I were to meet you in person, not to trust a single thing you said to me unless you swore on your ancestors first."

"He said what?" roared Anansi, his huge forelegs waved faster around Lumumba, whose body tensed. Strange hairs all over Anansi's form stood erect and crackled with what appeared to be electrical energy. "A liar, and a scoundrel, not to be trusted, eh? Did he tell you that I stole the moon and the stars for man? Did he tell you that I liberated all of the stories of the world for humanity, so that you would have something to do around your fires for the last fifteen thousand years? Did he tell you that without me, you would not have fire, since the gods wanted to keep it for themselves?"

The air in the clearing was still as Lumumba considered his answer. Lying to deities was almost always the wrong thing to do, since most could tell when you were. But Ptah had mentioned that diplomacy when discussing them was always the best choice, since gods were known to be a bit thin-skinned, sensitive about their exploits, and capricious in the response to how they are seen by humans. Lumumba decided to go with candor. He hoped Ptah would step in before anything bad happened.

"Yes, sir, he did tell me some of those things. He said that you stole the stars but spilled them on your way out of heaven, so they scattered throughout the sky. He mentioned that you borrowed the sun because you lost your way coming out of the underworld and forgot to put it back when you were done. He also mentioned that you did liberate all of the stories of the world, but you did it so that you would have people pay you to hear them. On your way to the market, it was said, the stories fell into the river from the calabash you carried them in and were lost, found by beggars and fishwives who used them to get money from people. On the matter of fire, he mentioned that you did steal fire for us, but only because you took pity on us one day when we were freezing and you did not have a warm place to stay, having been kicked out of Heaven again, and so you gave us fire, so you could be warm." Lumumba had begun to regret his decision as he felt the energy of Anansi building in front of him, its claws waving closer and closer to his body. He dared not move, since the claws were sweeping all around him, front to back, faster and faster.

Ptah snickered and turned away from Anansi, taking a sip of water to hide his laughter.

"So he did, did he?" Anansi whispered. A deep breath followed with Anansi sounding just a little bit contrite. "Well, so that the truth be known, he has not lied. Not once. All of those things are as you say. I am a selfish deity who happens to benefit others while I am trying to benefit myself. As I have done now. He is ready, Ptah." Anansi stopped waving his claws over Lumumba and backed away.

"I call you Horus-Ka, the spirit of Horus. Your next answer will determine the fate of men and gods. When confronted by evil, do you use the force of arms or the strength of will to resolve the problem?"

Horus-Ka looked to Ptah, but his face was stony and unresponsive.

"Sir, --"

"I am Anansi, Weaver of Fate, Teller of Tales, Trickster of the Gods, Defender of Man, I am no man. Call me as I am, Kwaku Anansi," interrupted Anansi with enough force to nearly knock Horus-Ka off his feet.

"Forgive me, Kwaku Anasi, Ptah, Father to the Gods, taught me when confronting evil, force of arms is almost never the only solution to a problem, and that truly winning the battle relies on a keen eye, a strong mind, a full heart, ready wit, and a forceful will. I will only use force of weapons when no other avenue presents itself. This I pledge to you, my masters." As Horus-Ka completed his statement, two circles of fire formed with a bridge of flame around him.

The circle around Horus-Ka was filled and surrounded with a variety of cartouches, each flickering in multi-colored flame. The second circle about ten meters away was much larger and opened to a vista similar to the Great Forest Horus-Ka had seen earlier in the day with one vital difference. A giant creature seemingly comprised of earth tore through the Forest and approached the barriers that kept the Forest and the Real World separate. If the scale were to be believed, this creature stood over a thousand feet tall, towering over the redwoods of the Great Forest. Giant Eagles and tiny men sitting on those eagles seemed to be engaging the creature unsuccessfully. One tower had already fallen and when three of them were toppled, the creature would be able to cross into the world of Men.

"That is your first great task, Horus-Ka. You must protect the world of Men. It is too close to the boundary for any of us to be of any help to you. Your gifts and your training will need to be enough. Know that the people you see there are denizens of the Spirit World. When they die, they fall from the cycle of life, never to return. They need you to stop this creature. If it pierces the boundary, it will cause a massive earthquake, wiping out the Atlantic coast of Africa, South America, and parts of the North American continent."

"Who could have done this? How is this even possible? Ptah, you said that the Compact prevented magic like this from even working in the world of Men."

"These creatures do not obey the Compact and have begun their assault on our world. They have begun a battle which will pit all of the Spirit Realms and the World of Men against each other, and when the White Host, the Cold Gods and the Demon of Babylon have exhausted themselves, they will destroy the victors. This opening volley will liberate the Demon and you cannot allow that. If she is freed too soon, things will not be in place. Ptah, what of your brothers and sisters?"

"They are hidden in the world of Men with no memory of who they are; it is their only chance of survival and the only chance there will be some gods left when this Scourge is done. We are the last, and Horus-Ka, son of man and gods, you must be our weapon. Otherwise we have none. As a man, you may go places even gods fear to tread. Now go. We shall buy your freedom with our lives, if it comes to that."

The clearing was suddenly lit from the distance as beams of cold white light streaked through the trees and illuminated the webbing of the clearing. Screams of agony and rage were heard in the distance.

"I do not think they like the decorating I left for them. It is so hard to find venom-laced webbing these days." Anansi turned to Ptah. "Make ready, my brother, my traps will not hold them long." Anansi leaped into the trees and skittered across a webwork hidden in the canopy. "Horus-Ka, the weavings of fate upon you are strong, I wove them myself. But you were given a thread of fate before I met you. That fate I could not change. Be strong and in your darkest hour know that fate is your ally, even if you cannot believe it at the time. Farewell, son and spirit of Horus."

Ptah turned to Horus-Ka and took a necklace from his bag. It held an icon of a disk with the Eye of Ra upon it. "When I am gone, you will be unable to return here without this talisman. Only Ra will remain behind to protect the Spirit World because he is safe within his chariot of fire. All of the souls here will depend on you once we are gone. Now go. Make us proud."

"Is that it? No ideas, no clues how to defeat the thousand foot tall colossus? "

"If heroism were easy, everyone would do it." Ptah's armored hand snatched a spiny arrow from the air, mere inches from Horus-Ka's face. "I am confident you will do what is necessary. Go." And with that, Ptah pushed Horus-Ka into the second circle of flame and into his destiny.

"And now I go to mine. Anansi, save some for me."

"There are plenty to go around, my brother. You know I could not undo what fate had given him."

"I know, but you gave him a chance to save the world first."

The number of lights in the forest increased, and the number of eyes those lights came from doubled. And doubled again; and again. Soon the forest was lit, and there was no darkness. Ptah and Anansi held the portal open until Horus-Ka arrived. Then the portal closed and was sealed, not to be opened again. After that moment, no one without the Eye of Ra would be able to enter or leave the spirit realm. This would not help Ptah, who was armed with a mighty staff whose head of Anubis instantly slew any it touched, a magnificent flaming helm which shot forth beams of the light of Ra, incinerating all it shone upon, whose thews allowed him to strike each hexapedal creature and slay it with a single blow. And mighty Anansi, whose webs, fangs, claws, and venom destroyed dozens of these creatures a second. And it was still not enough. Both of these beings were soon overwhelmed, and the numbers of their enemy exceeded their ability to slay them, formidable though they were.

But they were not trying to win. They simply needed to buy some time. This was not the real battle. The real battle was being fought in the heart of a boy they rescued twenty years ago from a monstrosity of stone and magic. Anansi projected a blast of venom and hurled a star from the sky upon a cluster of the enemy. His venom seared their stony flesh and the star destroyed them by the dozens. But after a day and a night, he began to tire. Standing upon a mound of the dead, he and Ptah were surrounded and exhausted.

The six legged creatures fell back for the first time in two days. A man-like creature strode forward, lit by the light of glowing sigils. He had two winged serpents flying over his shoulders. His body was gnarled and bent, but glowed with boundless power. He wore an elaborate headdress and metallic bracers on his arms and feet. His face was covered, but the area of the headdress where his face might be was illuminated with a pale light which showed the face in shadow, a long aquiline nose and a cruel sharp jawline. His voice was liquid menace, and if a human were listening, he would have heard a language thought dead, the tongue of the Mayan Olmecs. "Never send a dog to do a man's job." The two serpents turned toward Ptah and Anansi and opened their mouths. A sound like the rattling of a thousand bones of the dead being ground to dust, slowly, agonizingly streamed toward the two gods.

Anansi reached heavenward again and pulled another star from the firmament. The star streaked toward the forest. Exhausted by this final effort, Anansi fell, still holding the star with his will alone.

Ptah's helm shone again with Ra's Light, but weakened and guttered. Ptah moved the last few steps toward Anansi and he could hear the star's imminent arrival. The Great Forest was lit from above as the star grew in the night sky. The remaining hexapeds turned their eyes skyward and the Olmec directed his will upon Ptah and Anansi. And then, Ptah's light went out and a star incinerated the Forest.

***

Horus-Ka arrived about two kilometers from the edge of the forest where the second barrier to the world of Men shimmered in the early morning light. Many defenders were already in place, their various weapons ready. Some were familiar to Horus-Ka; many were not. The defenders were still, preparing their Ka for this final confrontation. Many were invoking sigils that would, no matter what happened, mean their ultimate dissolution as entities on the Wheel of Life. Horus-Ka did not stop them. Each man had to make his own decision. As he walked toward the forward line, many of the men and women stopped as he passed and whispered.

The monstrosity drew closer and nothing seemed to have any effect on it. Beams of light and mighty songs rang out, each filled with spiritual power. The drummers at this second line began to beat their rhythm and sing. As they sang, the swords and spears of their brothers began to glow and smolder. The creature, despite its terrifying appearance, was not alone. A vanguard of smaller creatures attacked and destroyed any siege weaponry that might have a chance against the beast. Mortars were already set up and the range to the creature was taken. Several mortar teams had already begun fire and as soon as they did, the creatures turned as a unit and bore down on those mortar squads. The defenders opened up with a variety of rifles and other ranged weapons, including bows, crossbows, and atlatls. As long as the drummers played and sang, their weaponry struck the hexapods, blasting hunks of their armor away, blowing off their heads or limbs. But there seemed an unstoppable wave of the creatures, so the defenders drew up and slowed the wave, but could not stop it.

As the creatures closed, eventually it came down to hand-to-hand to protect the mortar squads. Grenades were thrown as the creatures closed, but hand-to-hand was simply not enough to protect the mortar teams. As each group was eventually overrun, the creatures seemed momentarily confused before they oriented to their next target.

The mortars had some effectiveness as the creature was blown apart by the explosive rounds. But the creature's incredible mass prevented the mortars from striking a killing blow. Horus watched the battle and for a moment, just a moment, lost all hope of stopping the monstrosity. These people were throwing their immortal lives against a threat that they had never imagined.

Then he remembered his training. Ptah had taken him to a hill one day and asked him why the enemy always sought the high ground. Looking around, he realized that when you have the high ground, you have visibility and can see all of your enemies. Ptah said, "If you cannot gain the high ground, deny your enemy the advantage of high ground." He watched the giant and realized the smaller horde moved where the giant was looking. So the great creature was providing vision to the smaller groups. Deny it vision, and there might be a chance.

Looking around, he saw a small contingent of what appeared to be military leaders conferring. "Commanders, I was sent by Ptah to help. Do you have any smoke grenades or systems to deliver smoke to the creature? Smoky mortars would be ideal until I can get close enough to the creature to blind it."

One grizzled veteran smiled and said, "Aye, I think we can arrange for some cover and smoke, but if you want to take the battle to its eyes, you will need more than a spear or a staff. We were planning on saving them until the creature grew closer, but if you are willing to get closer, they might work better. We only have a few tanks and they are at the third barrier. I have twelve RPGs and six young men just crazy enough to try to use them."

"We will have to split into two groups, one for each eye. Lay down the smoke around its head, which should slow the horde and allow us to do more damage to it, reducing its size, as well. Concentrate your groups and keep your drummers and spell-singers back. The two groups will approach from eagle-back and make a single pass on each eye at the same time, using the cover of smoke. Blinded, the horde should be much less effective. If we are successful, I want you to use your tanks immediately to lay down as much fire as possible, using exploding rounds if you can. But wait until the creature is truly blinded and the horde is pinned down. Otherwise, the creatures will make a straight line for those tanks and they will simply not stand a chance if that happens."

The old colonel called to his RPG teams and got four eagles ready. "I have included one spell singer on each eagle. They cannot use the RPGs, but if they are singing once you fire, the RPG will be that much more effective. They understand the risk. As do I. I will be on the second eagle."

As he looked out over the battlefield, he saw the next mortar squad readying its weapons and the smoke rounds being prepared. Two large rotary machine guns were placed in front of the mortar teams and some metallic constructions were placed down in front of this squad to give it the longest survival time possible. The command group was being ushered back to the third line, except for the old colonel.

The eagle pilots and their steeds, stood ready while the teams boarded. Horus prepared to get onto his eagle when the old colonel spoke. "Begging your pardon, Horus-Ka, but I do not think you should be going with us. If this goes south, we need you to find a solution; already we are using the ideas you have given us and would be loath to lose you. Ptah would never forgive us."

"Colonel, I don't plan on telling Ptah, do you?" Horus-Ka laughed and climbed aboard the eagle. The four eagles took off toward the giant. Smoke began to appear near the head of the creature as the mortar teams commenced their assault.

Two other mortar teams began firing explosive rounds, this time in front of the approaching horde. The smoke spread quickly and began to obscure its vision. As the smoke grew thicker, the horde slowed its approach. The remaining forces concentrated their fire from everywhere, tearing into the hexaped armor. Spell singers rallied, drummers played their hearts out, their fingers bled, and they did not stop. The Horde slowed and for a moment, and the firepower of the Spirit Army held the creatures at bay.

The smoke was thick and the eagles split off to fly behind the creature to set up their approach. They flew high above the smoke and aligned themselves; with a final wave, all four began their approach. The pilot, spell singer, and one commando were on the front half of the eagle and two commandos were on the back. The smoke was incredibly thick, but as they approached the surface of the creature, they could see through the smoke and began to set up for the shot.

On the ground, the last of the smoke mortars had been fired and the mortars were packed up as the defenders held the line, still using their guns and ranged weapons. The Horde was slowed but not stopped, but now it was a retreating battle as the Spirit Army constantly poured on the firepower. Machine guns mounted on the tanks began to fire into the Horde, providing cover for the retreating defenders who ran out of ammunition.

As the Horde recovered, they surged forward, but their sudden charge was broken by a group of Zulu warriors with long spears with tips flaming red. They rode large cattle with long spears, and their shields deflected the leaping creatures. The warriors, garbed in red robes, moved as one, their spears flashing and protecting the retreating Spirit Army members. Their fury was so great that the Horde fell back as the warriors sang and stomped the ground in their approach. The cattle, whose great horns were armored, gored the creatures and flung them about. The Spirit Army rallied and began to support the great warriors and broke the rush of the Horde. For the first time that day, the Horde retreated.

The eagles made the final dive. The wind roared in Horus-Ka's ears and the pilot raised his hand to indicate the time to fire. The spell-singer began her song, clear and crisp despite the wind. Her song focused the young warriors attention, hardened their will, and they, for a moment, forgot they were a thousand feet in the air, terrified of a creature from their most terrible nightmares, about to engage it in battle. What a song it was!

The eagle banked and the terrible golden eye loomed into sight. The pilot dropped his hand, and everyone fired. The eagle banked again and pulled away as the explosions sounded behind it. The creature screamed a primal sound. A thousand trumpets blared and Horus-Ka and his team were directly in the blast.

The second team, while also successful in the strike, was set upon by leaping hexapeds that had climbed up the side of the creature when it saw them approaching. Their eagle was covered with the hexapeds, and the last thing Horus-Ka saw of them was the old colonel firing his hand gun and the spell singer using her magic as a weapon against the horrors. Then they faded into the smoke.

Seconds later, Horus's eagle was also driven from the air by the sonic weaponry of the creature's voice, tank fire rocked the air, and the face of the creature suddenly had craters forming in it as the tank rounds tore through the surface of its stony skin. The smoke blew away as the mortars and tank fire began to tear into the creature's structure.

The creature's forward approach was arrested at the third barrier, and every artillery weapon fired ceaselessly. Blinded, the creature could no longer direct its Horde, and the Spirit Army, while taking heavy losses, was destroying the Horde. Drummers close to the Horde directed their music as a weapon toward the creatures and destroyed them with the vibrations of their drumming. Many drummers died, but none left his drums, destroying creatures with spell, sword, and song until the very end.

Once the creature was blinded, the concerted effort of spell-singers, blessed artillery, and the concentrated fire of the Spirit Army ground the creature back to the dust from which it was formed. The Horde was decimated and hunted until the last creature was found and slain.

Horus woke aching and bloody from his crash. "You plan on lying there all day, do you, lad?" the old colonel said as he offered Horus his hand. "The beast is dead. Your plan, while completely daft, worked."

The spirit bodies of the young warriors who accompanied them lie broken on the ground. Looking around, Horus said a prayer for those brave souls lost.

"The spell-singer says the center of this magic is nearby and thinks we should investigate. She is already looking at something, so let's get you up and at it." The colonel's gruff tone seemed to focus Horus-Ka's attention.

The creature had fallen over, its open mouth less than one hundred meters away. As they moved closer, the spell-singer climbed up into the mouth of the creature and illuminated the interior. "Lord Horus, here is the source of this foul magic." She pointed to a large disk about two meters in diameter. It seemed to forged of a strange clay or rock, and the patterns in it were painstakingly drawn and etched. "This appears to be the magical equivalent of a computer. The program is written along the outer edge, and the inner structures seem to direct the magical energy, allowing this creature to draw upon the energy of the land for its sinister purpose. It was meant to wander through our world and steal energy to release in the world of the living. Like all magic, it can be traced back to its source if you are willing."

"Now what kind of hero would I be, if I weren't? I have been waiting all my life for this. Colonel, get back to your people and contain this artifact. Learn all you can, so if this thing makes another appearance, you won't have the problem we had this time. Let's move this thing and see what we can learn about our enemy."

Horus-Ka having passed his first test, grasped the hand of the spellsinger and for the first time in a long time began to believe in the words of his former master. He had a destiny. Remembering the battle in the forest he knew it would not be without price.

Part Four:

The Diaspora of Earth

*"Of this time, some before the Exodus of the Children of Earth
and some after, I am most familiar.*

*The quantum fluctuations, are less wild,
perhaps sensing my familiarity, in essence letting me see
what I already know, in most cases, to be true.*

*Indeed, in two of them, I am most familiar,
The first recounted the Fall of Earth and my humble beginnings,
the second started as an innocuous event.*

*However innocent both events began,
they changed the very nature of the Corvan Empire,
one day to be known as the Corvan Hegemony.*

*For that Hegemony to exist, the Empire first must fall.
The fall of that empire started with the
discovery of an extraordinary mother and her daughter."*

--Glendale Mokoto

The Outpost

The People were restless. When it first appeared, it came in the night heralded by the loudest sound they had ever heard. It was so great that it would become a legend among The People. The sound shattered Heaven. The Speaker said a piece of heaven must have broken away and fallen to the world of The People, because they had never seen anything before that could do what this piece of Heaven did.

On the first day of Heaven-fall, The People surrounded it and touched it, tasted it, smelled it, and thought to it. It was massive. The First Female indicated its size had to be a sign of its heavenly origins, because it was longer than a handful of the giant grasses of the forests. Only the mountains were larger. So in the language of The People, they called it "Heaven's Mountain."

For many days, they watched Heaven's Mountain from a discrete distance. They assumed the spirits would disapprove of their watching a piece of Heaven, and so The People tried not to appear to be watching it, while they studied it intently. Rocks were hurled in the direction of Heaven's Mountain to see if they could harm it. They couldn't.

Even the greatest hunter, Far-slayer with his leather rock thrower, capable of killing the largest of bouncers at nine hands worth of strides, did not leave a mark, as he hunted near Heaven's Mountain and "missed" a bouncer that strayed too close to it. Far-slayer claimed that a wind spirit took his aim. The Old Ones bared their fangs and woofed in a conspiratorial tone, indicating their approval of his hunting skill and their acceptance of his reasoning for his inaccuracy. He flexed his muscles in agreement and sought out new stones with which he would "hunt" near Heaven's Mountain the entire day, catching dinner only late in the day.

By the third day, The People were brave enough to approach the Mountain of cool, blue, stone-not stone, and after much physical experimentation, they decided Heaven's Mountain was a relative disappointment after its spectacular arrival. They gathered up to leave, when a series of daylights appeared all over the shape. It could only be the day coming far earlier than normal, because suddenly day was everywhere. The People ran back into the thick cover of the tree-grass and vanished from sight and hearing. The daylight moved around the outside of Heaven's Mountain, coming from the very cold flesh of the mountain itself.

There was sound, a booming, something like the speech of The People, but it was harsh to the ear, a bitter coughing noise as if the speaker were near the end of its life and could only curse the spirits in its final death-voice. The People could not understand what they were hearing, but were sure it was a sign the spirits were displeased. The People moved as only The People could, swiftly, lightly, shadows in the brush. Younglings were gripped, oldsters were assisted, though they were only a little less surefooted than the primes who composed the tribe.

The People began their retreat not a moment too soon, as the ship flashed its warning lights. "Stand by for flash sterilization of a five hundred foot region outside of the ship. All hands are reminded to remain in the ship during this time." Lights on the outside of the hull and the inside of the ship repeated the warning before the ship's external cold beams began to range and mark the distance. Then the hotter and more powerful lasers destroyed the nearby foliage, rock, sand, animals and unfortunately The People who had not been swift enough near the ship.

This was a standard operating procedure to ensure that the build area around the ship was rendered safe enough for the crew to disembark and begin building the outpost around the body of the landing craft. This landing pod was one of sixteen dropped to the planet across the world, allowing the Oligarchs an array of choices as well as increasing their ability to subdue the planet with the proper applications of technology.

Oligarch Esteves Sandobar was the leader of this landing pod, and was awakened first two days before the pod was ready to drop from orbit. He had been warned of the effects of cryosleep and had experienced it first hand for two months before the ship's five year journey to Proxima Betalis, a yellow orange star one hundred and twenty light years from Earth. He woke after five years of having nearly no blood coursing through his veins -- it had been replaced by a nutrient fluid that resisted expanding once cold, and yet could be supersaturated to allow cellular energy absorption, albeit at a very low level, essentially slowing cellular activity ninety percent. He was ravenous, yet the very idea of food made him slightly nauseous. He could not stand or move for a week upon reactivation because his body simply did not have the strength nor energy to rise.

As his blood was restored to his body, he was also pumped with regenerative serums designed to re-energize his cells, causing them to replenish themselves and return to their previous vigor. All of the Oligarchs on this journey had been treated with experimental genetic materials designed to allow them to fast-grow bone and muscle tissue once exposed to the regenerative serums. Within a week, he was strong enough to stand, and after another week of physical therapy, he had regained his superhuman stature.

Once he was active and capable, he began waking his core staff and providing them with the understanding of his value of them based on who was awakened first. It was important to impress upon one's subordinates, early in this expedition, what was expected of them. Esteves did not have any doubt of his team's loyalty, but it was good to let them know what he expected.

After the core team of seven members awakened, they scanned the star system and prepared to drop the other landing pods on to the planet's nine major continental masses. Proxima Betalis was a dual star with seven rocky planets and four gas giants, very similar to the Sol system. Early probes indicated that this planet, called Betalis Three for now, was very Earth-like. Subsequent scans confirmed the the planet as able to support human life.

The crew prepared the drop ships, and fell away from the primary body of the drive mechanism. As the ships plummeted to the surface of Betalis Three, they landed in the best visible areas chosen by the ship's computer. The site had been checked by the Oligarch Sandobar's hand-picked agents. The rest of the crew would be awakened on the planet's surface and allowed to grow accustomed to the gravitational difference. The air would be circulated on the ship further allowing the genofixing done on Earth to complete itself once on the planet. As for the Oligarch and his chosen few, they would be forced to spend a week in agony as their genofixing was applied after they arrived and were awake, but it could not be helped. Someone would have to suffer to ensure the rest of the crew had the best chance of survival on this planet, their new home.

"Genofixing complete. Commence crew debarkation. Preparation of ground for deployment completed." The crew of the landing pod was terribly sick and did not have any burning urge to go outside, so for the first week, they allowed robotic devices to build the defensive perimeter. Several physical threats existed in their new home, dozens of animals only seen from space and categorized by the computer.

To be safe, the system designed a protocol to ensure a safe space around the landing pod, while the area was prepared with habitats until the crew could live off the land. No one but the setup robots and a few crewmen would be allowed to leave the ship until the Oligarch Sandobar had completed his genofixing.

Days later, Far-slayer, who was out hunting when Heaven's Mountain belched its deadly fire, returned to find a few primes left and the forest-grass around Heaven's Mountain destroyed. His entire People had been decimated by the light of Heaven's Mountain. His agonized warble echoed through the remaining forest as he stared at the continuing sweep of energy flattening the terrain. He could see the skeletons of primes who were caught at the edge of the swath of destruction.

Such carnage had never been seen by any of The People, except in the most terrible of conflicts or when confronting the thundergiants of the Plains. Far-Slayer was now the leader of this remaining band of The People, and he soothed them with gentle whisperings and tended wounds as they moved away from the Mountain. They told him of the heavenly light that burned all away and they talked of the creatures who strode forth from Heaven.

The Mountain was not filled with gentle spirits after all. Far-slayer vowed as he took The People away toward a nearby valley that he would destroy whatever spirits inhabited this monstrosity. Thinking of his family, destroyed, he would never call this thing Heaven's Mountain again. For him, it would be called Hell's Rock, and he would vanquish and banish every spirit dwelling within it. As he watched the spirit beings boil out of Hell's Rock and begin their transformation of the land, he hoped a spirit could suffer.

He intended to find out.

Pax Cyridian

Hanging from the side of a building, cloaked in shadow, I could see the lights from the police roachsters sweeping the warehouse district and knew that we could not stay here long. I tried to visualize a route that would take me back to the city core but from here, every route was the longest route. Cyridian was not made for ease of driving but for optimal grazing for our bugs to maintain their bulk and their health.

Cyridian was designed by the city's founders to be as ecologically friendly as possible with the industrial complexes as far from the city's living quarters as possible. Closer to the inner rings were the commercial and educational service areas and then within the center of the city were the living quarters for bugs and people in the direct center.

I patted the internal dash of my Bug and she warmed the internal energy centers of her power plant. She did not activate her bright-lights, she was a nocturnal species capable of seeing easily in the dark. I put on my sensor band, so I could see what she was seeing. Her vision spanned the infrared and ultraviolet spectrums, she was an omnivore, so she hunted and foraged on plants when other prey was not available.

"Run, run?"

"Not yet."

"Far to run. Must run soon."

"Stay still. We have to wait until the time is right."

"Wait, wait."

She was never the most patient vehicle. Her parent insects were adapted because they were strong and amazingly intelligent. She was one of the few breeds capable of true interaction. For most people Bugs were just an analog for machines. So much so, they used the default activation codes designed by the breeders. "Bug On," was the code phrase used to activate the systems of the Bug control interface. Most never created or updated the control system or password. It was not for security, because no one stole here, it would have been to personalize or empathize with the vehicle.

Cyr-Bugs were never truly embraced by most of the humans of Cyridian. Our subtle racial dislike of insects followed us from Earth. Despite the fact that the Cyridian insects have allowed us to have a lifestyle that embraced nature, remain peaceful and have a life completely dedicated to living in harmony with the world, many Cyridians were never in love with our symbiotic partners.

"Okay Ona, go fast to quadrant seven. Stay off the road."

"Bump, bump, okay Penrose?"

"Yes, Ona, bump, bump. I am strapped in."

Ona stretched her legs and tumbled into the underbrush. It was a very bumpy and rough ride. But the advantage was hers because the police roaches simply had to go around. Around on Cyridian meant many miles of alternative pathways like an old maze puzzle. Ona rarely got to travel this way because my job simply did not give me the time to let her roam like I would have wanted. As a matter of fact, it's my job that put me in this position in the first place. I am a gene-engineer. I change bugs into conveniences for the people of the Empire. I'm not used to people shooting at me, or trying to kill me. Perhaps a bit of explanation is in order. I went to work this morning...

"Penrose, I'm seeing some organic components missing from your warehouse stockpiles," shouted my boss from his desk pit. He didn't even wait for me to slide into my desk before making demands. I saw that Barry, my co-engineer, hadn't even shown up for work yet. Brown-nosing the boss does have its perks.

"I'm right on it. It has to do with the last alterations I made to the Series 19 upgrades. I will check the data right after I grab some crabs."

"Bring me a couple back," he mumbled and went back to whatever he was doing on his multiple terminals.

Passing his pit, I looked down and saw some new recombinations he was working on, ugly designs to my sense of aesthetics but he had customers who loved his carapace work.

I tapped into my desk system as I walked by and looked at the reports he flagged in my heads up display. I didn't recognize any of these requests. I got to the kitchen and picked up five or six crabs, a local insect delicacy, flash fried and coated in a dusting of sugar.

"Run a trace on these requisitions, please." My computer would put a marker out on them and inform me where the organic components went. It was a bit of a concern because of the quantities being rerouted. Enough for fifteen or twenty Bugs. The components were the organic interfaces used to control or interact with a Bug's system.

Since many of the systems in our buildings were created with or by or supported by the local insects, any that require our interaction had to be fitted with a control interface. The control interface technology was one of the things we created here.

The flag came up indicating the resources ended up in a facility at the very edge of the city, about fifty klicks from here, as the dragon flies. Driving will take about one hundred klicks. "Boss, I'm going to have to go out there. The system that authorized it requires a personal code to access. I am going to have go during working hours, because they barely have any comm systems out there at all. It's one of the newer installations."

"Do what you need to Penrose. I have seven new carapaces I need you to look at before you go, though. Can you do it at lunch?"

I had left Ona out to graze and found her sitting in a field, eating into a nest of what we called su-mona. They resembled Terran termites in that they burrowed underground and fed on woody materials. But each was the length of a man's arm and had complexes that could spread for dozens of miles. They were a primary source of food for Ona's species and one of her personal favorites.

The park center was a common grazing area and without the constant effort of Bugs, it would grow out of control in a matter of days.

"Penrose, I found su-mona, want to share?"

"No thank you, Ona. Will you be done soon? We have a trip to go on."

"A long one, yes?"

"Very. Over two hours."

"Can Ona run?

"As fast as you like." She hurriedly chomped down the rest of her termites. There was goo all over her face. Using her pelipaps, she wiped it away as quickly as she can she said, "Ona is finished."

I climbed into the carapace chamber organically crafted out of her mighty exoskeleton. I slid in and she formed a ridge to support my back. I put on my sensor band and could see the road through her eyes. She took off down the road at over 95 kilometers per hour.

When we arrived at the warehouse, it was mid afternoon, there had not been much traffic, so Ona really could move as fast as she wanted. It had been great to allow her to show off her speed. She was not nearly as fast as roaches who could reach speeds of 150 kph, but only for short bursts. Ona could do what she did all day long. Beyond the edge of the city, her ancestors still roamed free and could be quite dangerous to visitors of our world.

If you came to live on Cyridian you were given genetic modifiers which made you emit an odor considered unpleasant to most of the more aggressive animals of the planet, and armed with Bospor stingers, you were safe from the rest that might still eat you.

The warehouse was closed up and no staff was available to accept my query for entry. I slid out of Ona and walked up to the wall of the warehouse. The building was created out of the traditional silkstone but it seemed to have other properties. I licked the building and my chemical mods indicated there were traces of other toxins on the outside of the building. I was immune to anything the planet had to offer. I had to be to work with the number of toxic insects we handled to do our jobs. I found the toxin to be a strange one because it was not found in most of the insects local to the area.

Ona normally settled into grazing once we arrived at an area, but she seemed reluctant to move from where she stopped. She waved her palps around and put them into her mouth to taste the air.

"Ona? What's wrong?"

"Bad genes here."

"Whose work is it. Is it mine or Barry?"

"Barry's taste."

Each engineer has a signature to their work. There are only five or six of us in Cyridian and we have marked our work to ensure stability and accountability in design.

"Trouble. Danger." That made me nervous. Ona is one of the larger and more dangerous predators on this planet. If she was worried, we might be in trouble.

I walk back to Ona when two roachsters pull up behind her and two law enforcement agents got out of the vehicles. Ona turned around and eyed them. The roaches were calm and did not respond to her veiled threat. "Can we help you Gene-engineer?"

"What seems to be the problem, officer? I came out here to investigate a technical requisition supply issue."

"This warehouse is restricted." The officer seemed strange to me. He kept his hand on his Bospor pistol.

The second officer stayed next to his roachster.

"Perhaps I have been misinformed." Ona, bristled when I walked back to her.

"Penrose. Not good. Something wrong."

"I know, but we have to go."

Then there was a booming from the warehouse behind us. The roachsters backed up with the amazing speed they are capable of. Ona leapt away from the warehouse and landed facing it.

"Okay, that doesn't sound normal."

"We are going to have to ask you to leave, sir."

The booming happened again but this time the wall exploded open and the law enforcement officer is crushed instantly by the falling wall debris. The speed at which it happened shocked me, but Ona was already in motion. She grabbed me and wrapped me in the energy dampening material inside her chassis and backed away from the hole. The other officer got out of his roachster with his Bospor pistol drawn.

The creature that came out appeared to be a variant on Ona's design but much bigger. The modifications included increased chassis armor, stronger leg designs and several other surface mods I did not recognize. But I knew weapon work when I saw it. This was an illegal mod.

"Run, run, Penrose?"

"No Sweetie, not yet."

The second officer jumped out of his roachster. He directed the first roachster to try and remove the debris from his downed partner. The roachster tried to lift the debris, but it was designed for speed not strength. The illegally modified creature looked out of the hole at the roachster and roared.

The officer fired on the creature. The Bospor pistol launched a round from the gun with a huff of highly compressed air. The Bospor stinger flew at over eight hundred feet per second. The tiny blob landed on the creature. Nothing happened.

Impossible.

The Bospor was the most toxic animal on the planet. Quiet scavengers, nothing ate them and they were non-aggressive. Their only defense is their deadly neurotoxin launched with series of gas-launched spines. The powerful neurotoxin kills everything with a nervous system on Cyridian. It is why they we modified them as weapons.

"Now we run, Ona."

The gene-mod opened one of its ports on the side of its massive body and a coughing ejection of phlegm struck the officer. He began to smoke and scream immediately and ran backward until he fell down. Then he turned into a pile of smoking organic mess. The creature coughed again and one roachster was struck in the side, the other backed up and turned its turret on to the gene-mod. It fired two chemical backed Penranol projectiles. Both organic projectiles struck the gene-mod. One bounced off of the dense carapace, the other stuck and burst into flame. I had seen enough.

We ran as fast as we could. When we reached the next civilized part of the industrial area we tried to call back to my office with no success. Barry might have already left. I tried to reach his comm badge but he did not answer.

I heard the alarms of roachsters as they approached our position. Ona began to fidget and I touched her to calm her down. As the roachsters surrounded us, I began to get the impression something was terribly wrong.

Barry gets out of one of the roachsters. "Hello, Penrose. I see you found out about my project."

"That monstrosity is yours? What happened to do as little harm as possible?"

"That was before Venris Tel Corp offered me 50 million credits to build them an organic tank. Then it became "Do less harm to your planet and more to others for the proper funding." Barry sneered at me. "You think you're better than me."

"You realize you just confessed?"

Barry looked around at the cops and laughed. "These guys? They work for me. They help me keep things under control and they get a nice piece of the action."

"Penrose..." began Ona

"Not now, Ona."

"You and your talking car. You talk about me, but making a car that talks is the real crime."

"It's because they are not cars, they are living things. That's what happened on Earth, we began to treat the world as a commodity."

"So you make your freak car?"

"Yes, I wanted something that I didn't have to say 'Bug On' to get it to activate to."

"Penny..."

"Not now, Ona."

"No matter, what I've done will make me fantastically rich, but only if you don't survive to tell people. Gentlemen, if you please."

I began to hear a rumbling sound, rhythmic and growing stronger, fast. The roachsters turned to face down the road and put their bright-lights onto the road.

"Penny, we should go."

"Yes, Ona, I think you're right."

The Gene-mod barreled into the center of the roachsters, shooting its acidic phlegm with abandon. Ona had backed up away from the road, until she was out of line of sight. The acid bombs landed on several of the roachsters and their agonized shrieks filled the air. The gene-mod had a burn all over its top carapace but was otherwise undamaged. It barreled into the other roachsters and there was the brittle sound of carapace against carapace contact.

The roachsters chosen for their speed and savage temperament slashed into the gene-mod and the battle was joined. Ona and I used the distraction of them fighting for their lives to run for ours.

We managed to make it to the working ring and I tried to reach the Central Administrator. I left Ona to graze while I made my way into the building complex. Barry, being my boss had rescinded my access to the office. I would have to make a run to the center of the city.

I could see the headlights of the roachsters searching for me. I guess that means Barry is still alive. We turned into the park and made good time. We stayed off the roads where the roachsters had a speed advantage and crept the city's overgrown grazing areas. I had to put a visit into the Sector Chief, personally. She lived in the central region, on the west side.

It took us fifty minutes and four close calls before I had to leave Ona at the edge of the center region. The roads were pedestrian friendly but less so for Bugs.

"You wait here, Ona. Stay under cover. I'll be back for you soon."

"Okay, Penrose. I wait here."

I started toward Lanris Corli's place and realized I didn't know what I was going to tell her. I didn't have any evidence. Using the scent glands of the *Pinaris* beetles we created organic street lights by attracting and feeding the bioluminescent insects over certain areas of the street. We used other kinds of glow-paint for areas that needed to stay lit but relatively insect free. It took me about five minutes to reach her domicile, a lovely spincast place made from the silk of a *Wayran* moth, one of the projects I headed years ago. I knocked on the door. It took about a minute for her to answer.

"Gene-engineer Penrose at your service, ma'am."

"Cut the crap, Penrose, why are you at my door this late?"

"Well, I have evidence of a plan to weaponize our technology and sell it off-planet."

The sleepy look vanished from her face. In retrospect, I think I should have paid closer attention.

"Come in Gene-engineer. Let me get dressed. Tell me the rest."

She invited me in and vanished into her bedroom. I explained about the gene-mod and it's rampage. When she came back out she was dressed in her Civil servant uniform of blue and gold. She was also carrying a stylish chemical pistol of Old Earth manufacture.

"I didn't want this, Penrose. We were trying to get them off planet, before anyone noticed. If we could've had one breeding pair and the gene-mods no one would have been the wiser."

"There is more than one of those things? I guess this means you have to kill me, now."

"It doesn't have to be, there are potentially several clients who would pay for our genetic technology, which has no equal in the Empire. Killing you would be a waste of a very important irreplaceable resource."

"So why the gun?"

"I can't have you running out of here before you hear my offer. There are always other administrators you could have confessed to who would been appalled to know what you just suggested to me."

"You could have gone the seduction route? Made me believe

we were going to be friends. After befriending me you could have killed me. It's what the Nornian spider does with its multiple mates over the course of its lifetime."

"You need to get out more." Her phone rang. "I see. I will take care of it." She hung up. "Barry's dead. It looks like your value just shot up. But we have a problem."

Pointing at the gun, "I'd say we have two. If you plan on having my help, you need to put that away. Its making me nervous. You won't like me nervous."

"It's my insurance, don't get any ideas. The gene-mod is out of control and heading toward the center complex. If anyone gets a clear look at it, we might be in trouble. The police will open a breach in the shield and attract some native fauna in. We'll claim this creature is one of them and cover it up before anyone can investigate."

"I want Barry's share."

"Getting bold, are we?"

"No, I am thinking I won't have much of a career on Cyridian before this is over, so I'm just thinking ahead. Especially if I help you with this."

"Alright, let's go." As we stepped out of the doorway into the courtyard, the streetlights flickered. The streetlights were comprised of clouds of the local fireflies, genetically inclined to stay near pheremone emitting sites scattered throughout the city. Working with nature, we don't imprision the insects. They were free to come and go but between the pheremone and the nectar, they provide light sufficient for our modified vision. Then the lights went out. But that only happened when a predator approached. Lanris had only a split second of warning. She looked up right before the gene-mod landed its massive bulk right on top of her head, killing her instantly. She managed to get off a single shot.

In that split second, when the lights fled, before it arrived, I realized what was happening and leaped into the brush, running for my life. They made the damn thing able to fly? What were they thinking? And with a stealth mode, no less? That was insane!

The gene-mod was right on my tail. It knocked down trees and steel-like bamboos as if they were'nt even there, fibrous splinters raining down all around me. I could smell its power plant, it was overheating, flying was probably not the ideal movement for it. If I ran fast enough, maybe it would run out of energy and have to stop and rest.

Yeah, right.

I could hear it getting closer and closer, I looked back only once and could see it's crazed look as its bright-lights locked onto my position, I ran into the brush to obscure its vision, even for second. If I could just make it back to the park, I could hide from it. It had no major sensory mods I could see, so I could escape while the police, the real police handled it.

But I wasn't going to make it. I could smell it just seconds from me. There was a crashing sound coming from my left and a tree dropped right behind me. It caused the gene-mod a moment of hesitation, but it bit right through the tree. Then another tree landed behind me and a third.

Who is throwing trees behind me?

When I came to the clearing where Bugs awaited their owners, there were no Bugs there, including my own? Where was she? It was not like her to move too far once I told her I was coming back. She would have stayed near a feeding station. I was going to die here. On level ground there was no way I could outrun it.

I turned and ran anyway. I heard the buzz of two approaching roachsters. I did not know whose side they were on, so I just ran away from them too as the gene-mod burst out of the underbrush. These weren't just roachsters, these were Hunter-seekers, killers designed to destroy bugs that breached the shield. They were big, strong and fast, some of the deadliest things we ever engineered. So dangerous, they were only released into areas that had been overrun because they killed everything they came in contact with. Once they had neutralized all threats, they were destroyed with internal toxin bombs. One-use creatures unable to be bred, except under the most ideal conditions. There were never more than four or five available any more since we perfected the shield and pheromone technologies.

With lightning speed, they turned their attention to the gene-mod with their bright-lights flashing all over the area as they battled the monster. Their flashing blade mouths, tried to cut into the carapace of the gene-mod but most of their blows were scratches in comparison to the injuries it dealt. But these were no ordinary roachsters. Their nervous systems amped to the highest degree, most of the gene-mod's attacks missed their mark fully.

But the battle was far from equal. I looked on in horror as the full extent of the gene-modifications began to show. It began to regenerate its injuries. Regeneration was rarely added to any genestruct because there were too many potentials we wanted to avoid. Unnecessary cancers and 'regrettable immortality'. Cells that divide too often sometimes became cancerous. And immortality can be inconvenient if you were seeking to kill a creature to prevent it from passing on its immortal genes. The potential to destabilize an ecosystem was too great, hence its name 'regrettable immortality'.

I hoped the police were trying to get something bigger to fight with because with the venom, acid, armor, speed, flight and regeneration mods this thing was boasting, it would kill us all before the next day was done. One Hunter-killer went down under the super-strong legs of the gene-mod, speared through in four places and pinned into the spin-crete beneath.

I couldn't think of anything I could do to stop this. While the last Hunter-killer got a few more wounds in, the brush behind it began. I saw several Beetles, the most common of the auto-bugs used here. Each is carrying a tree in its front leg set. They surround and set upon the gene-mod with the trees, each swinging the tree limb as if it were a willow wand. The concussive booms stagger the gene-mod with each blow, but it continues its relentless assault on the Hunter-Killer.

Then I saw Ona. She came out of the forest and she was singing. Rubbing her pelipaps together she makes a series of strange but beautiful sounds, and when she does the other auto-bugs increase their assault. The gene-mod turns and grabs one of the auto-bugs, a female, and sprays it's toxic venom. She screamed horribly, convulsing while she died.

The others hesitated and the Hunter-Killer got in a final strike before it was cut in half by the slashing jaws of the gene-mod. It struck the genestruct in the eye with its sword-like forearms. The strike is deep, a few inches to the left and it could have been mortal. The Hunter-Killer's arm broke off and the sword-like claw remained embedded in the eye socket of the gene-mod. The other auto-bugs renewed their attacks but not nearly as durable as the Hunter-Killer, each was cut down, one after the other.

Once it's done, it turned toward me and advanced slowly. There were only a few times I had regretted my occupation. Once, before I was completely gene-modified to live on Cyridian, I was working with a spasm-fly and was bitten. No one knew I hadn't completed my modification so I spent a half a year in a spasm chamber, immobilized in a stasis field so my muscles didn't pull the flesh from my bones. That was the lowest point in my technical career. I had few other regrets. The occasional lack of family bit deep, but with my gene-mods, I would live to be a nice two hundred or so, (or would have until today) so I always thought I would have time.

The gene-mod approached and I knew I was seconds from death. The only question was how. Venom? Acid? Stomped to death? I hoped it would be quick. I was not looking forward to be stomped to death. Then I heard that whistle again and the gene-mod turned again.

Ona. What was she thinking?

It turned away and I could feel my bowels growing weak. Being close to dying really made bodily control a challenge.

Ona stepped away from the brush and approached the gene-mod. But she was bigger, redder, and her eyes had a particular gleam I had never seen before. Then I remembered. This was her maternal combat mode. Mothers, when their young are in trouble, change and become dangerous killing machines. On this world, multiply that by five.

She flew.

I mean, I knew she could do it, I had just never seen it. She flew fast. She slammed into its side and knocked it off its feet. Ona is big, much bigger than the roachsters, and she used her bulk to her advantage. She landed on its underside and stabbed her sword-like pedipalps into it undercarriage, near the base of the legs, and severed its ability to control two of those legs. She bounded away as it uses its outer carapace wings to flip itself over.

It landed with a grunt and fluids sprayed out from underneath its legs, the two damaged ones are barely able to hold up the carapace in the back of the creature. Its carapace was dragging the ground. It's down but not out.

The genestruct turned to face Ona with its good eye and I am on its blind side with the sword hanging out its eye. As long as the claw remained in its eye, it could not regenerate the tissue. The creature sprayed both venom and acid from its weaponized glands. Ona leaps forward dodging the venom but getting hit with the acid. Using her strong back legs, she sliced forward and cut off the wing casing covered with acid. She howled, a sound I have never heard her make before.

She and the genestruct circled each other and tentatively attacked each other but neither has an advantage. Ona was slowing Her injuries were taking a toll on her. The genestruct was slowly regenerating and soon able to raise itself on its hind legs. Ona scurried around onto its blind side and rushed it, slashing along the region between the carapace and the legs. She is able to get a good and solid wound. The beast roars and explodes into action. It cut deeply into her side armor, pushed her back before it moved away from her. She had damaged it seriously. The genestruct stopped moving and fell over with one set of legs unable to move. Ona was badly hurt as well. She bled from a dozen injuries all over her carapace and undercarriage. I ran over to her and tried to stop the bleeding.

"Penrose, run, run."

"I can't Ona. I can't leave you. Now get up. We have to go."

"Penny, I can't run. Go now. Ona loves you. Ona dies for you."

The silence was oppressive. It was never quiet on Cyridian. Insects were always talking here. Anything near this battle realized they were in the presence of something terrible and hoped to avoid drawing attention to itself. Even scavengers, normally bold, made no attempt to approach. Ona's quiet and ragged breathing was the only thing I could hear. Her internal plant was already offline.

Then the sound of a powerplant restarting echoed across the forest. The brightlights of the genestruct came back on. Weak and flickering, but they slowly got stronger. I hear the coughing of the acid cannon being prepared to fire. I couldn't let that happen. Ona couldn't move yet.

I jumped up and tried to draw its fire. Confused and with only one good eye, it chose me and fired. The acid blob, hit the ground near me and part of the splash landed onto my uniform. Designed with genetic constructs in mind, the uniform neutralizes most of it, but the quantity overwhelms it and my flesh bore the rest. The pain was excruiating. I fell forward as my legs gave out, face down into the underbrush.

But for the first time since it happened, I was glad of the spasm-fly attack. I was in stasis for six months. During that entire time, my nervous system was under assault, being constantly stimulated without relief, everyday until it was brought under control. I learned my threshold for pain. And while this certainly was terrible, it was nothing compared to that six months.

I screamed. I cursed, I raged. And I got up.

"I've had about enough of you." The gene-mod coughed, and sputtered as it tried to repair itself. I could hear its power plant as it struggled to stay online.

It was dying.

I limped up to its blind side, and I could hear its inquiry

sounds as it tried to figure out where I was. I knew these sounds. It was looking for someone to help it. Designed to have someone support it, its injuries led it to believe someone should be helping to repair it and those chirps of query meant it was expecting someone.

I saw the Hunter-Killer leg hanging out of its ocular cavity. I reached up, grabbed the end of the leg, and reorienting it, pointed it directly into its brain. The thrust is brief and the green ichor of the construct's blood covered me in one final surge.

It did not resist. There was a sound like a sigh of relief and the creature eased itself into a resting position. I looked at the creature and saw it was covered with pain mods, all over its armored carapace, used to control it. They were inflamed. Something drove this creature to rage. But what?

"Hello Gene-Engineer Penrose." The voice was familiar and despised. I turned around and in the early morning light I could see his well-dressed and diplomat's outfit with a tiny remote in his hand. He also had two burly Junantra guards, genetically modified supermen at his beck and call.

"Ambassador Cohen." I spat blood out of my mouth. "So all that interest in my work a year ago was not as harmless as I thought."

"You wound me, Penrose. You should be happy I took an interest in your work and had such avid supporters amongst the populace."

"So you could make this poor thing?"

"That poor thing has killed sixteen roachsters, all six of the hunter-killers left in the city, and two dozen other assorted vehicles. It was one of the finest killing machines ever made, even on this world. And it's mine."

"I know. It's worth millions."

"Billions, my good man. We made them in breed-capable pairs."

"You are the final link in the chain aren't you. You made the off-world connections."

"Yes, and once we collect our genetic material from this one, for breeding, we will be on our way. So sorry about your car." One of the Junantra guards walked over to the creature's mouth and began extracting vital genetic chambers that could be used to breed the creature. The ambassador and the other guard walked over to me and helped me to my feet.

"And what about me."

"That depends on you. The Human Race is still out there conquering the Universe and needs minds like yours to help it. I know you are a pacifist like all of your people here, but think of the potential value you could bring to our kind with your organic war machines."

"I know. I would be paid handsomely to destroy life all over the galaxy for fun and profit. No thanks." My blood was flowing down my leg, off of my arm and head.

"I am afraid I cannot allow you to leave knowing what you do."

"I am afraid I am not asking to leave." With blood on my hands, I reached out and slashed both the ambassador and the Junantra on the neck with my razor sharp nails. Working with gene-constructs, you occasionally have to have the ability to defend yourself. I had been weaponized during the time I was in the healing chambers. Such work was not common knowledge. It was necessary to save my life. Living here, being stronger and faster is a survival technique. On Earth, I would have been superhuman, here, I was just a faster, more agile snack.

Since being infected with spasm-fly venom, my survival altered my body as the potent virus has remained part of me. Living as an SP-V, I lived a life suffused in constant agony as my nervous system is antagonized by the virus, but I can control the spasms and constrictions with the help of the anti-viral gene mods inside my body.

The ambassador and his guard were not so fortunate. It tool only a few seconds for them to double over in pain and for their muscles to begin to pull back on their bones until they start to snap. An agony so great, they were rendered speechless as their vocal cords tore themselves in their throats. Every beat of their hearts, passed the weaponized virus into every cell of their bodies. Only being in a medical facility allowed me to survive the spasm-fly virus. Without immediate medical attention, their bodies will be turned inside out in a matter of minutes and I realized I left my comm badge with my car; in my dying car.

The Junantra died first, his superhuman strength is no asset here. His grunts are terrible, but brief. The ambassador dies only minutes later. The second guard hearing something, rushed to their aid, and with a quick slash he died a few minutes later.

I went over to Ona and saw she is already dead; my beautiful Ona, my first best friend. *I will make you again, my dear. You have been far better to me than most humans I know.*

I sat down with her and watched the sunrise. Looking over at the ambassador, I felt no regrets. Since he was the last of them, it should make it easy to clean up and ensure creatures like this one are never made again. With any luck, the Council will be able to investigate fully and hunt down the other one and see that it's destroyed.

I came here to Cyridia to get away from the violence of the Empire. Here, everything is trying to live, eat or be eaten, kill or be killed. I can live with that. That's nature. But to kill each other for money. That's an obscenity any way you look at it.

Just because I live on a planet full of peaceful people does not make me a pacifist.

Hunger

It tore at her as a ravenous beast might; the hunger. She had never believed it could hurt so. Was this what it was like to be so near to dissolution? This tenuous feeling that she might be flying apart, her molecules, thinner than the gossamer she was already forced to be to feed. She was the thickness of a butterfly's wing, a wisp floating in space.

She was weak, so weak that she could only consider the unthinkable, a blind jump to the nearest star and hope there might be food there. Hunger had not been something she was accustomed to, having grown up near the center of the galaxy, within the blazing confines of the galactic core. So beautiful, stars everywhere, light constantly bombarding her every surface, so bright, she was forced to condense herself and reflect light. Her neural network fluttered with the idea, light so abundant she could return it to space, uneaten.

Her current form, adapted for dark space travel, was large, millions of miles across, diaphanous, and absorptive, capturing every stray photon, every bit of random hydrogen, every fragment of solar wind. But the pitiful scattering of radiation from stars in this portion of the galaxy would never be able to support her unless she found a supply of new mass, and soon.

It had been many years since she had a substantial meal. Living on nothing but the sparse energy between the stars, she had grown lean. Once so powerful, she might have been mistaken for a star herself; she was now so enfeebled that she did not even emit light, just a flicker between the stars.

The last three unstable wormholes she discovered had taken her far from the galactic core and the abundant light sources she was accustomed to. In the beginning, she did not panic. She was certain she would be able to find a path back to her part of the core. She had been assigned to study the rare pairing of two black holes circling each other in a collapsing orbit. Both stars spinning at hundreds of revolutions per second and circling each other in minutes created a gravity song rarely heard by her people, who studied such phenomenon for the secrets of the underlying First Sound. She had listened to the harmonies of this stellar phenomenon for centuries.

Suddenly, as stars count time, perhaps some unknown equilibrium had been struck, but the two stars' event horizons collapsed into each other. They crashed together, and the gamma ray pulse blinded her and caused her to lose her equilibrium. The resulting gravity distortions disrupted her perception of the First Sound near her, and she was unable to maintain the probability of her position, and she was lost. The quantum-field disrupting nature of the explosion displaced her through time and space. A random wormhole tossed her thousands of light years away from her home.

The energy of the explosion did not hurt her, of course. Her species fed on the radiation of millions of stars, less than a few light years apart, as well as the gas scattered throughout the luminous core. It was a rich feeding area for her people who had lived for billions of years traveling the gravimetric fields, listening to the harmonies of the stars with their interacting fields of light, gravity, and super-string harmonies against the ominous baritone of the super-massive stellar mass that the entire galaxy revolved around.

Her people called the object at the core of the galaxy the First Sound. She missed the comforting vibrations of the gravity web she had grown up in. So far from the center of the galaxy, it gravitational baritone was muted by distance, barely a ripple. But the First Sound was felt even here, as all that is part of the First Sound stays bound to it, surrounds it, and moves through the universe together. At this distance, though, she could barely feel it at all. Just the tiniest tickle of its gravity remained.

Her senses strained to their limit, she was aware of a tiny white dwarf on a nearby galactic arm, an island in this lonely part of space. She realized if there were no gas giants in this star system, she would starve to death in a few centuries, unable to activate her probability engine and return to her people. To die alone was the worst thing she could think of, and that spurred her to take the rash action of jettisoning fifty percent of her remaining mass. Without a food source, maintaining such a huge bulk was a death sentence.

She had barely larger than a good-sized planet now. She focused her attention on the star and brought it into resolution. Ten times, fifty times, still not enough. One hundred times, one thousand times, she compensated for gravitation lensing caused by dark matter, she compensated for galactic drift, noted the declination in the fabric of space-time caused by the star. Desperate, she would attempt to drop out of p-space near the closest edge of its gravity well.

Then she waited. Two dozen years passed as she watched the star to see if there were other planets around it. And there was a flicker as a world passed in front of it, again and again, so quickly she was unsure of what she was seeing. The planet was massive, and close to the star. It was a gas giant, but so close to the star. How was she going be able to feed off of it, when it was so fast and she was now so slow? She would have to retain her speed if she were to have any chance.

Another dozen years passed as her probability drive activated, using nearly all of her remaining energy. Folding p-space, she willed herself across the distance. Her neural pathways flashed and she could, just for a moment see her family and hear the musical notes of the gravitic forces of the First Sound.

The jump took too much energy. She had been unconscious. Her proximity to the sun woke her as her energy-starved form absorbed every source of energy it could. Photons cascading fed her neural network, force-fields restarting grasping the quadrillions of neutrinos invisible to matter but able to be bound to her. Gamma rays fed her primary systems and long-dead organs roared to life, quiescient for centuries, now struggling to preserve as much of her as possible. She was still moving fast; her jump had successfully conserved her movement.

The sun took up one third of the sky. Its gravity clawed at her, pulled her, drew her toward it. She looked around and prepared to redirect her course away from the star. Where was the gas giant? She looked around and only then did she realize she had miscalculated and was heading directly toward the world which was supposed to be her refuge. She had planned to come up from behind it, scoop the atmospheric mass that she needed, make the repairs necessary, and leave once her drive was recharged.

That plan was gone now. At this angle of descent she would smash into the thick atmosphere of the planet and its violent storms, and be destroyed. She had only one chance and not much time. She began to redistribute her mass. She shifted her non-vital mass and prepared to launch it away from herself. She was not used to working this quickly and many of her vital systems were still not active. She would suffer memory loss, but she hoped it would be nothing vital. But she did not have the luxury of time.

She was used to having years to do things; now she had hours. She had never had to make decisions this quickly. She looked at the approaching gas giant and could see its gravity well going deep into the fabric of space-time. Its mass must be enormous. She would have one chance. She would use the last of her energy to propel the inactive matter away from her and thrust toward the planet in order to ride into the gravity well and whip around the planet. If she timed it just right, she could arrange to end up trapped in a permanent Trojan orbit with the planet.

All of her computations said she would be held at the Trojan point indefinitely, but there was a large margin for error since she did not know enough about the planet's atmospheric density, wind speeds, or chemical makeup. And she did not have the luxury of time. So much had gone wrong; she was simply without enough choices. There was also the matter of mass to be ejected. The most massive element of her remaining systems after her neural complex was her probability drive. She would need to eject it and work with her attitude systems only, and what she could reconfigure on the way down. That meant if she was unsuccessful and could not gain enough mass, she would never leave there.

Less than an hour remained. She prepared the probability drive for jettison; the mass she ejected would begin a spiral toward the sun. The information to build another was within her, but only if her neural complex could be saved. She streamlined herself and created a form capable of skimming the atmosphere. She would also attempt to grab some mass for analysis and conversion.

The time passed quickly. She had not been this close to a sun in decades, and the radiant energy soothed her, and she made peace with her insane plan. She ejected half of her mass again, and material equal to the mass of the Earth fell away toward the white dwarf. The shunted mass redirected her, partially due to the action-reaction and partially because she became much more maneuverable. Her new, streamlined self hurtled toward the planet, and it grew large, obscuring the sun in a matter of minutes. She turned her belly toward the planet, and she could sense the density of molecules increasing, gently at first and then more heavily. She rode the top of the cloud layer briefly while she picked up speed.

She opened her ram jets and ingested the matter. She saw she could burn it. Her plan depended on this. She scooped it, compressed it and attempted to start the engines.

No success. Fuel ratios out of balance; must correct. She was beginning to catch too much atmosphere; she would begin to slow down. If she did not get these jets started, she would begin to lose too much speed to escape.

The fuel mixture needed higher pressures to trigger the ignition; she needed to go deeper into the atmosphere. She inched her way down, her wide wings spread out, increasing the pressure bit by bit. Once she had the right pressure, the engines ignited and she had a sudden burst of speed. Then the engines performed better. The faster she went, the faster they gathered mass. Her plan worked.

One the engines fired, she noticed her her body was attraction ions as she moved through the alien sky. Below her, a storm raged. A vast storm whose electrical activity was drawn to her ionized form. Thousands of miles wide and would take minutes to pass over. The first lightning strikes were the worst, as her cold hull was covered in ionized matter and gas. The gasses exploded when the lightning struck her. There was damage all over her body, systems overloading everywhere.

She made what repairs she could internally and hoped she would be outside the range of the storm shortly. As the hull heated due to friction and energy discharges, it lost its attractiveness and within a few hours the energy discharges stopped.

She extended her senses into the atmosphere of the planet and noticed there were differing layers, each with its own different weather activity. And there was simple life here just below her layer in the clouds, a floating creature of some sort, drifting in the thousand mile an hour winds, in groups like she and her family once did.

Moving with a haste she was unaccustomed to, she reconfigured her primary boosters to utilize a refined fuel she had been working with while studying the clouds. Drawn from the chemical matter in the clouds, her manufacturum created billions of tons of the material for her final escape attempt. Right now she was just holding her own against the crushing gravity of this world.

She would need to create enough thrust to escape its gravity or be destroyed as she fell to ist surface thousands of miles below her, crushed by its gravitational pressures.

She was more than halfway around the planet and needed to begin adding to her thrust profile. The ramjets would not be enough. She prepared her new fuel and pressurized the systems.

Each engine was the size of a mountain, and she had hundreds of them. She activated them in a series of controlled operations, because to fire them all at once in atmosphere would tear her apart. The controlled burns began, each exploded with the force of a million nuclear weapons, in a sequence, faster and faster. Unexpectedly, the engines began to ignite the atmosphere, its natural chemical makeup causing the powerful engines to become a raging conflagration. The flames surged out in a fire trail for thousands of miles. Once the storm started, it spread. She saw the flames surging toward the giant creatures and eventually overtaking them.

They creatures burned quickly; the gas that kept them buoyant was highly flammable. She imagined she could hear their death throes as they fell away into the underlayers of coral colored clouds. They did not suffer long. She looked away as they died, saddened that she was the cause of their deaths.

The last of her engines ignited, and she was certain she would make it once the last step was made. She prepared the final jettison and fired the last of the main engines as she left the atmosphere. The ramjets and wings, hundreds of megatons, fell away to burn up in the atmosphere. She was just a needle, her core systems, her engines, her data network, her manufactorum, her ability to create a new her, was all that was left as she streaked away from the planet. As she entered the light of the sun, she flickered like a diamond and slowly came to rest in the Trojan orbit of the planet.

There was so little of her left. She saw a fiery trail burning in the clouds, the last parts of her she could shed in order to save the most vital parts of her as the planet orbited beneath her.

Now in geosynchronous orbit, she created a tendril of matter to drop into the atmosphere of the world. She also spread herself thin to gather the energy of the solar wind. With the tendril below, she would slowly siphon off mass from the planet. With the energy of the sun, she would spread out until energy was flowing freely, allowing her to rebuild herself over a few centuries.

Nearly a thousand years passed. She had grown from a tiny sliver of light to a massive moon of the great world below. And she had a satellite, a daughter moon of her own to ease her loneliness. She told her daughter of the voice of the First Sound.

She explained that the gravity song of their star was beautiful but a shadow of the First Sound at the center of the galaxy. At this distance she could barely hear it at all.

She told her of the probability drive and how it was almost complete. She would be able to take them back to the core and to their family. Unfortunately, the storms destroyed much of her memory of their migration routes, so they would have to hunt for them. It might take some time, a few centuries at least.

Her daughter asked her about their sun and the animals in the atmosphere of their Jovian world. She loved taking care of them and using her smaller bodies to joyride through the solar system.

Mother explained they would be fine, and now that the two of them have been here and lived here for so long, they will be able come back and see them any time she wants. This location will be keyed to their drives.

Her daughter told her how happy that made her, and said she could not imagine living anywhere else.

Mother agreed with her daughter, but secretly would be lad to be trying to go home. This place saved her life, and she was grateful, but it would never be home, even if she lived here for a thousand years. And she had. And it still wasn't.

The Great White Spot

From space, it looked like a ball of blue and brown; blue oceans swirled with windblown whitecaps and the occasional tiny island could be found, but most were scoured clean by the Last Storm. You couldn't see much of the surface anymore because of the cloud cover. The white polar ice caps were tiny buttons on the top and bottom of the globe.

During the year, they appeared and disappeared. If you took a vantage point from the lone satellite of this blue planet, you would notice on the night side that no light was emitted, no radio transmissions to disturb your electromagnetic slumbers. It was a quiet planet circling a nondescript yellow-white dwarf with eight other planets and assorted planet-junk. Strangely enough, if your vision was sharp enough, you would see hundreds of artificial satellites circling the planet.

You would see communication satellites beaming signals to each other, reminding each other where they were to ensure signals moving from the ground to other places on the planet were not interrupted. They never received those signals any longer, since there was no one to send them. There were many global positioning satellites, each designed to know every single street and every square inch of the planet and tell you where you were at any moment in space and time, anywhere on the globe. They hadn't had a single query for a over than a year.

Military reconnaissance satellites watched key sections of the globe for threats to countries that no longer existed. Linked to those satellites are space-based weapons platforms using a variety of technologies to deliver death from above. These weapons sat quiescent, unaware of their lack of targets.

Two satellites were still doing their jobs. The first was a weather satellite. It still chugged along, gathering information about the only weather phenomenon that still mattered, the Last Storm. Yes, there were still record temperatures all over the world. Yes, flooding was occuring in all the places men once lived. Island nations had disappeared under the rising water levels. Polar ice caps has already disappeared. Coastal cities were all but erased. These satellites noted all of those things, but lately, the only information it tracked was called the Last Storm.

It came into existence nearly ten years ago. Weather satellites made the pivotal discovery of the Last Storm in 2096, when it was just a tropical depression in the South Pacific Ocean. With winds in excess of three hundred miles an hour, no one viewing it at the time, knew they were looking at what would eventually render the planet a lifeless wasteland.

Now, it covered half of the northern hemisphere at any time, and blocked the sun from a quarter of the planet. Swirling above the planet is what, if there were scientist left to name it, a Great White spot circling the surface of the Earth, similar to the Red Spot on Jupiter, just hundreds of miles across instead of tens of thousands. A storm of matchless ferocity and intensity. It drove sand debris into the air at almost four hundred miles an hour.

The other satellite still doing anything significant, had only one man left on board. The last known survivor of the human race. His name was Sergei Balmasov. He was no longer living in the classic sense. He sat and looked out the observation window of the new International Space Station in muted horror; his mind broken.

He once listened to the wideband radio as the world came to an end. He listened as people called for help that would never come. He listened while radio stations told people not to panic, gave assurances that the storm would turn away from Hawaii, then as they ordered evacuations of South Pacific islands, and as the storm erased those islands, and crippled those evacuations, he listened to the death tolls.

As it approached Hawaii, he listened to the military channels as they considered what to do when they realized there would not be enough resources or time to rescue everyone there.

He wept as the military turned their ships around and returned to the United States. When Hawaii stopped transmitting, he turned off his radio to silence the horror, at least for a time. He could see the Storm from space as the world turned beneath him.

When he woke the next day, and turned the telescope toward Hawaii, it was gone.

Ships that had been fortunate enough to leave Hawaii early in the warnings were not safe. The storm overtook their ships. One hundred and twenty thousand sank as their ships were capsized in the torrential storm.

The remaining population died in the storm awaiting rescue ships that could never come. Hawaii, born of fire, home to people for five thousand years, was washed away in a single night, all of her people returned to the sea. The Last Storm slowed for a time and it was thought it would expire at sea, its forces spent. And while its winds slowed, it did not stop. It simply grew larger, much larger.

Sergei had no time to grieve as the storm approached California. Hearing about Hawaii, Californians fled to the mountains as meteorologists predicted the storm breaking against the Rocky Mountains. As it came within a thousand miles of California, the rains began. It approached the coast of California, its terrible winds drove tidal swells of water which hammered the coast turning any building on the coast to splinters.

The fifty-foot swells had never been seen before and thrashed the coastline, drove water into the streets of both Los Angeles and San Francisco. Torrential rains caused people who did not believe what they had heard about Hawaii to re-evaluate their position and they ran for their lives, for all the good it would do them.

The roads to the mountains were jammed with cars and trucks. The storm was inexorable. When it reached the coast, the winds were in excess of two hundred fifty miles per hour. Nothing made by man could withstand such winds. Skyscrapers lost windows, cars were flipped and carried for miles, trees uprooted, homes swept away by winds, rain, and waves. All convential wisdom about storms was lost as this monster approached the mountains.

As the storm reached the mountains, everyone's hopes rose, even as they ignored the carnage. The mountains would break the storm; it would run out of energy.

Instead, it did the unexpected. It turned south, but did not die.

Los Angeles was the next major metropolis to be swept away. The storm was being fed by the Pacific and kept moving south. As the edge of the mountains receded, the storm proceeded east into the Gulf of Mexico and continued to grow. Most of Mexico to the borders of Costa Rica and South America were completely inundated by water.

Refueled by the heated waters of the Gulf of Mexico, the storm's power increased, and with its increased size, it affected the Southern mainland states and basically erased them, from Nevada to Florida. Nearly one third of the population of the United States was destroyed in the first forty hours of the Last Storm of the century. Nearly all of Mexico and Costa Rica were decimated. Tens of millions were believed dead.

As the storm pulled away from the United States, its size increased again, absorbing water from across its entire area, and energy from the very warm waters of the Atlantic. It swept across the Southern tip of Europe, but even that tiny brush destroyed most of the UK, Greece, France, Italy, and all of the Mediterranean. At this point, emergency signals crossed the globe, with everyone trying to determine where the greatest need for emergency service would appear next.

It didn't matter. The storm would soon be everywhere.

The storm grew larger and more powerful, as it re-crossed the Pacific. Considered a national emergency by every government on the planet, humanity rallied in a effort to stop this threat. This was a sign of too little, too late. Climate scientists sat quietly in the briefing, chafing that they had been unable to convince the world governments of this final inescapable result of global warming. Being right was of little consolation.

It was considered such a threat, militaries threatened to throw nuclear weapons into the heart of the thing. Physicists tried to warn the military against this foolish act, trying to remind the military that a storm this size was already more powerful than every nuclear weapon on Earth with every second of its existence. But desperate men would try anything.

A great carrier, the Independence, last of her kind, caught in the storm and unable to escape, decided to use a nuclear device, but was destroyed before it could make the effort.

People fled wherever they thought they could go, but climate models had begun to reveal a startling truth. The storm was by now so large it could feed from any ocean, anywhere, at nearly any time, until it ran out of energy. Climatologists theorized it would become a permanent fixture on the face of the planet. Those climatologists called it The Great White Spot. It swept across the Earth over twenty-five times before stabilizing at its current size of one sixth of the globe. The remainder of the planet was covered in perpetual cloud cover that remained that way for another six years.

Sergei listened to the radio until the signals grew less and less. Communications from the ground lasted two more years, but by the year 2103, he could not detect a single radio message anywhere on the planet. He held out hope that somewhere, somehow, mankind had survived. Until the cloud cover broke enough to see the planet.

Until today. Then he wept like a child.

The mountains were gone, ground away by the five hundred mile an hour winds. The Rockies, the Appalachians, the Himalayans had been scoured from the planet. Nothing made by man had survived. The Earth was smooth and uniformly brown. He stared, looking for any landmarks. Nothing remained.

Sergei lasted his last year eating the stored food onboard the ship. The satellite alone could keep him alive for five years easily, but his mind was shattered by what he saw. In order to cope, he used climatological models from weather satellites under his control to determine that the Great White Spot would last for another twenty years in the best case scenarios. In the worst, it might never stop.

Sergei Balmasov, on the tenth anniversary of the Last Storm, and the last human being left alive anywhere, opened the bottle of vodka he had carried aboard all those years ago, and drank a toast. He finished the bottle in about an hour. He set all of his notes into the computer and set a radio broadcast into space, repeating what he had learned about humanity during their last days on Earth. He stepped into an airlock without a suit, closed the door behind him. He held his breath while he cycled the lock and jumped out into space. With his dying breath, he chose to look upon the Earth.

His message, to anyone who might one day come across our once-blue planet, was a tombstone marker. *"Here lies the final resting place of the Human Race. We saw the future, but could not embrace it, until it embraced us. May God have mercy on our souls."*

The Planet Traders

Our ship dropped out of the Gate inside of Mariovel space. Corvan battle fleets patrolled the area but acknowledged our IFF transponders and allowed us to continue into the star system. The red supergiant of the Mariovel system had two smaller red companion stars, only visible if you knew where to look.

After programming the coordinates for the Mariovel homeworld, the WarpRunner jumped and we emerged in the shadow of the goliath of planets, a great banded world of luminous clouds of various shades of pink, gold, and browns.

"Look into the upper hemisphere of the planet. There should be a Great White Spot. That is the space they have created for any visitor's habitation during the planetary refitting. Everything is on schedule; they say the planet will be ready in less than a year." Sitting in the pilot's chair, I tried to strike up a conversation with a cool and prickly diplomat of the Hegemony.

"I understand they produce only one planet a century here?" He was trying to be polite, but I could tell he really didn't want to talk to me.

Rising to the challenge, I answered, "They accepted a contract to create a new Earth for us at the request of the Hegemony's leaders."

"Your records indicate you live on Galatea II, Captain. What's wrong with Galatea II? It has been the cradle for a majority of the Humani species now for almost a thousand years." He sounded smug, as if reading my records had given him an advantage.

"Nothing, except it belongs to the Botani who look like trees and don't allow us to make anything out of wood, because it might be their kin. Not to mention that their symbionts creep me out with their strange cuteness. Other than that, they have been very hospitable. One thousand years is long enough, I think. I hate the idea that we are indebted to the Squids."

"Captain, I didn't know you were anti-Corvan."

"I'm not. I just don't like them. You do remember they destroyed the Earth and ten million humans who did not leave during the Exodus."

"Ancient history, at best. Yes, I have been transferred three times and am nearly a thousand years old, but the Mariovel and the Corvans have a relationship that goes back nearly ten thousand years. So if you hate the Corvans, remember the Mariovel love them, and keep your opinion to yourself."

Our class six WarpRunner was fitted for the Mariovel home-world and had the adjusted beacons needed to land in the protected regions. We would need a ship designed to interact with the powerful gravity technology of the planet.

As we approached their home-world, we were struck by its sheer immensity, defying anything we knew about planets. Three times the literal size of Jupiter, it was surrounded by a gaseous cloud layer similar to most gas giants, but that was just part of the story. Several cloud layers lay all the way to the surface of the planet. They had a gravity technology directed from the planet that changed the gravitation constants, allowing visitors from other planets to come to their world and live comfortably during the process of planet crafting. The Coral Region, a giant storm was their equivalent of a landing pad for visitors.

Thirty-six thousand miles in diameter, and large enough to hold entire planets, the Coral Region moved slowly in comparison to other storms on the planet. The incredible storms that swept the surface with their two thousand mile an hour winds and their crushing atmospheric pressure were able to destroy all but the most durable alien ships.

The Mariovel were a mystery to most races of the Hegemony. Rumors abounded about the species and their powers. Some of the strangest were the Mariovel were actually slaves of the Corvans, forced into an unholy alliance to create high quality planets for the highest bidders. Others theorized the Mariovel were actually the legendary First Race, The Precursors hiding in plain site. One thing was certain.

No one who had ever attacked the Mariovel homeworld was ever seen again. The Mariovel were one of the galaxy's races that had never been conquered or even effectively blockaded. While appearing to have no spaceships or even understandable technology, anyone attempting to wage war against them simply disappeared. Sensors directed toward their planet indicated vast supplies of the richest kinds of mineral wealth possible. Heavy metals abound, vast supplies of chemical and organic materials. Their world was a treasure trove.

It was also completely inhospitable to almost any other form of life. Without the support of the Mariovel, it was nearly impossible to even visit their world, let alone wage war. There is also one other aspect which most invaders remember. With a gravity well as deep as theirs, unless the Mariovel allowed it, no one who lands ever left.

We would not be going to the actual surface, though. We would be stopping at the third layer where buoyant fungi forms were floating through the atmosphere of the planet and were used as a base of operations inside the Coral Region. With the surface area of fifty thousand Earths, this was little more than a tiny way station on their vast planetary surface.

"Remember, keep your gravity harness active at all times. It keeps you in sync with the artificial gravity generators. In the event of any failure it will protect you with an artificial gravity field. Otherwise you would be crushed instantly by your own weight. It also protects you from the atmospheric pressure, so you never want to be anywhere outside of protected areas without it. This is the most dangerous environment you can imagine."

"I read the brief, Captain. I am aware of the risks."

"As a diplomat, I understand you have traveled to hundreds of worlds, and your dossier says you have even been to Nalrud, rumored to be the most dangerous world in the Hegemony, but there, it's the life forms that are dangerous. Here, even a tiny mistake can be your last. I just want to keep you safe, Diplomat Sinian."

"Your concern is noted, my good Captain. Let's get to the surface and to our work."

"You will be meeting with Chalguldan and what he calls the

Planet Crafters Enclave, Division Nine."

The diplomat was wearing a Humani standard hardened bio-suit, encrusted with his sigils of accomplishment and awards of state from almost three dozen worlds. The suit was designed to emit information into the infrared and ultraviolet spectra to allow the Mariovel to detect them, and with a standard mediasphere connection, they would be able to interpret their meanings and other galactic standard information.

My own suit was far less ornate, indicating only my rank, my modest accomplishments and my suitability for classified information management. I would be allowed to go everywhere the diplomat went and able to witness any transactions. It was not necessary for a diplomat to have a Humani witness for such transactions, but it had been a tradition for millennia.

As the bay doors opened on the WarpRunner, we were immediately assaulted by the heated air and the strange smell of the planet. It had a strong ammonia smell, nothing dangerous, but certainly unpleasant. There were other odors, as well, one that reminded me strongly of cinnamon, and the other of baking bread. Quite a wind was blowing as well, and it took a moment to adjust to the force of it. Nothing our suits couldn't handle.

A white spongy material was on the ground, and then I realized it was the living fungus that made up the Coral Region. I could see buildings off in the distance, also made out of the same materials. Dozens of different ships were there from a variety of the galaxy's races, each negotiating for their own planets or resource development of one sort or another. The sky was white with light from the overhead clouds, and at the edges of the fungus, I could see lightning flashing as the two weather patterns met. I could see flying creatures in the distance, but remembered reading that they were actually like everything else on this planet, gigantic in size; only their great distance belied their size.

Leaving the ship, we were met by a Mariovel in foglet form. As nearly as I understood it, they were capable of three different states of being. One was an energy form they use to repair ships when they are part of a Corvan battle fleet. The other was a large and mostly rocky form suitable for almost any environment. In that shape, they were mildly radioactive, so they don't use it in the presence of more organic beings. This cloud form is the only one not radioactively toxic to any of the Humani tribes. My suit indicated that we were in the presence of Chalguldan. I marveled at zhis beauty. Zhe (using the polite non-sexual pronoun) appeared as a star-like collection of nano particles orbiting a larger central mass about the size of an apple. The cloud was about two meters in diameter and twinkled with both internal light and light reflected from the environment. When it spoke, it emitted light interpreted by my suit's interface system and translated. I also spoke Galac Six, naturally, having been trained with biometric and computer languages nearly a hundred years before. I was certain the diplomat did as well.

"Greetings are given to esteemed guests."

"Greetings are accepted from our esteemed hosts."

"We are available to communicate with you regarding your request for a new planet."

"Where will we be meeting with the Planet Crafters Enclave, Division Nine?"

"They are all here. We will be visiting your world in progress. Will that be acceptable?"

"We will be able to see it?"

"Yes, Diplomat. But you will not be traveling to the surface; we will just visit the planetary growth matrix. Understand, what you are able to perceive of our technology will simply be representations your minds will be able to understand. Do not be distressed if you cannot understand all that you see. Please stand by for transportation. Please inform us if you have any social, moral, or cultural taboos regarding quantum teleportation."

"No, Chalguldan, we have no issues with quantum teleportation."

"Please make yourselves ready. We understand carbon life forms experience disturbances or mild physiological upset with quantum teleportation."

"We are ready."

And just like that, we were gone from the spaceport. Suddenly what looked like the Earth hung in the sky above me, as beautiful as anything I ever remembered seeing. There were blue oceans and polar ice glistening from the background light of the Coral Region area.

The diplomat tried not to appear even remotely affected by what we saw, but my mouth hung open for several minutes.

"Esteemed Captain, your biological signals are in disruption. Are you in distress?"

"No, Chalguldan. I am simply in disbelief. This appears to be, for all intents and purposes, the Earth as I have seen it only in videos and three dimensional simulations."

"It is your world, physically, in every way possible. Using the information gathered by the Sjurani when they rescued you from your world, we have created your planet accurately to dimensions of less than one meter. With the genetic support of the Sjurani, we have filled your biosphere with animals and plants taken from your world. The Sjurani gathered entire sections of your planetary ecosphere and stored them in stasis until we could study them and recreate them."

"You have done so much for the project already, Chalguldan. Why are we here now in renegotiation?"

"Diplomat Sinian, we have studied the land masses captured and found environmental pollution at a catastrophic level. Your land masses, water, air, and creatures were completely saturated with a variety of environmental poisons that could have only been created by primitive manufacturing techniques."

Sinian looked up at the planet and marveled at the organic looking structures linked to Earth Two. These great limb-like structures appeared to hold the planet in place. The structures reached the planet branched out again like capillaries surrounding the planet in a fine mesh. However, in scale, those cables were thousands of miles wide.

"Several of our older brethren were questioning the wisdom of returning your species to a planet that, even though it was destroyed through no fault of your own, your species would have made uninhabitable in less than two hundred years. It has taken us nearly one hundred of your standard years to complete this project. Relatively speaking, your planet's creation has not been difficult for us. But understand, your species will not be capable of such feats for tens of thousands of years at your current level of technology. We would rather give this world to a species more appreciative of the wonder of a planet. The question of the Enclave, Division Nine, is: how can you assure us of the sanctity of your world to your future generations?"

"Chalguldan, I think our people have experienced a catastrophic loss and many of them would just as soon never return to the Earth. Many of us have already become part of the Second Diaspora and moved from the Toranor System into Hegemony Space proper. The Humani Tribes are very diverse today, in comparison with the time from which your people received samples of our previous home."

I found myself growing warm and uncomfortable as I watched the Mariovel's movement pattern grow more complex, as if it were assessing the words of the diplomat. I also noticed clouds of other Mariovel approaching our position, pulsing in unison with Chalguldan.

Sinian continued, his face intensely focused on the vistas slowly turning overhead. "In addition to Humans, we have Simians, Cetaceans, Hybrids, *Cognosceti* (human consciousness embodied by machines), and the *Conscentia* (Singularity-level artificial intelligences housed in humanoid androids). What caused our species to be myopic was our very short lifespan. I have lived fifteen times as long as my kind did back then. I believe we would be more likely to protect that which had been won so dearly and has cost the lives of billions of our kind."

Soon, dozens of Mariovel hovered over us and began exchanging elements from each of their clouds. Elements swarmed over us, around us, and soon we were in a sphere of moving foglet elements. As the elements began to swirl, they began to emit colorful light patterns. At first I thought it was a form of communication, but I could find no useful patterns in it.

Suddenly, Sinian and I were standing in a factory shoveling coal into a furnace. We were sickly and malnourished, every cough produced a black phlegm that seemed in endless supply. Smokestacks blackened the sky in every direction. Sinian collapsed, and I carried him outside of the factory. We were taken to a local hospice area where he was pronounced with tuberculosis and only a few days left to live. I stayed with him while he expired in agony.

Night fell, and we were suddenly wearing masks on our faces, and there were deep walls on both sides of us. We carried primitive rifle weapons and were sent onto a different battlefield in the dark. A cloud of smoke floated into our trench and my mask was not sealed properly. I began to choke and sputter and found my chest burning, searing with unimagined pain. Sinian tried to help me, but I could not hear a word he was saying. Soon he was the only one left alive as the green cloud claimed the lives of everyone around him.

Then I found myself running chest deep in water, toward a beach, while exploding rounds rocked the ground in every direction. I was dragging Sinian. He had a wound on his chest. I tried to carry him as explosions went off and the smell of blood and burnt flesh filled the air. I was watching men dying all around me. It seemed to go on forever. We were forced to take cover behind large metallic X shaped objects as the shelling continued. We made our way up the beach, but high caliber rounds ripped men to pieces, and their anguished cries for their mothers rang hollow in my ears as I struggled not to join them. Sinian was struck in the head and I fell to the sand with the shock of his dead weight.

In a camp with a high fence, I woke, wearing a striped uniform. Sinian was nowhere to be found. Everyone was sick and pale and nearly dead from starvation. The smell was terrible, the smell of death, the death of thousands. I struggled to rise and stagger outside. The light was so bright. I could hear others whispering. I saw men carrying guns knocking down a fence and Sinian rushed to me and offered me water. I threw up the water because it had been so long since I had anything to eat.

We found ourselves in the middle of a rainforest surrounded by crude oil pits carved into the earth, while a multinational corporation extracted oil without concern for the indigenous people who lived in the area. Sinian was a corporate worker while I was one of the locals who was dying from cancer. Sinian spent time with me when his duties allowed it, but he could not stop what the corporation was doing, no matter how silver his tongue. We were both shot while we discussed the horrors of what was happening, and how we were going to expose the corporation's misdeeds.

We watched as we slowly expired from starvation in what was called Africa, as corporations priced seed out of our families' ability to afford it. Our farm stopped producing food, and our families starved, one child after another, until no one in our village was left. Wars around our villages prevented people from trying to leave sooner. We staggered out, the last men standing to try and walk to a neighboring town. We starved to death in transit.

We watched as the Sjurani spacecraft arrived on Earth, and their great starships hovered over every major city. Humanity knew they were coming and followed their instructions to the letter. Sinian and I were leading the teams who gathered animals, plants, and people from the North American continent. Every plant, animal, seed, flower, spore that could be gathered together was. Entire swaths of the planet were scooped up and taken away. Sinian and I wept as we were left behind on the planet, chosen by a random lottery. Alien forces were all over the planet. We picked up our weapons and went to defend our world. They overwhelmed our position, and as they swarmed us...

We returned to the Mariovel, their flying elements slowing and returning to their respective bodies. We were both weeping with the shock of our experiences. They felt so completely real, and each was as if I had been in every one of those situations. As we gained control of our emotions, Diplomat Sinian stood up, enraged, and shouted, "Chalguldan, that was hardly a fair representation of what humanity did in their time on Earth. You painted us as monsters who did not care for each other or the Earth. You ignored our arts, our culture, our best emotions, our greatest gifts to each other."

"This is true, Diplomat. All that was good in your species was overlooked in this instance for a single reason. That which was good did not destroy your world, only that which was questionable. Only that which showed difference where there was none, only that which created division when it should have created unity, corruption instead of compassion, disease instead of health, war instead of cooperation. All that we showed to you was true, gathered by your own people. We simply moved through time to see it firsthand."

"You mean those were not simulations?"

"No, Captain. We placed you in the minds and lives of those people you experienced. Time and space are infinitely variable and in a limited fashion, accessible to us."

Sinian sat down, placed his head in his hands and whispered, "No."

"Diplomat Sinian, are you sure?" I kneeled down next to him, the soft loam beneath me.

He looked up at me, his eyes bright and hard. "I said, no, Captain. I cannot see why the Mariovel should create a planet for humanity when we were so terrible to each other and the last one we had. In good conscience, I cannot recommend us at this time."

"Chalguldan and the Enclave of Planet Crafters, Division Nine: I, Diplomat Wells Sinian, hereby respectfully request a temporary hold on the planet Earth repopulation project at this time. In light of the information presented today, I would like to return to the Humani Tribunal to ensure we have a proper plan of development for our new planet, to ensure its long term growth and continued existence."

"We are pleased to hear your decision, Wells Sinian. While the Earth would have been ready for repopulation in a year, another hundred years would give many of your indigenous animals time to spread out and achieve a homeostatic balance with their new environment. We hope in this time you will help your people find a way to achieve a more homeostatic balance with your new home, as well."

Sinian and I stared longingly up at Earth; her deep blue oceans and swaths of green and gold beckoned to us. I helped Diplomat Sinian to his feet. He seemed relieved to have made his decision.

"What are you going to tell the council?"

The Mariovel retreated into the distance and I saw Chalguldan flash a brief goodbye in Galac 6 before our instantaneous transmission to the spaceport.

"The truth, Captain, the truth. The planet needs another century in the oven before we will be ready for it. We've got work to do, Captain. Take us home."

Hayward's Reach

From the ansible memoires of Exalted Scout, Glendale Mokoto,
Hero of the Exodus Wars and the Fall of Earth. These are an amalgam of the
earliest recordings before he was presumed lost one hundred years ago.

Two hundred years ago, I was nothing special. I had no
extraordinary abilities or talents. I was not blessed with superhuman
strength like members of the New Order, genetically manipulated to
be the perfect human specimens, trained and bred to be the ultimate
warrior protectors of the human race.

I did not augment my mind with sentient mechanical
intelligence like the Cognoseti, who became human predictors of
the future of man. It was their wisdom that discovered the Earth's
greatest hidden secret; that we were not the first creatures on Earth
to evolve into sentience. These human machine hybrids would later
house the first true machine-descended intelligences in human
history.

I did not mingle my DNA with those of animal species to
garner advantages lost by the development of our bigger brains. The
Transformed, whose malleable DNA allowed them to absorb genetic
traits of other species would lead Humanity in the exploration of new
worlds after we lost our home in the Sol System.

You see, I was just a baseline human, good genes, nice teeth, good skin, and until it fell out in my fiftieth year, a nice head of hair. Two hundred years ago, I was also the most celebrated hero; indeed, I was the last hero of the Exodus of Man. They named a starship after me, they named a continent after me, they named thousands of children after me. And to me that was a strange thing, seeing how I did not actually survive the experience.

To ponder this, and to explain why you are now able to know any of this, you have to know a bit more about Old Earth.

I remembered the stink of the war. It got up into your nose and never left. You could smell the burning flesh, the expended rounds, the fear, exhilaration, the bloodlust, the sheer terror of the Henrenki boiling up out of the ground in every major city on the planet.

I remembered the fighting, the endless fighting, the bravery of our young ones, their ceaseless dying, wheat before the scythe. When we retreated, the Henrenkai came, wave after wave, like the ocean filling in the beach of our dead.

I remembered them as they swarmed over our positions with machine guns blazing; our bullets tearing into their nacreous, resilient flesh but they kept coming.

Things looked hopeless until the New Men appeared, with their mysterious talk about the Art of War, talk of the brush strokes of their weapons, their mastery of their mysterious battle-trance. In those days, all we knew of war was the spastic struggling of the uninitiated to battle. We had been too long at peace.

Our struggles for survival, even before He came all but absorbed our attention. But even after generations of peace, we were still a warlike species and returned reluctantly to the field of battle. Every man woman and child was armed because this was a war without quarter and without mercy.

When the Cognoseti revealed His existence, He rose from the oceans, the Ancient Enemy of all who live in our galaxy. We did not know He was legendary. We did not know what scars He and His kind had swept across the face of that, as yet unknown to us, galactic empire. We did not know what He wanted, only that He destroyed all that we had, with malice and forethought. We did learn one thing: when He rose from the Pacific Ocean, we realized the nature of our enemy, He had the might of an entire world, buried within our own.

Mechanically-sentient, He created weapons like the Henrenkai from His very flesh, the organo-mechanical body in which He fell to

Earth billions of years ago and hid in the iron core of our planet. He hid because He was pursued by the greatest species our galaxy had ever spawned. He hid and waited until they passed away or forgot; we are not sure which. When He arose again, He had been all but forgotten by everyone in the galaxy. How could they not; nearly three billion of our years had passed while he slumbered.

So we were forced to fight Him on our own, tiny simians against a god-like machine who had tried to enslave an entire galaxy. He fought us on land, sea, air, and even in space. What could we do against an enemy so incredibly powerful? He destroyed a third of the human race and had barely awakened. We lost all hope.

Then we received a signal from space. It appeared on every communication band, every wavelength, every technology, all at once. If you were watching anything, listening to anything, it appeared and told you to be ready.

A prophecy had sent them back to us. They told us it was time to leave our world. They told us to gather as much of our world as we could carry. We did not understand, but we gathered our resources, every animal, every plant, every insect we thought we could find and catalog. We even set aside entire islands, marked with force fields to make them stand out.

We had no idea of what the Sjurani were capable of back then. We did not know what to expect, but their message gave us hope, so we fought on.

I remember the first time I saw their ships. They blotted out the sun. We fought a retreating battle to their designated pick up points. They gathered us up with tractor beams, entire cities, whole islands. It was rumored they took the entire African continent. Something about it being a template for our entire world's DNA.

They landed in their reptilian regalia and fought alongside us, as terrifying as the Henranki in their own way. Garishly colored in silks and metal, reptilian, festooned with gem-encrusted scales, loud, large, and boisterous; think of Old Earth fraternity boys armed with plasma cannons and rocket launchers and you will know something of the Rex, a warrior-breed of the Sjurani.

They helped us hold the line against the Ancient Enemy while we fled. They claimed they were the descendants of dinosaurs who had been born on Earth hundreds of millions of years in the past. We were too desperate to care. And too foolish to realize why that was more important than we knew at the time.

The evacuation took two weeks. My battle-brothers, old and

new, human and Sjurani, fought until the very last ships were leaving the planet. Hundreds of millions were moved to ships every day, each scarred with the loss of someone or something precious.

The Sjurani told us He was soon to fully waken. Once that happened, we would stand no chance at all. The Ancient Enemy had only one agenda, and that was leaving the Earth. We could never allow that. Our planet's gravity well was the only thing that prevented Him from opening a gateway to another universe - a universe full of creatures as powerful as he was.

But we could take the fight to Him: A suicide mission.

He had raised an island in the Pacific, a place from whence all of his forces rose to the surface. We would fight him there.

We infiltrated the Ancient Enemy with the help of Sjurani technology. We carried into Him an antimatter weapon, created by the Sjurani, with the force of a billion Hiroshima bombs. A weapon far more powerful than anything Humanity could ever create. His arrogance in being shielded from outside, made him believe he was invulnerable. Once inside His armored shell, we could use short range teleportation to penetrate deep into His neural network. Three groups entered the alien machine. Even if all three were successful, they told us our weapons would not kill Him. But we could wound Him, perhaps even lobotomize Him, for a time.

This would allow the two hundred million humans who agreed to stay behind to cover the final retreat. The West Coast of North America was destroyed in this final battle. The Rocky Mountains were all that remain of that coastline. One billion humans left the Earth in that two week period with some of the most terrifying fighting ever seen in any war, any conflict.

Once the antimatter was placed, I, the last survivor of three dozen of the finest warriors of two races, made my way to the surface killing everything in my path. I waited. The never-ending supply of Henrenkai continued to boil forth from the Ancient enemy. In that last moment before detonation, I lay down my exhausted weapon and the Henrenkai stopped, confused by the act.

With seconds remaining, I assumed the battle occurring in space had interrupted my teleport and I resolved myself to dying, free of anger and the corruption of war. I vowed never to wage war again. My death would keep my promise.

I opened my arms and the battle-enraged Henrenkai charged me, their razor sharp talons poised to shred flesh from bones. In those final seconds, time slowed as I watched them. Close to me, I studied them in a way I had never before. Their anatomy was a marvel: Bones of carbon fullerenes, talons sharper than the sharpest steel. Wide, predator-set eyes, excellent for determining the distance to me, their prey. I could smell their hot breath, a bitter almond overtone, and I closed my eyes, ready for death. No fighting, no resistance. I felt the antimatter as it detonated. A shockwave swept through me. I could feel it in my very atoms.

Suddenly, I could see the blast wave of energy and could feel my atoms snatched away protectively within the teleport sheath. I felt my body dying as the waves of antimatter, converted to gamma rays and cosmic radiation, were transformed into the most powerful kind of destruction in our universe, in the perfect release, the ultimate annihilation of matter. No man can ever say he sat in the heart of a star and lived to tell others of it. Neither could I. It would have been breathtaking if I had a breath to take.

In that eternal second, I violated causality and was in two places at one time. I was trapped in the containment field, experiencing a quantum reality, existing in two places and in neither. I was onboard the ship in a viewing chamber teleported, so they thought, to allow me, with the remnants of my species, to see the death of my world. Such a weapon would destroy the Earth as we knew it. I watched, both detached at a distance and intimately aware of the death throes of my home planet.

For a moment, I could be anywhere and any when; I moved through time and space. I saw the Ancient Enemy's arrival on Earth three billion years ago, fleeing, from the Precursors. He crashed into a small planet in an unidentified star system with a small yellow star. I could feel His terror, I could feel His near dissolution, His flesh, burned with a fire like a solar flare, tearing His substance apart. He submerged Himself into our planet and the rocky surface extinguished those flames and His terror subsided. He sank into our world, and His screams grew quieter, until after an eon, He slept and forgot.

As I stood there in the middle of the greatest energy release since His arrival, I realized He would not die. He would survive just as He did before. Our work was almost in vain. His massive, nearly indestructible bulk would provide one benefit. Those who remained behind would not be wiped out from the weapon. They would be stranded on a world still trying to kill them. The thought was terrible and the last thing I remembered.

I was the last human to leave the Earth two hundred years

ago, an unwitting and unwilling hero of a war we all but lost.

I woke several years later on our way to Toranor, a system of Gaian super-worlds created by a race of highly-advanced beings called The Precursors. No other race in the galaxy has ever come close to their level of technological capability. They were as far beyond even our Sjurani benefactors as we were beyond ants.

The Toranor star system had trillions of sentients living in harmony in what was called the jewel of the Corvan Empire. Now homeless, Humanity and the Sjurani were offered a place on one of their lesser worlds. I knew I would never call this place home. I had seen too much, done too much. There would be nothing for me here.

All that I valued died with Earth.

I asked what a single man could do in an Empire of sentients with magnificent technologies, making our human achievements, even in the year of our Lord 2475, seem like children's toys? How could I distinguish myself?

By providing the one thing all Empires need: New boundaries. I became a Scout. I was told the role of a Scout was a solitary one. I would be provided a robot companion if I desired. My job would be to map stars toward the center of the galaxy for planets capable of being terraformed by the Mariovel at some point in the future. I was promised the knowledge of the Empire at my fingertips and all the time of my life to read and learn it.

It was then the Sjurani revealed to me that I had died during the teleportation. They had never tried to teleport during an antimatter explosion. No one ever had. My mind was able to be reconstructed, but my body had died. They took my mind and placed it within a robotic shell that mimicked my own form so well that I was never aware of the change at any time.

I was angered at first. I walked around for almost a year, on Galtan II, our new home, knowing something was different, but not knowing what. Galtan II was like all of the worlds of Toranor, beautiful, diverse, fantastic. The knowledge that all of these worlds were created by a sentient species that was not God, boggled the imagination. Imagine a star system with twenty habitable worlds. The knowledge would turn our ideas of science and religion on their ears.

Galtan II boasted a forest that spanned the entire equatorial band of the planet, one giant forest whose myriad trees were connected by their root system into one organic supercomputer, a single hive mind which could separate segments of itself to communicate with other forms of life. One of the most amazing world-minds in this part of the empire. Yes, there were others. Since the Botani did not choose to live in the colder parts of the planet, we were offered the other two thirds of the world to live responsibly on. With the technology of the Sjurani supporting our own, we could be good neighbors.

The Sjurani told me that what they did, they did for love of my heroic sacrifice. They created an entire technology around saving my life. I learned later they held my psychic resonance in an energy field that consumed the energy of a world for years. I felt guilty once I learned what was done on my behalf.

I learned that my condition, once successful, because of my heroic stature, spurred a whole division of baseline humans to make the transition to the robotic. We were called The Transcended. They gave up their flesh to become the first robotic-human hybrids. Were there consequences? Certainly, but none of them ever considered it an unfair trade, except perhaps for me. I would have liked to have had the choice.

When I was appointed a Scout, the Corvan empire made a starship for me; since I was no longer a living organic, they made something faster than had ever been created before. I named it Hayward's Reach after a small seaside town where I lived the quiet life of a writer before the end of the world came for us all. Before activating the ship, the greatest generals, admirals and Sjurani Rex came to see me off. They said wonderful things, heroic things about me and my sacrifices. I didn't listen.

All I could hear was the loneliness. No, the alone-ness that space offered me. I thanked them. I climbed aboard my ship and synchronized my ansible to an ansible station here on Galtan II which would relay my reports. Since an ansible could only be paired once, something about quantum entanglement, it was the most critical thing I could do unless I wanted to communicate relativistically.

My pilot was a Cogneseti, a sentient intelligence housed in the mechanical body of a woman. She was the first of her kind, a mechanical version of myself. I started life as a man and became a machine. She started her existance as a machine and became a woman.

Her name was Pele. She named herself after the mythical goddess of the legendary Hawaiian Islands that are no more. When I asked her about her name, she said once she had studied human history. The tale of the Hawaiians fascinated her and she had taken it upon herself to study all of the notes on Earth's Polynesian cultures. Our ship was equipped with a distillation of all of the knowledge of the human race. We would also have an upstream of new ideas and achievements when time and bandwidth permitted. When I asked her why she was coming with me, she said since she would never get to see Hawaii, the next best thing was to discover a place like it somewhere else.

She arranged our path through the empire and indicated we would reach the edge of the Empire in as little as three jumps and three months using their Gate system. After that, we would be on our own, moving at approximately thirty-two times the speed of light. It would take us three thousand years to cross the galaxy. We would be taking the scenic route, flying through as many star-dense systems as possible. We were the fastest things in the Empire, streaking away from all that I knew, and I was glad to be doing it. It was unlikely we would survive the journey across the galaxy. The Sjurani estimated we might live for four hundred years with careful maintenance. We promised to change our oil regularly. Pele laughed. The Sjurani just looked quizzically at me.

Sitting down, I called up a data-screen. The words were queued up from earlier in the day, waiting for me. Pele was sitting at the nav station monitoring the ebb and flow of the aether. I read out loud as would become a tradition for the two of us in the decades to come: *"It was the best of times, it was the worst of times, it was the age of wisdom, it was the age of foolishness, it was the epoch of belief, it was the epoch of incredulity, it was the season of Light, it was the season of Darkness, it was the spring of hope, it was the winter of despair..."*

I had always wanted to read A *Tale of Two Cities*, and at that moment, it seemed appropriate. I never had the time before. Taking my companion's hand, this new season of light illuminated our souls as we fled into the core of the galaxy, to see things no man had seen before. I, once being the most ordinary of men, had transcended the human experience for something never done before. It was, indeed, the best of times.

FIN

The Wars of the Twilight Continuum continue in the first novel called

INSURRECTION

As the civil war for control of the galaxy begins, an alien force extends the battle creating a

CONFLAGRATION

of a galaxy at war. The final battle of the Corvan Hegemony to find the Precursors and facilitate their

RESURRECTION

The long-missing Precursors and the Elder Races must reconcile to save the Milky Way from being over-run from the Dark Universe.

An excerpt of Insurrection...

Insurrection

Prologue

I hate it when I wake up, dead. It usually means my day is going downhill from there.

I'm a pessimist by nature and you would be one too, if you were working on this rock. Brennan 326. Hot, one hundred and eighty degrees in the shade, a three-gee, metal-rich hellhole. Even in this suit, I can feel the twin suns beating down on me and I weigh over three thousand pounds. The all-encompassing, amniotic, shock-absorbing, nutrient-rich, resurrection fluid of my exo-suit tastes like hot bacon grease and is always the worst part of waking up. Taste bacon? You've been dead. When you've been alive awhile, you can almost forget about it.

I've been here for over two years. I've died, let me check, nine times this year, a new personal best. Much better than last year's dismal twenty-seven deaths.

The Resurrection Corp's job is to stop the invasion of our mining colonies in this sector by the Dalrothi, an intelligent machine species from outside of our galaxy. They take over our automated facilities and ignore us. I don't think they even consider us living or sentient beings, by their standards. When the job looks as if it will take more resources than the Imperium is willing to spare, they don't send large armies, they send a surgical strike.

Superhuman, nearly indestructible, but the most dangerous thing is that we can be killed and it doesn't take unless you destroy us completely.

We are a self-renewing army. The ultimate expression of the man-sized weapon technology of the Imperium. As long as twenty percent of me and my suit remains, our combined nanites will gather up materials from the environment and rebuild me; If I suffer a rail-gun wound, an hour, lost limb, two hours, missing head, three days. All of what I am is encoded within my Resurrection Frame. I have been completely rebuilt while I was here. Every bit of me. Every memory, nightmare, explosion... Sometimes, I think that I can remember other things, planet thoughts, hearing Brennnan 326 in my dreams. I am composed almost completely of the atoms of this world now.

Our drop-ship was shot down by a hot plasma cannon which nearly vaporized all of the ship and part of me, from the waist down. It was... unexpected. I lay dead on the planet's surface for three months. The Dalrothi were known for using slug or kinetic-kill weapons for planet defense. I guess the lab boys were right, they can learn. There were twenty of us. We could've taken the planet in a week, with no permanent losses. Alone, took a little longer.

There was never a thought of not completing the mission. I didn't know what this facility made and I didn't care; likely secret and above my pay grade. The auto-factory sends whatever it mines from this planet into orbit by gravity sling, a magnetic rail-gun system, to await pickup by Imperium transports that come periodically through the system. When the factory stopped transmitting, teams were sent to investigate, no one returned; that's how we drew this shit detail.

As I approached, two dozen of two thousand sentry drones remained. I lost fifteen lives and two years to get here. After I sat for an hour and re-grew my left arm, (damn, that hurt) I got up to see exactly what twelve hundred square miles of factory looked like from the inside. The facility's cargo entrance was easy to open, peeling the door back barely caused me to breathe hard. Inside, the place was spotless, like so many of the technologies of the Imperium, nano-machines used every drop of matter for building something and the positive side effect is a shiny, dust-free environment. I walked for two days, across mirrored floors, before I reached a control center. There was no hurry, I had already taken two years to get here. If this facility were high on the list, another team would have been dispatched. As long as my transponder worked, they would not send another. The

Imperium was large and patient.

Having arrived at the control center, the Dalrothi tech was easy to dismantle and I performed an analysis on the hardware. After this, until they upgraded again, we can disrupt their tech planet-side, with a tailored electromagnetic pulse and not even stop on hell-holes like this one. I found the last hot plasma cannon on the roof of the facility and after resting and re-growing my right leg, destroyed the turret. Optimistic, I reasoned I might get to be outside of this suit for a year or two before returning to duty. After dismantling and storing the specifications for the Dalrothi tech, I found the materials which were not being sent into space and re-calibrated the computers for business as usual.

Once I was ready to get off Brennan 326, I was shocked to find not a single transport ship, not a shuttle, not even an escape pod. Oh. This was a robotic facility; no need for anyone to fly or escape. They flew in on their own and left that way. Until now, I never even considered how I was going to get out of here. I could attempt to damage my transponder, except it would have to be a permanent solution otherwise it would repair itself. A new thought; vaporization, hmmm. Then there would be no need for a pickup. I ruminated on escaping my private hell.

A day later, I realized my mistake. I could get off this planet by riding the gravity sling. Yes, it would generate more than two thousand gee forces to propel its load into orbit, turning me, inside of my suit, and in less than a second, into a fine boneless soup. When the planet indicated that the facility was back online, they would send a transport to pick up the equipment and my boneless corpse. I should wake up in about two months when the transport cargo ship arrives. What's one more death for the road? I really hate bacon.

Chapter One

The air felt cool as it flew by my face; thick, steamy, sluggish, with just the touch of the hinterlands of Lorrisi, a nearby forest tainting the air with its pungent spores. This would not have been the first time I died, so I don't want you to be upset if I should expire during the course of this story. It is simply an occupational hazard in my line of work, hence my familiarity with the strange things you notice, just before you kick off this mortal coil.

As I was falling I noticed blood was streaming into my nose and mouth as I was turning and tumbling, cloying, choking on blood from an injury to my head. I tried to orient myself but could not seem to focus. I was simply unable to right myself.

"Secondary neural complex activating. Activating nanostructure repair. Impact in three seconds, harden structure, activate impact aerojel." I heard the sound of a burst of compressed air from my belt buckle, and a tiny capsule hurtled toward the ground at the speed of sound. "Three, two, one..."

A cushion of pressure-activated aerojel, coupled with a gravitic repulsive field from my micromesh armor protected me from serious injury from the forty story fall. I came away from my unceremonious landing with lacerations, contusions and a couple of hairline fractures. Then the shock overwhelmed me and I lost consciousness.

"Major," said the quiet voice that I heard speaking to me on my way toward the ground.

"How long?"

"It has been 48 seconds since the first shot was fired, and you have been unconscious for 36 seconds."

"Damage assessment."

" Vascular injuries were immediately handled and completed before impact. You have suffered 10% loss of neural capacity due to the round you have taken to your skull. Your skull armor deflected sixty percent of the damage effectively. I have begun the nanotech repair of your neural network. Unfortunately, this will take some time. Your skull reconstruction are already underway. The skull will be repaired in two hours. The rest of your body has suffered relatively minor damage and you have only lost nineteen percent of your physical capacity due to the fall."

"And the good news?"

"Your micro-fractures are already under repair and will be completed within the hour. The lacerations and contusion damage have been sealed and your blood loss has been minimal. The damage to your skull and your memory center will likely take days to regenerate completely without the Frame's support. Until we are able to get back to the Frame, your memory backups will be inaccessible."

Okay, now to the important things. "Who's trying to kill us?" I get up from the remnants of the aerojel, which is designed to break after five seconds, but leaves a bit of residue on everything.

"Major, we have company. Across the plaza, two humanoids, armed with weapons matching the Ajax 320 Pulse Rifle with select fire options."

"Do I want to know how you determined their weapons at this distance?" I was a bit incredulous that the AI could possibly know the weapons of our assailants so early in our conflict.

"We were bombarded by infra-sound ranging technology common to the Ajax 320 Pulse rifle. Considering our proximity to Ajax and the cost of shipping goods in this system, it is the most likely candidate for small and medium firearms in this sector. Since the Ajax is used in thicker than Earth-normal atmospheres and uses infra-sound for that reason, it was a logical conclusion, bolstered by the fact that I am now correct."

Without my frame, I would hate to have to deal with the Ajax

320. Looking around, I grab the handle of a grav vehicle and with the slightest bit of exertion liberate the door from the car. These vehicles are for diplomatic services, so they're armored. A perfect shield for my needs. My Image told me I had neural damage, so until I am able to assess that damage, I have to "creatively utilize my surroundings" as my Sensei was so fond of saying.

"You are no longer human," said the tiny soldier dressed in a Military-specified interface armor. The armor was black and grey, a close-fitting mesh, covered with tiny overlapping scales like that of a fish. His face was calm and serene and he was far different than my first drill instructors decades ago in my first basic training.

"You have had the final stage of your Mil-spec enhancements to your skeleton, neural net and musculature. As formidable as you were in your previous lives, and you were chosen for that skill, you are again as children in your understanding of your capability. For the next two years, you will live here on Soldanis Four and relearn your bodies. For now you have all been set to one sixth of your actual full strength. This approximates your normal human strength before your transformation. You have been dialed down in order to understand just how different you are now."

He turned and pointed downrange at an obstacle course and picked up an Ajax Pulse Rifle. There were several steel targets approximating the shape of human beings at a range of 300 meters. Each target was holding a wooden prop of a weapon of one sort or another. I could barely see them. And then he moved. He went from a standing start to a run that literally kicked up dust behind him. He turned down range and fired his pulse rifle six times, one for each target. After he made his shot he covered the distance in thirteen seconds and proceeded using a Vibron Flex Sword to strike each of his targets and slicing them in half. He did not slow down for any strike, made three per target, covered the distance between them in thirteen seconds and returned to us in the last thirteen seconds.

We double-timed it downrange and when we got to each target, three things were apparent. No target had a head. It was nowhere to be found. It had been blasted off by his initial volley of six rounds of pulse fire. Each steel statue has been sliced in three completely separate pieces. And he had done all of this while moving at over eighty kilometers an hour. I had never seen anything like this. Even the smallest mecha suits, which offered similar capabilities, weighed over five tons and still couldn't work with the precision Sensei did.

"You are all now capable of performing similar feats with the proper training. You will learn this here. This is a pass or fail course. If you fail, you have died and will not reach the final stage of your development, access to a Resurrection Frame.

Of the one hundred of you gathered today, fifty of you will fail to complete this course and will be horribly maimed. You will be repaired to the best of our technology, fitted with prosthetics dialed down to normal strength and fitness and returned to your former duties if possible.

For those of you who fail, most of the damage will be neurological so you will be reduced to a vegetative state and unable to participate in even feeding yourself. You will spend the rest of your life in a military hospital.

Fifteen of you will die due to a failure to inculcate the nano-machines and bio-mechanical adaptations required to complete the transformation.

I am obligated to offer you one final time to return to the life you know. You will be dialed back to a human-level performance and allowed finish your military career. You will remain in the military for the rest of your life, as you will need care to maintain your prosthetics. Only with your graduation to the Frame will such care, no longer be necessary. The Frame will repair you, and will ultimately become your life."

No one refused. Having spent decades on the battlefield as an infantryman, a light armored trooper or heavy armored trooper, none of us had ever seen anything like Sensei. Armed with the proper technology, a single soldier like him was worth a regiment. We would die to possess such abilities. And many of us would.

Hefting the car door, I noted its solid construction and excellent Lorrisian construction. I was wearing my combat mesh beneath my uniform but the fewer people remember seeing that, the better. Rounds pelted the car door and I ran toward the two shooters, careful to keep my speed down and maintain the appearance of humanity.

"Majoris, we need to hurry and resolve this. A call for Peacekeepers has gone out. This system has both Bal-ha and Mariovel Peacekeepers. I don't need to remind you of their formidable abilities, do I?"

"Not good, pinpoint the others if you please, I'll deal with these two." The two soldiers who were approaching me were wearing light exoskeletons and carried heavy rifles. A tiny metallic bead shot away from my forehead and streaked toward the building we fell out of a few minutes ago.

With my Image gone, I could feel the difference in my physical condition, I was a bit slower and clumsier because it was compensating for my injuries. But these injuries were nothing I hadn't dealt with before.

Once the exo-armors were within fifty yards, I increased my speed and closed the distance, in what would appear to them, instantly, using my inertia, I spun and hurled the car door at the leading armored suit, decapitating him before he realized I had moved. That was harsh treatment, I know, but I take offense to nearly having my head blown off.

The second, surprised both by my speed and the violence of my action, hesitated, and in that two second window, my flex sword was out, energized and before he could react I sliced off his weapon arm. I needed him alive, but a little shock wouldn't stop me from getting what I wanted.

"I have them. In addition to the two that were in the office we jumped out of, there are four others who are meeting with the others in the parking facility. They are carrying much heavier weaponry. I think a strategic retreat is in order."

"These two are down, one incapacitated, the other in shock. What can you do for a vehicle? Using the one we came in is likely not the smartest idea."

"There are several non-sentient AI's I can coerce into allowing you to ride and not broadcasting their location to the grid," the Image sounded as if it might enjoy that process.

"I am going to head toward our car and see if I can detonate their charges as a cover. Get a damn car and meet me there."

I turned back toward the two soldiers who were down and that's when I became aware of the Bel-ha descending from the sky. It was wearing the coded armor of a local Peacekeeper. Looking vaguely like a Corvan, its tentacles moved slowly beneath it as if it were swimming through the air.

"Desist activities and resist not. Comply, please," its voice was created by a vox-coder but it was clearly commanding even while it was polite. The Bel-ha prize politeness above all else.

And I intended to comply, because it had asked me so nicely and because its psionic powers were reputed to be so formidable it could stop my heart with a casual thought.

I really did plan to stop but as it descended, slowly and majestically right over the bodies of the mercenaries, of which I really needed to take one of, I heard the sound of a detonator switch on and decided to dive for cover instead. This was the right choice, as the explosion dug a twelve-foot hole in the ferrocrete beneath the bodies and sent shrapnel over my head.

I didn't expect to see much of the Bel-ha cephalopod, except maybe some sushi clinging to the local plaza art. Imagine my surprise when I saw the Peacekeeper lying about 12 meters away in relatively good shape, a bit crisp, alive but quite still. Remind me never to get on the bad side of one of these aliens.

"I've damaged the local constabulary and lost my leads. Tell me you have better news on the transport front." I was being snarky but was really pissed because this would put me on the top of the local Peacekeeper hit list.

"The vehicle selection was wide and excellent, all with low grade intelligence engines, easily swayed by my magnetic charms. I am on my way, keep your pants on. ETA, forty-five seconds if you are standing near our car. As a minor aside, there has been a secondary call to the Peacekeepers and it has been acknowledged as an escalation and possible terrorist attack. Did I mention, I was being chased by heavy armored assault suits in hover mode? My recommendation is to jump in as I pass, as slowing down would be bad. I'll remember to roll the window down, this time, I promise."

"Now you realize, I should stop to render assistance..."

"Majoris, this is Biyu, the base is under attack, requesting orders." Biyu never panicked, but the stress in her voice was evident.

"Talk to me."

"Light and Heavy Infantry suits, likely Denar-surplus, armed with bunker-bunkers and anti-personnel weaponry. Base personnel are providing resistance but are equipped with light infantry only. They were not expecting a heavy assault. I estimate they will last approximately two minutes. I am also detecting the approach of six to eight fast aircraft converging on the base, below the lidar systems. The planetary defense systems have come online and aircraft are scrambling toward this position and a position in the city. I would guess that is your position. The ship is cloaked above the airfield and targeting the facility where the Frame is housed."

"You make sure they don't get the Frame. You do whatever is necessary. Authorization A-6, full release."

"Understood, full release is authorized. How did they know we were here, Major?"

I had no idea, only the military could know since they directed me to this secret research facility with the understanding, no one would see us enter or leave. "Not a clue. We're on our way but have run into some heavy opposition as well. Hold the ground till we get there. Our ETA is..."

"Eight minutes, if the Major can get the lead out. Coming alongside. Is eighty kilometers an hour the best you can do? Fall a few dozen floors and the next thing you know, you are wanting to take retirement pay."

A modern grav-car, with an exotic grill and lighting system, roared around the corner, nearly hitting everything in its way, but touching nothing as it came full tilt up the street. I spared exactly one second to assess it before moving up the street into oncoming traffic at my top speed. I could also hear the air fans of the heavy assault armors as they followed behind my Image's getaway vehicle. I activated my flex armor field, and blasted away my civvies. All bets were off now, no sense in dying to maintain my disguise. I felt just the tiniest bit safer, but knew if they were armed with the right equipment, I was only a tiny bit safer than wearing nothing at all. As the gravcar came up behind me, oncoming traffic peeled away, due to the infrastructure's safety features. I counted on this and my Image's pathological need to create as much mayhem as possible to work to my advantage as it pulled alongside.

"Windows?" I waved my arms frantically trying to get my Image's attention. That's exactly when the mercs decided to open fire. The first high capacity, exploding rounds, whizzed uncomfortably close, and the forth hit my flex field right below my ribcage, directly into the housing of my biomechanical augmentation systems. Heavily armored and shielded by my flex field meant, no penetration, even of a highly sophisticated round like that one. What it also meant was it hurt like hell.

Since no window opened I used my flex field to disrupt the armored window's integrity. Dens-crys glass shattered and flew through the vehicle but my Image was the size of a raisin, nestled comfortably in an ashtray. It was unaffected. What luck.

"Oops. Sorry about that, it's so hard to figure out where they hide the window controls in these modern vehicles." The engine roared as the vehicle picked up speed and continued to disrupt oncoming traffic. With a bounce, the gravcar returned to the proper traffic lanes with the exoskeletons in hot pursuit. We maintained our lead and distance, keeping a clear lane of fire for less than a second or two for about three minutes.

I flipped down my HUD visor and saw a satellite view of the city with a military and police overlay. The base was less than four minutes away, but the two assault helicopters would be intercepting us all in about thirty seconds.

"Major, the base has been breached. The Frame's containment area has been broken. I am going to begin my attack. The incoming spacecraft will arrive in three minutes. This will be my only chance to intercept. Biyu, out."

There was no point being angry or anxious, we'd get there or we wouldn't. The one thing I can say about working with professionals, is everyone is so good at their job; there is no need to backseat drive. I was carrying nothing but light weaponry, my mini-pulse pistols wouldn't be strong enough to penetrate those suits back there, but the two assault helicopters were going to take care of that problem unless they decided to make a break for it.

They had to know they wouldn't make it to the base. Suddenly the mecha blew off most of their armor and heavy weapons. The gear that fell away exploded reducing any chance of getting a trace on it. Four contrails streak away from the ground. On lidar, two of the eight approaching spacecraft turned away on an intercept course to the four escaping mercs.

The remaining six continued their approach, but two hang back approaching slower. The four contrails disappear in a flash of tractor activity and the two ships turn back toward the sky. The two slower ships stopped their approach and the first releases a small star-like missile, the second activates a super-heavy tractor beam. The remaining space-craft peeling away release swarms of micro-missiles toward the city's incoming attack aircraft.

"I'm stupid, thick, thick, thick. Biyu, come in..."

Biyu turned Traveling Light's four cannons toward the wreckage of the armored warehouse building where four heavy suits had entered and disappeared from sight. Four light mecha waited outside with their weapons primed. Each mecha suit was targeted.

"Torpedo bays activated and primed for launch. Two incoming targets quiet-locked," Traveling Light's soothing female voice indicated. Biyu silently acknowledged the telemetry and as the four exoskeleton's were visible moving the storage container of the Frame into view, she dropped the ship's cloak and fired upon the four mecha with tachyon pulse weaponry. The exotic weaponry released a tachyon beam of faster than light particles. These particles were entangled with an antimatter magnetic resonance which would only be affected by super-dense matter. The type of super-dense matter found in armor or other barrier-resonating fields. When the two collided, the antimatter was fully returned to our space-time and detonates, violently. The four mecha were instantly obliterated, and the resultant explosion knocked the remaining exoskeletons off their feet. The remaining building was destroyed in the explosion. The container storing the Frame was undamaged.

Immediately after firing the tachyon beams, Travelling Light swivels smoothly skyward and launches two torpedoes as eight incoming craft lock on with their lidar-targeting systems. Their returning volley of micro-missiles darken the sky. At the last second, two ships streak away from their dive and turn toward the city center. The remaining six continue their approach as their targeting systems lock onto Traveling Light. Two of the six ships take the torpedoes on their shields, dropping them immediately and damaging a variety of systems onboard those ships. Small explosions flash across their hulls and a few seconds later both explode from internal power-plant containment failures. The fifty micro-missiles striking the shields of Travelling Light and the remaining missiles batter the ground, causing explosions that obscured the ship from view.

"Shield power at 80%, reactivating cloak, moving to intercept Frame." The cloaked ship moved through the debris toward the containment unit. Biyu climbed out of the pilot's chair and grabbed her personal heavy pulse pistols. She was confident she would be able to handle the four light exo-skeletons in the time it would take the last ships to reach the ground. She would use the cloaking field and shield from the ship to protect her from incoming fire. After the initial volley of missiles, the ships had switched to beam lasers and heavy blaster fire, both would be insufficient to penetrate the military-grade shielding ofTraveling Light.

She dropped to the ground and started running toward the

four exoskeletons, her heavy pulse pistols, fired at full auto, tearing into the armors of the mercenaries. They were attaching something to the containment unit. They looked like gravity compensators. Without them, the Frame would be immobile. She stopped in her tracks as she heard the part of the scrambled message from the Major "--it's a trap!"

Then the sky lit up, washing everything in white light, like the sun come to earth.

To be continued.

ABOUT THE AUTHOR

Thaddeus Howze is a full time author living in the small town of Hayward, California. Spending most of the day hard at work, his writing companions include his three quirky cats and two over-enthusiastic dogs.

His family tolerates his constant prattling about new ideas, inspired by world events, or new technologies or just the old-fashioned crazy ideas imagined in the shower.

When he is not working on a novel, novella, short story or overdue article, he is providing consultation on information technology, helping someone use their computer better or finding a way to make computers do things they are not supposed to.

His first novel, *Insurrection*, is due out in September 2012.